CAN

what's yours
is mine

TESS STIMSON is the author of six previous novels and two
works of non-fiction, and writes regularly for the *Daily Mail*
as well as for several women's magazines. Born and brought
up in Sussex, she graduated from Oxford before spending a
number of years as a news producer with ITN. She now lives
in Vermont with her American husband, their daughter and
her two sons.

www.tessstimson.com

Tess Stimson

what's yours is mine

PAN BOOKS

First published 2010 by Pan Books
an imprint of Pan Macmillan, a division of Macmillan Publishers Limited
an imprint of Pan Macmillan Ltd
Pan Macmillan, 20 New Wharf Road, London N1 9RR
Basingstoke and Oxford
Associated companies throughout the world
www.panmacmillan.com

ISBN 978-0-330-45854-2

3 5 7 9 8 6 4 2

A CIP catalogue record for this book is available from
the British Library.

Printed in the UK by CPI Mackays, Chatham ME5 8TD

Visit www.panmacmillan.com to read more about all our books
and to buy them. You will also find features, author interviews and
news of any author events, and you can sign up for e-newsletters
so that you're always first to hear about our new releases.

For my daughter

Lily Jane Isabeau:

the sweetest gift

1

Grace

For most of my adult life, thanks to my sister, I've been terrified of getting pregnant. I've taken a belt-and-braces approach to contraception: condoms and the Pill; the patch and an IUD; the safe period plus a diaphragm (after I hit my thirties and began to worry about blood clots and heart attacks).

The joke is on me, it seems.

'No chance?' I ask, to be quite clear. 'Absolutely none at all?'

'I'm so sorry, Grace. Perhaps if you'd come to me ten years ago, we might have been able to do something, although I doubt it even then. If you or Tom have any questions—'

I stand, terminating the conversation before Dr Janus' professional pity embarrasses us both.

'I think you've explained it all very clearly, doctor. Thank you,' I add.

His secretary presents me with a sealed cream envelope on the way out. I drop it into my Birkin without opening it.

Fourteen months of tests and thousands of pounds to find out that *relaxing* and *giving it time* were never going to work. No amount of zinc-rich foods and leafy vegetables, chasteberry tincture, red clover, acupuncture, hypnotherapy, B6, B12, noting my temperature, propping my pelvis up on a pillow for twenty minutes, no amount of *enjoying the practice* or *letting nature take its course* – none of it, nothing, will ever give me a baby.

I stop a moment on the surgery steps to pull myself together, holding my Birkin against my chest like a scarlet shield. I'm rather more shaken than I thought I'd be. I shouldn't be: unlike Tom, I had a feeling all along something was wrong. Susannah's life is a car crash in motion, but Tom and I are perfectly placed to have a child: strong marriage, secure jobs, a beautiful home in the Oxfordshire countryside with plenty of trees to climb. Naturally I'm the sister who can't get pregnant.

Already I'm mentally searching for a loophole: a way out, a solution. My mother says I think like a man, and she doesn't mean it as a compliment.

I can't believe this is the end of the line. For more than a year, I've formulated Plan Bs for every eventuality: if I don't get pregnant in six months, I'll see a specialist. If they can't fix what's wrong, we'll try IVF. If Tom's firing blanks, we'll use a donor.

After our first consultation with Dr Janus – the one where he referred to my thirty-seven-year-old eggs as 'geriatric' – I quietly researched clinics without telling my husband, evaluating those with the highest IVF success rates, and efficiently setting money aside so we wouldn't have to wait on the caprices of the NHS. Whatever the problem was, we'd find a way round it. We'd keep trying, however long it took.

It never occurred to me that the problem might not be fixable.

Dr Janus briefly mentioned surrogacy at our first meeting, but I'm not prepared to take the risk that the surrogate mother would refuse to hand over the baby at the end. You read such tragic tug-of-love stories in the papers. Adoption is a non-starter, too; I looked into that months ago. Tom has a heart defect. He was born with it, and the doctors say he'll probably live to a ripe old age, but as far as Social Services are concerned, he could die at any moment. They won't let us adopt in this country, and we're not rich or famous enough to go off to Africa and start a rainbow family.

There must be a way. This can't be over. Think laterally, Grace. Work the angles. I'm a forensic accountant; I'm trained to find loopholes. *There must be a way.*

I back up against the Harley Street railings as people bustle past me, their heads bent against the biting February wind. I'm always calm in a crisis, I'm known for keeping my cool, but suddenly I can't think straight. I don't know which way to turn. Literally: I'm standing in the street and I can't even decide whether to go left or right. I don't know what to do next. My mind is blank.

No, not blank. So densely over-written it just seems that way.

A tangle of thoughts ticker-tapes through my head. *Congenital uterine malformation . . . exposure to diethylstilbestrol . . . no one could have known . . . incompetent cervix . . . impossible to carry a foetus to full term . . . additional factors . . .*

thirty-seven years old, PCOS, endometriosis . . . harvesting eggs not an option . . . very sorry, extremely unfortunate . . .

Tom. My poor Tom.

That huge house; four bedrooms. I've kept my Lego all these years. And my wedding dress. What will I do with my wedding dress now?

Mum. She'll be devastated. She's already lost two grandchildren, thanks to Susannah. She's pinned everything on me making it right again. Now, for the first time in my life, I have to let her down.

No chance.

The words echo on the wind. A bus vibrates with them. Stiletto heels tattoo them on the pavement. *No chance no chance no chance.*

A freezing sleet starts to fall. I'm blocking the street; shoppers bang their bags against my legs, to make the point. A bundle of foreign students sweep noisily along the pavement and, as they pass, I blindly allow myself to be carried along in their wake, my afternoon meeting forgotten.

I'm aware I'm in shock, but I'm powerless to do anything about it. My future has just been eviscerated. It plays in my mind's eye, a montage of failure. There'll be no Christmas stockings to put up, or paintings in primary colours on the fridge. No bucket-and-spade holidays. No Mother's Day cards, no first day at kindergarten. No homework to help with, or rows about messy bedrooms and exorbitant phone bills. No first kisses, first dates, break-ups, weddings, grandchildren. No one to come after me, no one to listen to all I've learned.

Just Tom. And me.

I'm an amputee, staring at the place where a limb used

to be. Knowing that soon it will hurt beyond imagining, and that its loss will ache forever, but unable to feel anything yet.

The tide of pedestrians surges to an abrupt halt at the edge of the pavement. I look up and realize I'm at Oxford Circus, the opposite end of town from where I need to be for my meeting. I should turn round, retrace my steps, hail a cab. I do none of these things.

Impatient shoppers jostle from behind as we wait for the lights to change, and I stumble into a woman laden with plastic shopping bags, nearly knocking her into the road. I apologize and stand back, allowing the crowd to shove past me. A pushchair wheel grazes my ankle, laddering my tights. A small child bats a stuffed toy against my knees; a girl, I assume, from the bubblegum-pink anorak and purple jeans. I have no idea how old she is. Is that something that comes naturally, once you're a mother: the ability to judge a child's age?

I can't tear my eyes from her. She isn't pretty. The wind has whipped her plump cheeks red; two train-tracks of mucus dribble from her nose and her hair has been flattened against her head by the rain. Her eyes are too close together and she has scabbed patches of eczema around her mouth.

I never thought I'd want a child. Growing up, Susannah was the one who brought home stray kittens and pleaded to adopt a puppy. I was the clever one, the one who'd go to university and have a career. Susannah was the earth-mother type. My mother often said so. She'd be the one with four children and an Aga and dogs asleep in the kitchen. Not *Grace*. Grace couldn't boil an egg!

It never occurred to me, then, that my mother was trying

to give Susannah something to be good at. Something I hadn't already claimed.

For years, I bought into the accepted family version of history. I wasn't domestic; I couldn't cook; I wasn't good with children. I was good at passing exams and earning money and achieving professional success. Even when I met Tom, and discovered that I could, after all, whip up an omelette and manage a vacuum cleaner, the thought of children still terrified me. Until, all of a sudden, two years ago, it didn't.

The little girl drops her stuffed animal onto the ground, and reaches impotently for it, fat starfish fingers opening and closing in frustration. Her mother ignores her, drifting towards a shop window a couple of feet away. She presses her palm against the glass like a Victorian street urchin at a bakery and gazes at the display of studded urban jeans. She's little more than a child herself, scarcely out of her teens. Her hair is scraped back from her face by a white plastic hair band and she's wearing a short, tight cotton skirt and pink denim jacket, both far too thin for this weather. A large blue-and-green tattoo of a dragon snakes around her bare calf. She reminds me of my sister.

I don't often think about Susannah. To do so is to give in to the regret and guilt that have stalked me every day for the last five years; to admit that, despite everything my sister has done, all the hurt and pain and damage she's caused, I still miss her.

The signal beeps, announcing it's safe to cross. I glance round for the little girl's mother, but she's chatting to a boy sweeping the shop doorway and hasn't noticed the lights have changed. The crowd behind us plunges across the road, swirling around the pushchair and kicking the child's toy out of sight. Her face crumples as her mother is blocked from her view, and she strains against her safety harness, her body arched in a rigid, distressed bow.

I reach beneath the pushchair wheels and pull out the flannel rabbit, dusting it quickly. 'Here you go, sweetheart. Is this what you wanted?'

She flings it away, screaming red-faced for her mother, who's still too busy flirting to pay any attention to her child.

Anger whips through me. Some women don't *deserve* to have babies.

The toddler's heels drum frantically against the footwell of her pushchair. No one even gives her a second glance as they hurry past. How can her mother leave her like this? Her pushchair is just inches from a four-lane road. It could roll forward into the path of the traffic. No one's watching her. Anything could happen.

I tuck the soft toy into the basket beneath the cheap pushchair, and jiggle the handle, murmuring soothing noises. The little girl's face is shiny with tears. What kind of woman would abandon her child to the mercies of a stranger? Doesn't she know how precious her baby is? Doesn't she realize there are women who'd give anything to have what she has?

No doubt she sees her child as an inconvenience, an obstacle to her social life. I doubt the baby was planned. Her mother's probably palmed her off on anyone who'll keep an eye out for half an hour ever since she was born. It's only a matter of time before she abandons her child altogether.

I'll never forgive Susannah. Never.

I stroke the poor mite's frozen cheek, wiping away her tears, and then tuck a threadbare fleece blanket around her, trying to protect her from the freezing rain. She deserves so much better than this. What chance does she have in life? A different roll of the dice, and she could have had access to private schools and gymkhanas, ski trips to Italy, a mother and a father who put her at the centre of their world. Instead, she'll be lucky if she isn't pregnant herself by the time she turns sixteen.

The child sucks in a ragged breath, hiccupping, and her sobs slowly begin to taper off. The traffic starts to flow again, and a new crowd of impatient shoppers builds up around us as we wait once more for the green man.

Her mother glances briefly in our direction, carelessly catching my eye, and then turns back to the handsome boy who is making her laugh. I'm sure she loves her daughter, in her own way, but don't babies need to be loved their way, not just on your terms? They can't come second to nights out and strangers in shop doorways. If this precious little girl were mine, I wouldn't leave her side for a second. I'd put my business on hold, hire a temp, spend every second with my daughter, teaching her what it means to be loved.

I don't suppose this mother would even really miss her baby, as long as she knew she was safe. Susannah never did. She's only a teenager: she'd probably be glad of the break. She could spend as much time as she wanted flirting and having fun. Poor kid. It's not really her fault any more than it was Susannah's. She's just not ready for the responsibility.

If someone were to . . . take . . . the child, they'd almost be doing her a favour.

I don't stop to think. This time, when the green man beeps, I seize the handle, reach down and gently release the brake on the pushchair.

2

Susannah

It's lucky Dex's prick isn't half an inch shorter, or we'd both be shit out of luck. Having sex standing up isn't as easy as it looks. Frankly, it's one occasion where size matters.

He's still inside me when my mobile rings. Instantly, he flings me against the alley wall, practically breaking my ribs. 'Babe! Turn that fuckin' thing off before someone hears it!' he yelps. 'D'you want everyone knowin' our business?'

He says it *bidnizz*, like he's 50 Cent or Ja Rule. Seriously, who does he think he's kidding? He's a preppy white kid from Boston who drinks Diet Coke and worries about his pension. Talking like Ali G and wearing his pants so low he looks like he's crapped himself when he walks doesn't make him black. The other inkslingers at the shop call him Wigga, and, trust me, they're not laughing *with* him.

I push at his chest for air as sweat trickles between my breasts. Even in February, the Florida humidity drives me nuts. 'Call me crazy, *dude*, but I think they may have guessed about us.'

'Who've you told? If my wife—'

'Gimme a break, Dex. This place isn't exactly private. There are five people working here. When two of them sneak out the back door for a quickie, it's kind of notice-able.'

'Do you have to be so crude?'

'Do you have to be so anal?'

He pulls out of me, and wipes his dick on his satiny red shell suit. *Nice.*

I check my phone to see who called, but it just says *private number.* I chew my lip. I skipped the last couple of car payments, and it's been four months since I even paid the minimum on my credit cards. But I reckon I've still got a bit of time before they get break-your-legs serious.

I pick up my knickers, shove them in the pocket of my denim miniskirt, and push through the back door without bothering to wait for Dex. Nipping into the staff loo, I chop out a quick line of blow on the cistern, check my nose for residue and then hustle back into the shop.

Oakey's working on some guy's sleeve near the window, and there's the usual cluster of curious looky-Lous peering and pointing through the glass. He puts down his tattoo gun when he sees me and comes over.

'I'm outta goo. You got any?'

I rummage around the shelves beneath my workstation for the cream we pass out to all our customers after they get inked. 'Here. How's it going?'

Oakey rolls his eyes. 'Dude's a total Michelangelo.' He adopts a narky tone. *'Use the passion red. I think the wings should be turquoise.* Got to give the asshole props, though. He's taken a beating today.'

'Anything lined up for me this afternoon?'

I'm asking more in hope than expectation. Getting inked isn't like having your hair done. We hardly ever take bookings, except for really complicated work. You never turn a customer away, but no one likes a closer who walks in thirty minutes before we shut up shop and demands a two-hour tatt.

'Sorry, doll. Your B-back with the red hair from yesterday stopped in again, though. Wanted to take another look at your flashes. Said she'd come by sometime Saturday – I told her you'd be here.'

'No shit. I didn't think she'd show again.' Buzzed from the coke, I check out my design samples, displayed on the wall behind me. 'Which one was she interested in?'

'The Mucha.'

I raise my eyebrows. 'Sure she don't want to start with something smaller?'

'Said she was into that one.'

'Fine by me. I could use the cash.'

I grab an elastic band from my drawer and tie back my blonde dreads. Behind me, Dex swaggers to the front of the shop and starts acting out for the tourists. Loser. I'd never have fucked him if he hadn't threatened to shop me to Immigration for working without a permit.

'You got time this evening, I could work on your shoulder,' Oakey offers. 'Bronx cancelled on me, so I got some spare hours.'

Oakey's the only person I trust to ink me these days. He's better drunk than anyone else stone-cold sober. We met four years ago at the Inkslingers' Ball in Hollywood, where I'd fetched up after my last divorce, and briefly hooked up. Didn't take us long to work out we'd be better off as friends. We've hung out together ever since, working our way east from California down to Florida, never staying anywhere longer than a few months. He's come up with a really smokin' new design that'll cover my right shoulder and blend into the crappy half-sleeve I had done when I ran away at sixteen. I took off with some guy to Brighton and got inked every day, until my mother found me. Took her ten days, by which time the whole of my upper right arm was a pre-Raphaelite Lilith. Mum was pretty pissed, but it was Grace who had a total shit fit. She'd just got into Oxford, and no one even noticed, because they were all so busy freaking out over me.

Oakey reaches behind the register. 'Here. You got some mail today.'

I kick out the stool at my station and flick through the stack of envelopes. I don't need my dickhead landlord holding my post hostage when I'm late with the rent, which is like every month, so I use the shop address.

I toss aside three airmail letters from my mother (she's never got the hang of email) and rip open the official-looking envelope from the Department of Homeland Security. My buzz evaporates as I read it.

Damon, you bastard.

I was still married to Marty, my second husband, when I met Damon in a club in Brixton about five years ago. After Marty found out about us – well, OK, after he walked in on us in bed together – he hit me with a quickie divorce, which meant that by the time I found out what a triple-A-rated freak Damon was, I'd already married the loser, *so* burned my bridges in England and followed him to his hometown of Kalamazoo, Michigan.

Needless to say, the marriage didn't last long. One hundred and fifty-nine days, to be precise. I don't mind a guy screwing around on me, so long as he uses protection, but I draw the line at teenage boys.

When Damon and I split, we made a deal: he'd help me get a Green Card so I could stay in the US, and I'd keep my mouth shut about his chickens and make sure he never laid eyes on me again. I've kept my end of the bargain.

I screw up the immigration letter. I didn't take a fucking penny from him. All he had to do was sign a few forms. Bastard. Now I've got thirty days to leave the country or I'll be deported.

Nervously, I twist the ring in my lower lip. I could go off the radar, but it'd mean quitting my job, and these days it's not easy to find one without papers, even in this business. No work permit's one thing; not having a visa is something else. All those damn security checks and penalties for hiring illegals. I won't be able to rent anything more than some cockroach-ridden slum if I can't provide references, and that's going to be impossible without a bank account. No credit cards or health insurance, either.

'Bad news, doll?'

I smooth out the crumpled letter and hand it to Oakey. 'I'm screwed. No way will I get a work visa now Damon's pulled the plug. Tattoo artists are hardly top of the heap.'

'Can't you call them and explain?'

'Doesn't work that way, Oaks. Shit. If you weren't a Kiwi, I could marry you instead.'

'So what you gonna do? Go back to England?'

I grope for my packet of lights, ignoring Dex's filthy glare from the other side of the shop. He really is a prick. 'Life wasn't exactly a roaring success before I left, and that was before I pissed everyone off. There's nothing back there for me. I'll be stuck in some crappy council flat if I'm lucky, with no job, no money, no friends and fuck all to look forward to.'

'Don't you got family you can stay with?'

'Are you kidding? I'm public enemy number one. They'd probably shoot me on sight if I came within a hundred feet of the family home.'

'That all was five years ago, doll. They've probably forgotten all about it. I bet they're missing you as much as you're missing them.'

I suck in a lungful of nicotine. *What you've done is unforgivable, Susannah. There's no going back after this. I don't ever want to see you again. As far as I'm concerned, I don't have a sister.*

I know Grace. Once she makes up her mind, it's over. She won't back down. I don't suppose she even gives me a second thought these days, much less misses me.

I wish I could forget her as easily.

I'm sketching out some new designs when a kid of about nineteen or twenty strolls in through the door just before lunch. Dex is all over him, but the kid isn't having any of it. 'I'm looking for someone called Zee,' he calls out.

'Yo, man, I kin help you—'

'Sorry, dude. Mace said I should stick with the girl.' He points to one of my flashes on the back wall. 'Like, can you do that on the back of my neck?'

I squint at the design. 'Yeah. It'd fit better on your shoulders, but I can do it on your neck if you don't mind me changing things up a little. You been inked on your spine before?'

The kid bristles. 'I can take it.'

I take the sample off the wall, and work it up a little to fit the confined space on the back of the kid's neck. It takes me half an hour, and then I transfer a preliminary outline onto his skin and show it to him with the aid of a mirror. He's already got an armful of badly drawn tatts, inked by scratchers like Dex who go in too deep or at the wrong angle and end up blurring the outlines or scarring the skin. A really good tattoo should last a lifetime and look as clean and clear on your corpse as it did the day you got inked.

I'm not surprised when the kid faints in the chair as soon as I get near bone. It happens more often than you'd think, and the bigger and tougher the guy getting inked, the louder he squeals. Girls never complain.

We close at eight, and Oakey inks me for a couple hours. I turn down his invitation to hit the bar afterwards and drive home alone along the beach road. The seatbelt digs into my raw shoulder, but I daren't risk taking it off and getting stopped by the cops. My insurance lapsed two months ago, and I'm behind on my car registration too.

A warm breeze blows in off the Gulf as I park beneath my apartment block, and I turn off the engine and stare out across the black ocean. I don't like thinking about home. It brings back too many bad memories.

I get out of the car, but instead of going up to my condo, I head out across the dunes onto the white sand. Late night joggers thud along the beach, swerving around couples holding hands and watching the horizon. A few kids kick a ball around by moonlight, and several families are sitting round camp-fires, toasting marshmallows and making s'mores. I go down to the water's edge, then slip off my flip-flops and allow the silver waves to lap gently over my feet. I'd strip off and go in if I wasn't so shit-scared of sharks.

Fuck it. I don't want to leave all this. Florida suits me: nobody belongs here. We're all from somewhere else –

tourists, retirees, drifters. What's waiting for me back in England?

Maybe I'll head down south to Miami, talk Oakey into coming with me. His reputation will open a few doors. I'll have to work on the downlow, which means I'll get paid a pittance, but I don't need much out here to get by. If worst comes to worst, I can always sleep on the beach.

As I cross the boardwalk back to my apartment, a red Mustang pulls into the parking lot. I duck behind a concrete pillar, but it's too late.

'Hey! Punk girl! I see you!'

Reluctantly, I step back out. 'Mr Varthaletis. I was just coming to—'

'You owe me rent! Three weeks overdue!'

'Yes, I know, and I'll get it to you, I promise, but—'

He pokes me in the chest, copping an eyeful while he's at it. 'I come back tomorrow! You give me rent, or you give me keys, OK?'

'Look, I'm not sure I can do it tomorrow, but I'll get you the money soon, Mr V. I swear. If you could just give me a little more time—'

'Maybe we come to arrangement, hmm?' His sweaty hand slides up the back of my thigh beneath my miniskirt. 'I do you a favour, and you do me a favour. We scratch each other's backs.'

Fucking pervert. His poxy apartment isn't worth shit. I don't have to take this.

I have no money, nowhere to go, and thirty days before I've got to hit the road or leave the country. I *so* have to take this.

'No panties,' the landlord pants. 'Dirty bitch. *Dirty bitch.*'

He shoves thick fingers inside me. I force myself to stand

still and concentrate hard on a crack in the concrete pillar behind him. It looks like a serpent's tail. I imagine it in green, coiled around a shoulder or forearm, its scarlet eye unblinking. Grace hates my tattoos and piercings. She calls them tramp stamps. When she first saw the thick metal hoop in my eyebrow, she slapped my face. She always wears a pair of neat diamond studs that Tom gave her on their first wedding anniversary. I don't suppose she's ever gone out without knickers in her life.

She would never end up in a situation like this.

I swing back my hand and whack the pervert's cheek hard enough to leave a red skull-and-crossbones imprint from my ring.

'You little whore! You give me all money you owe, tomorrow, or I call the cops!'

'Fuck you and the horse you rode in on,' I retort.

He spits on the ground, but backs away towards his Mustang. I flip him the bird, then storm upstairs to my apartment.

There is *no* way my day can get any worse.

3

Grace

Tom is stirring the contents of a large zinc pot on top of the Aga, looking like one of the witches in *Macbeth*, when I push open the kitchen door a little after seven. Steam fills the warm room, billowing around us like a thermal spring. His face is red and sweaty, his fox-brown hair plastered to his head.

I toss my Birkin on the kitchen table, and shrug off my sleet-frozen coat. 'What colour are you doing this time?'

'Kelly green,' Tom says. 'What d'you reckon?'

I glance over his shoulder into the pot. 'Nice. Matches your eyes.'

'Thank you kindly, ma'am. I thought I'd do those canvas trousers with the grass stains.'

We smile as our eyes lock, remembering a long, lazy afternoon by the towpath, two summers ago, when we still just made love for the hell and pleasure of it.

Bleakness washes over me. Deliberately, I break the moment, leaning forward and stirring the bubbling green cauldron on the stove top. Tom watched a programme about recycling a couple of months ago and has been on a kind of *Good Life* conservation kick ever since, saving every twist of string, displaying his (rather fine) legs in cut-offs like a gawky eight-year-old, and brewing his own beer. A. N. Didron's quote, 'It is better to preserve than to repair, better to repair than to restore, better to restore than to reconstruct,' takes pride of place on the kitchen notice-board.

I'm rather enjoying his conservation efforts. The other night, he came to bed in a pair of glorious purple pyjamas ('I think there was still some red in the pot when I added the blue'), and a number of his more psychedelic tie-dye efforts have added a certain character to our washing line, the energy-guzzling tumble dryer now being off-limits.

'You're later than I expected,' Tom says, giving the pot a final stir and turning it down to simmer. 'How was the dentist?'

My body floods once more with nervous adrenalin. Only I can ever know how close I came to doing the unthinkable this afternoon. *Oh, God.* What if I'd pushed the little girl's pushchair in the opposite direction today? What if I'd walked away from her mother, and kept on walking until we were lost from sight, instead of manoeuvring the pushchair through the crowds towards her and explaining that her daughter had been crying, frightened by the crush of people?

The young mother had just shrugged and gone back to her conversation. She didn't even bend to comfort her child.

I can't believe what I nearly did. I always thought people who gave in to their impulses were fundamentally different from me. I suppose I thought they were weak. Lacking in discipline and control. I thought they were people like Susannah.

It's a shock to know they're just like me.

'Tom. I need to talk to you—'

He's running cold water into the sink, ready to set his green dye, and he cups his hand to his ear to indicate he can't hear me. I feel sick at the thought of what I have to tell him. He's a paediatric anaesthetist, for heaven's sake; he chose to spend his life working with children. Why must I be the one to deny him the chance of his own?

How will he feel about me, once he knows?

I turn off the running tap and suck in a deep breath. 'Tom, I wasn't at the dentist.'

He looks surprised, but waits for me to continue.

My nerve fails me. How do I even begin? First, I have to tell him I went to see Dr Janus without him. I know Tom will be hurt by that, though it'll be as nothing to what comes next. But even though he's my husband and this affects him deeply, it's peculiarly my tragedy, not his. I didn't want him there because I knew it was going to be bad news, and I didn't want to have to bear his pain and disappointment along with my own.

For a fleeting moment I wish Susannah was here. As if she could help. I haven't talked to her in five years. I don't even know her phone number.

My fingers dig into my palm. 'Tom—'

The kitchen door opens, and Blake, Tom's best friend and the husband of mine, blows into the room on a gust of sleet and sexual energy. I don't know whether to laugh or cry at the reprieve.

'Fucking freezing out there,' Blake says cheerfully, flinging himself sideways into a kitchen chair. 'Claudia'll be along in a minute, Grace. She's just putting the girls to bed. Next-door's babysitting for an hour. Any danger of a beer, Tom?'

'Been waiting for you to show your face,' Tom grins, disappearing into the basement. His voice echoes sepulchrally up the stairs. 'Got this new brew I've been working on. Should be about ready now.'

He reappears with two pint glasses filled with equal parts sea-foam and cloudy amber liquid, and hands one to Blake. They raise them in mutual salute, then take healthy gulps.

Even with a foam moustache, Blake exudes a raunchy glamour. I've had a bit of a crush on him for years. Tall and rangy, all angles and tousled dirty blond curls, he looks like a rock star on his weekend off. He was born in New York, and although he was raised in England from the age of two, he's somehow managed to retain that indefinable American gloss. Even in the depths of an English winter he has a tan that sets off gleaming white teeth just crooked enough to be sexy, and eyes the soft slate-grey of the sea after a storm. He just has a way of . . . *noticing* you. I don't know how Claudia manages him.

Tom drains his glass, then fishes in his cauldron with a pair of huge laundry tongs, and heaves the emerald jeans into a bucket. He staggers across the kitchen and dumps them into the cold water in the kitchen sink. He looks like Widow Twanky.

There's a sudden tightness in my throat. His old pink shirt may be tight across his stomach these days, rather than his chest, and the boyish features have blurred, but he's still my Tom, still the man I've loved for the better part of two decades. He doesn't have Blake's flashy charm or movie-star good looks, and after all this time together, there are few surprises left. But he's my best friend. I trust him completely. I know where I am with Tom.

If that sounds unromantic, it shouldn't. A good marriage, like a good business, is outwardly ordinary. Tom and I have grown up together. We know each other inside and out.

We met seventeen years ago at the start of our second year at Oxford. It took me a little while to find my feet at university and, though I had some good female friends, I was still painfully shy with boys. Claudia, one of the eight students with whom I shared a house, had decided we should throw a Halloween party, and I'd volunteered to man the front door, since this enabled me technically to participate without actually having to make much conversation beyond, 'The kitchen's through there.'

Tom was unfashionably early. I had a fleeting impression of a russet-haired boy with green eyes and unexceptional looks, before he dropped his bottle of cider – that Eighties student party staple – at my feet, showering the two of us with shards of glass and sweet-smelling alcohol.

'You're the girl from the library,' he gasped. 'You spend every Tuesday morning in the Duke Humfrey Reading Room with the hippy black girl. You get out very dull books about Anglo-Saxon literature, and then spend most of your time reading your friend's history books. You had a birthday three weeks ago – I saw your friends' cards sticking out of your bag.' He was smiling now. I liked his smile. 'You always leave just before twelve and go across the road for a hot chocolate.'

No one had ever paid me that kind of attention before.

It wasn't love at first sight, but it was *something*. Recognition of a kindred spirit, perhaps, of someone just as unsure and uncertain and determined as I was. We dated earnestly for three months, and then I woke up one morning and realized I couldn't imagine my life without Tom in it.

The following weekend, I lost my virginity to him. Tom was scarcely more experienced than me, having had the benefit of just two lovers, but we applied ourselves diligently to the task of learning our way around each other's bodies, and experimented freely. We'd soon graduated to the advanced chapters of *The Joy of Sex*, and congratulated ourselves on our racing start. Certainly, if my friends were to be believed, we were more adventurous than the average novice, and were in the happy, if unusual, position of finding that familiarity with each other in bed bred satisfaction rather than contempt.

It wasn't long before we'd become one of those ampersand couples: Grace&Tom. A composite, the sum greater than its parts, long before Brangelina.

At the start of our final year, we moved in together, sharing a narrow terraced house with six other impoverished students, Blake and Claudia among them. After Tom and I graduated with our respective Firsts, there were a few years of commuting between my flat in London and his digs near Edinburgh's Medical School, which was a little trying, but eventually Tom returned south to take a job at the John Radcliffe Hospital in Oxford, and later in London. By then, I'd had time to establish myself as a forensic accountant and was in the process of setting up my own independent consultancy. Marriage seemed the next logical step: we were both twenty-nine, and had got any playing-the-field impulses out of our systems; although, to be honest, neither Tom nor I had ever been what you might call wild.

Six years later, when I turned thirty-five, we decided it was time for a baby. It never occurred to either of us that it wouldn't happen. Why should it? Neither of us had ever failed at anything before.

Claudia arrives just as Blake disappears down to the cellar to fetch a second round of home brew. I suppress a sigh. It's not the smell of Tom's beer that bothers me (though the entire house now smells, not unpleasantly, like a rotting apple orchard) so much as the unfortunate effect it has on his digestive system. You could power the south-east of England with his farts.

Claudia unwinds her scarf and takes up her accustomed position perched on the closed stove lid of the Aga. She's like a cat, always seeking a warm place to sleep. She blames it on her South African heritage: her mother is Sowetan, her father Boer. They fled to England before Claudia was born to escape a regime that deemed inter-racial relationships not only illegal, but a sin against God. In vain do I point out that I'm always cold in this house too, and you can trace my genes back to our fog-bound island's indigenous Celts.

'You do realize your moat has actually frozen over, Grace?' she complains, wrapping her arms around herself and tucking her hands beneath her armpits. 'Everyone else's daffodils are out, but you're still stuck in the Ice Age.'

'We have our own micro-climate,' Tom says blithely. 'When global warming turns the rest of Oxfordshire into a desert, you'll be begging us to let you move in.'

Tom and I live in a marvellous example of a Victorian folly: a miniature Gothic castle, complete with rounded turret, gargoyles, stone battlements and, yes, a moat; all this despite the fact that the entire property is no bigger than your average four-bedroom semi. It was built smack in the middle of a quaint Oxfordshire village on the site of a fourteenth-century cemetery by a nineteenth-century entrepreneur. He'd made his fortune selling armaments to both sides in the American Civil War and had little regard for either superstition or history.

It's bizarre, impractical, monstrously expensive to run, and Tom and I both fell in love with it the moment we saw it, a year after we married, driving back to London from a paediatric conference in Oxford. It wasn't officially for sale; we'd stopped at the pub across the road for a quick bite, and couldn't resist strolling over for a closer look. At which point Fate took a hand: the estate agent who'd just been saddled with it after the death of the previous owner (penniless and in debt to the tune of hundreds of thousands of pounds – something we didn't discover until it was far too late) happened to be there, walking the property. He must have thought his ship had come in when we turned up before he'd even had a chance to write up its particulars.

We agreed a price that at the time we thought was a steal, and in retrospect turned out to be daylight robbery. In the five years since then, we've replaced the slate roof (twice; the first builder used tiles that didn't conform to its Grade II listed status), dredged the moat of bicycles and beer cans, spent three months camping out in Claudia and Blake's spare room while the asbestos lagging on the pipes was replaced, woken one Christmas morning to find eighteen inches of raw sewage in the basement after the cesspit overflowed, rewired the place from top to bottom, and coped with a thousand minor inconveniences from backed-up lavatories to rising damp. It's cost us everything we made from the sale of our London flat, plus Tom's inheritance from his parents and a small legacy from my maternal grandmother, but it's been worth it. I love this house. I want to grow old here.

The only room we haven't yet touched is the third-floor turret nursery, which came to us complete with an original carved Victorian rocking horse. We were waiting to see if we needed to paint it pink or blue.

Blake clatters up from the basement, but instead of two glasses of Tom's brew, he's clutching a bottle of champagne from their last boys' booze cruise to northern France, which he and Claudia store in our wine cellar.

Tom looks confused. 'Cracking open the bubbly? Am I missing something, mate?'

Claudia smiles secretively, and her hand flutters to her stomach. She doesn't know Tom and I have been trying for a baby. It's always seemed too private to share; something that belonged only to Tom and me.

She's my best friend, and I love her, but oh, God, *it isn't fair*.

Later, after Blake and Claudia have left, awash respectively with champagne and delight – 'I know we said no more babies until the twins were at school,' Claudia whispers, as she hugs me goodbye, 'but we just couldn't wait' – I finally sit Tom down and tell him about my conversation with Dr Janus.

And Tom doesn't mind. He's upset for me, of course, because he truly loves me and he knows how much this means to me, but he's not upset for himself.

I should be pleased, relieved, even, that my husband

finds me enough. He wanted children, certainly, it was his decision to try for a baby as much as mine, and he would have been an involved father, a 'hands-on dad', but it seems he's equally happy now to adjust his ideas of the future to focus on just the two of us. But I'm not pleased or relieved. I don't feel thankful he feels this way. I'm hurt and angry. His stoicism seems like a betrayal. How can he not grieve the way I do? Why isn't he railing against Fate? How can he just *accept* this?

'One thing I don't understand,' Tom says, as I sit on the bed and furiously brush my hair. 'If it's inherited from your mother, why didn't it affect Susannah?'

The million-dollar question.

Carefully, I put the brush down, fighting the impulse to throw it at the wall. 'The drug was only prescribed until the early Seventies, to prevent miscarriages and premature babies. My mother had lost two babies before she had me. But by the time she was pregnant with Susannah three years later, it'd been taken off the market.'

'You're going to be all right, though?' Tom asks anxiously. 'You're not going to get sick, or anything?'

I want to scream. No, I'm not going to be all right! I'm *already* sick! My mother took a drug which has robbed me forever of my chance to have a child, and it wasn't her fault, of course it wasn't: I know that, and I wouldn't wish this on anyone, but if it had to happen to one of us, if it really *had* to happen, why me? *Why not Susannah?*

I was the *good* daughter. I was such a careful, conscientious teenager. I didn't stay out late, date unsuitable boys, shoplift, play truant. I never gave our parents a moment's worry, other than fear that I'd collapse from studying too hard. Susannah's the one who messed everything up. She was just thirteen when she ran away the first time; less than ten years later, she'd already been married and divorced. She never even wanted children. She's lied, cheated and betrayed everyone who ever loved her to get what she wanted. I could never rebel because Mum and Dad needed to have one child they could be proud of. So why, then, am *I* the one being punished?

I say none of this aloud, of course. I never do.

Tom hesitates a moment, then sits down beside me, the bed rocking gently under his weight. My tears splash on his green-dyed fingers as he takes my hand. 'Have you spoken to your mother yet?' he asks softly.

'I wanted to tell you first.'

It's not quite the whole truth. I'm not strong enough yet to deal with my mother's disappointment on top of my own despair. She's rung my mobile three times this after-noon, and for once I've ignored the calls. I *will* talk to her. Soon. When I've had some time to get used to this.

When I've stopped feeling *so fucking angry*.

'Grace, there are other options,' Tom says carefully. 'There are so many children out there who need a home. We could give them a good life. I know you probably don't want to think about it now, but later on, perhaps—'

'We can't adopt, Tom. I've already looked in to it.'

'Oh, come on. We're not too old, surely? We've got enough money, and I'm sure we can round up a few deluded souls who'll say we'd make great parents—' He stops, and his smile suddenly fades. 'Oh, I see. It's *my* fault.'

'No more than being barren is mine,' I say bitterly.

Tom pulls me into his arms, and I tuck my head into his shoulder with a sob. 'Grace, Grace. I love *you*. I married *you*.

If children had come along, that would've been great, but it's you I want, it's you I've always wanted.'

I raise my chin, and he kisses me, his tongue slipping between my lips, warm and sweet. I'm surprised by a sudden flare of heat between my legs. Sex between us has become so laden with expectation since we started trying to conceive, there's been no room for anything as simple as desire.

Now, though, I'm consumed by a hot, unexpected, animal need. I wrap my legs around his waist and fall back on the bed, taking him with me. I physically ache to have him inside me. My fingers tangle in his thick curls as I press his head to mine, my kiss hard and demanding. Tom's response is just as heated. Lust races between the two of us like a prairie fire. We bite each other's lips, claw at each other's clothes. Roughly he frees my breasts from my night-dress, and I groan with pleasure as he bruises my nipples with quick, hard bites.

I pull up his shirt and yank at his belt buckle. My hands corkscrew around his cock, but as I reach to guide him inside me, he pushes my knees apart and slides down between them instead. I buck as his tongue finds my clitoris, flicking back and forth across it like a serpent. In a sudden shower of sparks, I explode, my orgasm sheeting across the surface of my body like a summer storm at sea.

Tom covers my body with his own, pinning my arms on either side of my head, and pushes himself inside me. I tilt my hips to meet him, using my thighs to pull him deeper into me. Sweat drips from his hair into his eyes; darkly intent on his own need, he doesn't even blink. The naked lust on his face is startlingly erotic. I find myself in the grip of a second orgasm, more intense than the first, and lose any semblance of sense or control. With a hoarse cry, Tom comes with me, pounding into me with something that feels very close to fury.

Afterwards, we lie side by side for a long time on the rumpled bed, without touching. Tom's breathing slows, and gently settles into the rhythm of sleep. No longer warmed by our lovemaking, I shiver in the cold room, and pull the edge of the duvet across me.

The movement causes Tom's flowback to trickle wetly between my legs. *Tom's seed, falling on barren ground.* Seared with misery, I leap off the bed and run into the bathroom, scrubbing and scrubbing at my thighs until no trace is left.

Bones and heart aching, I climb back into bed. I close my eyes, praying for sleep to come quickly.

But I'm still awake when, at 3.48 a.m., the phone rings.

4

Susannah

You'd think she could've sprung for business class. After all, this whole dramatic race-and-rescue nonsense was her idea. I'm like a bloody battery hen stuck back here in economy, with all these screaming kids and sunburnt tourists in tracksuits and 'comfy' sandals. And they have the cheek to look at me like *I'm* the freak they don't want to sit next to.

'I've arranged for you to pick your ticket up at the airport,' Grace told me bossily last night, without bothering to check if I *wanted* to come rushing home. 'It's all paid for. And make sure you bring enough clothes for at least a couple of weeks. I don't know how long you'll need to be here.'

I didn't bother pointing out everything I owned could fit into a single suitcase.

'It's not that easy for me to drop everything,' I said perversely. 'I'm an *artist*, Grace. I get paid on commission. If I don't work, I don't eat. And if I just up and leave without notice, I may not even have a job to come back to.'

'This is an emergency, Susannah. How can you even think about money?'

'Because, unlike you, I *have* to.'

A long-suffering sigh, then, 'Fine. I'll look after things while you're here.'

Oh, I'm so grateful. Like she couldn't afford it. Mind you, it'll be for rather longer than she was thinking, given that after leaving the US I won't be allowed back in without a visa; Grace didn't need to know that yet.

'You'll have to stay with us for the time being,' she added crabbily. 'Obviously Dad won't have you, and clearly you can't afford a hotel.'

'Can you send me some cash? I'll need a taxi to get to the airport—'

'There won't be time to make a wire transfer before your plane leaves in the morning. I'm sure you have *someone* who could give you a lift,' Grace said, meaningfully.

Bitch. She's right, though. I always have *someone*.

I was about eleven when I noticed I possessed a certain something that set me apart from other girls my age; something quite important. It wasn't just that I developed proper breasts while they were still stuffing tissues in their training bras, or that my periods started before Grace's (which *really* pissed her off). Boys liked me. I mean, they *liked* me. Men, too. I saw the way my father's friends looked at me, then looked away, shocked by their own response.

Whenever we played It, I was the one the boys chased. They jostled me to the ground, even when I yelled *pax*. They snatched my lunchbox and held it over their heads, so I had to wrestle them to get it back. It seemed there was always a knot of boys hovering near me, drawn like bees to a honeypot; or, as Dad charmingly preferred to put it, like flies to shit.

I quickly realized the boys' attention gave me status among the girls; even with Grace, who pretended hard not to notice. So I began to egg them on. I stole Coke-flavoured lip gloss from Woolies, and undid an extra button on my school blouse. I was the first girl in my class to have a boyfriend, and – at fifteen – the first to let him go 'all the way'.

The sex was crap, of course; frankly, it usually still is. It doesn't matter. As far as I'm concerned, sex is just a tool: something you trade for something you want. I've rarely had an orgasm I didn't give myself.

OK, I wasn't exactly a class act, but let's get real: I had precious little else going for me. Following in Grace's golden footsteps was *such* fun. Little Miss Perfect. My big sister got straight As, won the county general knowledge quiz five years running, was a whizz at tennis, became head girl, won a scholarship to Oxford, and generally Made Her Parents Proud. She even found time to raise money for the Anthony Nolan Bone Marrow Trust (for which she was featured in the local papers under the highly original headline 'Amazing Grace'). The only thing I ever aced at school was human biology; and we're not talking about the exam.

From the day I started kindergarten, all I got was, 'You must be *so* proud of Grace.' After thirteen years of full-time education, half the teachers still didn't even know my name; I was forever Grace Latham's sister.

But the weird thing was, I didn't hate her for it. I *was* proud of her. I'd never tell her in a million years, but I was her biggest fan. I once got suspended for a week for punching another girl who'd been badmouthing Grace. I never told anyone why I did it, of course. I always acted like being her sister was the biggest bore in the world.

She thought she was looking out for me, but the truth was, *I* protected *her*. Without me, the cool clique at school would have made her life miserable. Poor, geeky Grace. Tall and clumsy, she didn't have a clue how to dress; she refused to shave her legs or get her ears pierced until she went to university, like being a virgin at eighteen was a point of *pride*. Her eyes were too narrow, her nose too big, and her long hair (which she flatly refused have highlighted) was thin and mousy. Back then, her only really good features were her mouth, which was Julia Roberts-wide and full and sexier than she realized, and her hands: elegant and graceful, with long pale fingers and perfect oval nails that she always kept neatly trimmed and painted with frosted pink polish.

If you asked *her* what her best feature was, of course, she'd say her mind. Which just goes to show how little my big sister knows about men.

The flight crew turns out the cabin lights, and I pull my eye mask down, trying to find a comfortable position in this miserable coffin of a seat. The combination of three vodka tonics and a Xanax is finally beginning to kick in. I close my eyes and yield to the warm fog enveloping me.

Despite the shitty things we said to each other last time we met, I'm looking forward to seeing my sister. I'd do anything for Grace. Not that she'll ever need me to. I don't think Grace has ever needed anyone in her whole life.

I trundle my luggage trolley through customs, jonesing for a cigarette as I wait impatiently for the fat tourists ahead of me to get out of the way. For fuck's sake, why'd they have to ban smoking on planes? If there's ever a time you need a smoke, it's trapped in an airborne cattle truck for nine hours with hundreds of sweaty tourists. I'm tempted to ram the swollen ankles of the morons in front of me. Nicotine rage.

'Excuse me, miss?'

Christ al-fucking-mighty, what now?

The customs officer smiles blandly. 'We need to check your bags. It's just routine.'

Routine my peachy ass. I don't see them stopping Mrs Apple-Pie Mom in her twinset and pearls over there. Hmm. We have a choice: the pretty Stepford wife in ballet pumps and Boden, or punk girl with dreads and tattoos. Goodness me, who *shall* we pick?

I fold my arms and scowl as the customs guy hefts my canvas holdall onto his table, and unzips it with the reverent care of a new father changing his baby's first nappy. Anyone'd think it's packed with Semtex. They're not going to find anything. Oakey made me get rid of my stash and then put all my clothes through his washing machine before I left, to make sure there were no traces of anything left behind. I just hope I can find a dealer in darkest bloody Oxfordshire. I'm going to need some serious pharmaceuticals to survive Grace.

I try out a smile, making sure he catches a good eyeful as I lean towards him. 'Look. I've been stuck on a plane all night and I'm dying for a cigarette. Is there *any* way we could hurry this along?'

He delivers a pair of grubby black Converses from the belly of my bag, then pulls out a pair of handcuffs and dangles them meaningfully from his index finger.

'I just use them in bed,' I say crossly. 'If I was going to hijack a plane, they wouldn't be fur-lined. Look, I'm not a terrorist. I'm not smuggling drugs, and I don't have any ivory hidden in my knickers. My sister's out there waiting for me, and we haven't spoken in five years. If I don't get a smoke in the next five minutes, I'm going into a complete meltdown.'

He nods towards a screened area to the side of the hall. 'There's no CCTV over there. Sit on the floor and blow the smoke down, so the detectors don't pick it up. And if anyone catches you, I never saw you, OK?'

I sneak behind the screens and slump on the cold marble floor, sucking in a lungful of nicotine with something akin to ecstasy. I wish I'd brought a couple of vodka miniatures off the plane too. I really don't need to be sober when I face Grace.

Five minutes later, the customs officer hands me back my bag and my boarding card with his phone number scribbled on the back. I promise to call him, and bin it the moment he's gone.

My stomach is a knot of excitement and nerves as I walk into the arrivals hall. I spot Grace before she sees me, though for a moment or two, I don't recognize her. It's not so much that she's changed since I last saw her; more that I still think of her as she looked at eighteen. She's had her hair cut shorter, which makes it seem thicker, and coloured it a deep chestnut that warms her face and brings out the hazel lights in her eyes. I don't know much about designer labels, but even I can tell her high-heeled boots and nipped-in cinnamon suede jacket are expensive; I wouldn't mind betting her jeans alone cost more than my entire wardrobe. She's got that sort of glossy sheen about her that only money can buy. She's still not pretty, but she makes you look twice now. Mum always said Grace had the kind of face she'd 'grow into' in her thirties. For the first time, I can see what she meant.

Tom, on the other hand, hasn't improved with age. He's got really chubby since I last saw him, and his brown curls are too thin these days for him to carry off the hippy drummer look. Mind you, I wouldn't kick him out of bed. I've always had a bit of a thing for Tom, but maybe that's just because he belongs to Grace.

Grace strides forward as they catch sight of me, her boots clicking briskly across the concourse.

'What happened?' she demands, without a word of greeting. 'It's been an hour since your plane landed. Everyone else came through customs ages ago.'

'I got stopped—'

'Well, I'm not surprised, dressed like that.'

Tom kisses me on the cheek. 'Good to have you back, Zee.'

'Thanks, John.'

'It's Tom,' Grace says crossly.

'I knew that,' I smile.

Tom takes charge of my trolley. 'Did you have a good flight?' he asks kindly.

'I got a couple hours' sleep, but you know what it's like on planes.' I shiver as I follow them out to the car park, pulling my leather jacket up around my ears. 'God! I'd forgotten how bloody freezing it is in this country!'

'You'll catch your death of cold if you don't put on some proper clothes,' Grace sniffs. 'It's February, Susannah, you can't just wander around in a miniskirt.'

'There's not much call for sheepskin coats and fur boots in Florida, Grace.'

'Well, you chose to go there.'

I want to hit her, but I keep my cool. No point winding her up before we've even got out of the airport. I'll cut her a bit of slack because of Mum, but she'd better not push it.

Tom leads the way towards a gleaming black 4x4, but just as I'm about to make some wisecrack about his carbon footprint, he stops beside a tiny little hatchback and unlocks it with his remote. 'You own a *hybrid*?' I snort.

'Nearly sixty m.p.g.,' Tom says proudly. 'More when you're on the open road.'

'What happened to "a man's Land Rover is his castle"?'

'He's still got the bloody thing,' Grace says tartly. 'It's parked behind the garage. He's keeping chickens in it.'

'Be fair, darling,' Tom protests. 'Only the chicks. It's easier to keep them warm, and it stops the other birds attacking them.'

My sister and I exchange a glance. She gives me a brief but real smile, and helps me load my bag into the boot while Tom returns the trolley to a bay at the end of the car park.

'How's Mum?' I ask.

'No change since yesterday. The doctors say she could be in this coma for weeks. Until she comes out of it, there's no way of knowing how much damage the stroke has caused.'

'But she's not going to die?'

She sighs. 'I don't know, Susannah.'

Grace *always* knows. All my life, she's known what to do next. It's the only certainty I've ever had in life, next to death and avoiding taxes.

I clamber awkwardly into the back of the hatchback, wondering for the first time if her insistence that I come home wasn't just because Mum needs me.

'It wasn't easy to track you down,' Grace says suddenly.

'Even your ex-husband didn't know where you were. In the end, I had to call Donny to get your number.'

'Donny?'

'Your son,' she snaps.

'Yes, I know who Donny is, thank you very much. I just hadn't realized you were in touch with him.'

'Why wouldn't I be? The boys need to know they have some family left.'

'I call them—'

'Donny says the last time you bothered to ring was over a year ago.'

I pick at my nails. 'It's not easy, what with the time difference—'

'They're your sons, Susannah. The least you could do is call them and see how they are, even if it means you have to get up in the middle of the night. You *are* going to see them while you're here?'

'The social worker said seeing me might stop them settling with their new family.'

'That was five years ago, Susannah. They're not kids any more, they're fifteen and twelve. They understand who their family is. But you're their mother. You *owe* them.'

'Don't call me Susannah,' I say childishly.

'Why not? It's your name.'

I'm on the verge of climbing right back out of the car, but then Tom returns, cheerily complaining about finding the right change for the car park meter. His amiable perkiness is almost as annoying as Grace's constant bitching. But, short of breaking a window, I'm trapped with the pair of them. Who am I kidding anyway? I can't go back to Florida: I have no money, and nowhere to go. Like it or not, I'm stuck with Grace, and she's just as stuck with me.

The traffic out of Heathrow is heavy, and as soon as we reach the M25, it grinds to a complete halt. I'm too wired to fall asleep, so I lean forward between the seats. 'OK if I light up?'

'No, it's not—'

'Grace, give her a break. We can open the windows.'

Grace shrugs and turns her back on both of us; quite a feat in a car this small. Frankly, I don't know how Tom puts up with her. Half an hour in her company, and already I want to top myself.

'Can I get to the trunk from inside the car?' I ask Tom. 'I've finished my cigarettes.'

'*Trunk*?' Grace snaps. 'We all know you've been living it up in Florida, Susannah. You don't have to show off. We're not impressed.'

'*So-rr-eeee*,' I retort.

No one speaks for the rest of the journey. I finally manage to doze off, and when Tom shakes me awake, we're in an underground car park outside the hospital. I stumble out of the back seat and follow him and Grace towards the lift. My head is thick with tiredness and too many vodkas and Xanax.

'She's in intensive care, Susannah,' Grace says abruptly. 'You need to be prepared for what that means. There are all sorts of machines and tubes. She's on a ventilator at the moment, which is doing her breathing for her, though they're hoping to take her off that soon. They've put her on an IV, and there are all sorts of monitors keeping track of her heart rate and blood pressure. It's not like it is on *ER*,' she adds thickly. 'It's so much worse.'

'Is Dad here?'

She hits the call button for the lift again. 'I should think so.'

Tom casually drapes his arm round Grace's shoulders as we ride up to the ICU on the fifth floor. I watch her lean into him with a sharp pang of envy. I've been married three times, and screwed more men than I can remember, but I've never shared that closeness with anyone.

Grace buzzes for entry at the door to the ICU. I reach nervously in my jacket pocket for my cigarettes, then remember where I am and put them away.

'It's going to be OK, Zee,' she says unexpectedly.

I nod, my throat suddenly tight. Grace can be beyond annoying, but if Mum . . . if anything happens to Mum . . . she'll be the only person left on the planet who even remotely gives a damn about me.

A nurse in pink scrubs pokes her head around the door. 'Mrs Hamilton? The doctor would like a quick word before you see Mum. If you and your husband could come with me, he'll be here in just a minute.'

I start to follow, but the woman blocks my way. 'I'm afraid it's still family only—'

'What am I, the hired help?' I demand.

'It's OK,' Grace sighs. 'She's my sister.'

I shove past the old bitch, fighting the urge to slap that snotty expression off her face. I *really* need a fucking cigarette.

We're shown into a cramped waiting room furnished with cheap beige cube sofas, fuzzy beige carpet tiles, and beige-painted walls. If you weren't depressed before you got in here, five minutes should do the trick. A potted plant in the corner has simply given up the fight, its dusty green leaves slowly turning brown as if to match the rest of the miserable little room. The only window is set six-and-a-half feet up in the wall, adding to the sense of incarceration. It's like something out of *Prisoner: Cell Block H*.

Ignoring Grace's disapproving glare, I pull a low coffee table over to the wall, climb on top of it and force the window open. Then I pull out my Marlboros and suck as many carcinogens into my lungs as possible. I'm just stubbing the butt out on the sill when the door opens again, and my father comes into the room, followed by a man in a white coat who may or may not have come to take me away.

My father nods briefly at Grace as I jump down from the table, and looks straight through me. *Gee, Dad. Thanks for the prodigal daughter welcome.*

'Are we all here?' the doctor asks. 'Good. Shall we sit down?'

'I'd prefer to stand,' Dad says stiffly.

'Well, then. As you all know, Catherine is very sick. She's survived the initial stroke, but we have no way of knowing what damage has been done until she regains consciousness . . .'

He starts in with the *ER*-speak, but loses me at *vital signs*. It's weird to hear Mum called Catherine, like she's a kid or something.

I sneak a sideways look at my father. You'd think he'd joined the military, he's so stiff-backed and stiff-necked and stiff-upper-lipped. I'm shocked by how much he's aged. But then I haven't set eyes on him in more than nine years; our little falling-out goes way further back than my bust-up with everyone else. Pretty much back to when I was born, if we're being honest here.

'. . . Mr Latham, we may need you to make some very difficult decisions,' the doctor is saying. 'I know this isn't something you want to think about, but it's best to be prepared. Of course we'll do everything we can, but you may decide at some point that it's time to let her go. As her next of kin—'

'Dad,' Grace says, 'Dad, you won't let them just *stop*, will you?'

'Has Catherine ever discussed her wishes with you?' the doctor asks. 'Did she sign an advance decision – a living will?'

'She's fifty-nine,' Dad says. 'She isn't even old enough to retire.'

'I realize how hard this is, Mr Latham, but if your wife—'

'Dad?' Grace says, tugging at his sleeve like she's five again.

'I'm not making any decisions now,' Dad says, pulling himself together with an effort. 'I'm not having you write her off. She's a fighter. She'll come through this, I know she will. I want you to—'

'Actually,' I say clearly, 'actually, Dad, it's not up to you.'

They both jump, as if they've forgotten I'm here. For the first time since he walked into the room – the first time in a decade – my father turns and *sees* me.

'What the hell do you mean?' he grinds out finally.

Oh, I've been waiting a long time for this.

'Mum came to see me before I left England five years ago,' I say, unable to keep the triumph from my voice. 'She gave me something. A power of attorney, in case anything happened to her. It's not you or Grace who gets to decide what to do. It's *me*.'

5

Catherine

I feel fine. The nagging headache that's been plaguing me for the last couple of days has finally gone, and so have the beginnings of that sore throat I thought I had coming.

In fact, I feel *better* than fine. At fifty-nine, you get used to aches and pains shifting around your body from one day to the next, like mercury in a glass phial. One morning it's backache, the next you can hardly bend your knees. But this morning, I don't feel any pain at all.

Voices murmur in the hospital corridor outside my room. I sit up, straining to hear. I do hate all this *fuss*. I had a bit of a dizzy spell, that's all. There was no need for David to call an ambulance! I can't believe the hospital admitted me. I'm not *sick*. I probably just turned the central heating up too high again.

I slide off the bed, smoothing my grey wool skirt and checking my hair in the tiny mirror above the sink in the corner. I must have slept well, because I feel better than I have in weeks. I'm lucky to have got a private room, with the NHS being what it is these days.

I turn round as the glass door whooshes open, and a nurse in what look like pink pyjamas pushes a small trolley into the room.

'Excuse me?' I say. 'I don't suppose you know where my husband David is?'

She's so focused on her other patient she doesn't hear me. 'How are you feeling, love?' she asks the woman in the bed, reaching up to replace her IV bag. 'Caused a bit of a stir, you have. Your family have arrived; they're worried sick about you. Be nice if you could sit up and give them a smile when they come in.'

She scans the clipboard on the foot-rail, and then checks the monitors hissing and beeping to the side. I don't want to interrupt, but I'm getting slightly anxious to see my husband. I cough politely as she adjusts the straps holding the patient's ventilator mask in place. 'I'm sorry to bother you, but if you could just tell me the way to reception, I'm sure I'll manage to find him.'

She must have heard me, but she doesn't even look up. Is she deaf? Or just plain rude?

'I know,' she sighs kindly, straightening up and patting the woman's still hand. 'You'd wake up if you could.'

I'm in front of the door. She can't ignore me now.

She pushes the trolley right through me.

I feel dizzy, as if I'm standing too close to the edge of a cliff. Behind me, the ventilator hisses rhythmically. It sounds as if someone is breathing in my ear.

This is a private, single room, but there's a patient in the bed. *The bed I just got out of.*

On the green visitor's armchair by the window, someone has carefully folded a neat pile of clothes: a dark skirt, a pink-and-grey striped blouse, a pink pullover. The toe of a pair of charcoal tights peeks out from beneath the pile. Under the chair, two black driving shoes are neatly lined up side by side.

The same clothes I was wearing when I came into the hospital. The clothes I'm still wearing now.

You'd think I'd be frightened, but I'm not. I know I'm not dead. The machines tell me that. I stand at the foot of the bed and look down at myself. One breathes for me; another measures every heartbeat. I'm not dead. But I'm not *here*.

At my neck – at the neck of the woman on the bed – the gold crucifix I inherited from my mother catches the light. I haven't taken it off since the day she died, seventeen years ago. Automatically, my hand goes to my throat, and closes around its echo. It feels real – *I* feel real – to me.

I don't know if I'm going to die soon. I don't know if there will be a white tunnel and light; or if I can still . . . *go back* . . . into my body. I don't know how long I have to choose; or if it's even up to me. But if I am going to die, I have to see David first.

The door swishes open again; you wouldn't think a ghost – or whatever I am – could jump, but I do.

The nurse is back, a white-haired doctor in tow. With them is my family. David, Grace and Tom I expected, but I'm startled to see Susannah. I thought I was the only one who even knew where my younger daughter was. She telephones me every six weeks or so, and I wire her money. I haven't told David, of course.

Grace must have tracked her down somehow and flown her back home. Which means I've been sick longer than I thought. How many days have I been here? What's wrong with me?

I call their names, but of course they can't hear me.

Oh, David. He looks tired and anxious as he goes to the bed and stares at the woman lying there. I touch his face, but he can't feel me. And worse: I can't feel him. My fingers stroke his cheek, but it's as if I'm smoothing air.

He grasps his wife's hand, and suddenly I yearn desperately to be able to feel his touch. I close my eyes, and will myself back in my own body. I open them, and I'm still here, in limbo.

I'm brought up short by the thought. Is that what this is? *Limbo?*

Long-forgotten phrases from my schoolgirl Catechism come back to me. *Limbo is the border place between Heaven and Hell where dwell those souls who, though not condemned to punishment, are deprived of the joy of eternal existence with God.* But it refers to children who haven't been baptized, or those who lived before the birth of Christ, not adults, practising Catholics like me.

Not limbo, then. But . . . perhaps purgatory.

Purgatory. For those who must atone before they can be forgiven. It's not fashionable to talk about purgatory any more; these days it's all about tolerance and loving the sinner, if not the sin. But that doesn't mean purgatory doesn't exist. Is there something I need to put right before I can move on? Something I need to stay for?

I look at my daughters, on opposite sides of the bed, unable to come together even now, at a time like this. At my husband, who hasn't spoken to his younger child in nine years.

I'm ready to die. Not eager, certainly, but ready. I believe God is waiting for me. I've been lucky enough to know love in my life: the love of a good man, and the love of my children. There isn't really much more to say about me; I didn't have a career, or change the world. I was happy to stay at home and look after my family. I think girls these days have it much harder, despite all their washing machines and expensive clothes. All those *choices*. So much easier in my day, when you knew what was expected of you and how to give it.

David will survive without me. He'll grieve, of course, which is as it should be. And then he'll recover, and live the rest of his life, which is as it should be too.

But I worry about my Susannah. She still needs me so much.

I follow her as she stalks over to the window, peering through the slatted blinds with one finger. I can tell she's itching for a cigarette. Gently, I stroke her hair, though of course neither of us can feel it. Such pretty blonde curls she used to have when she was little. Now look at it: thick, matted rat's tails reaching halfway to her bottom, tied back with an old elastic band. And the way she dresses these days. Like an emu, Grace says it's called. No: an 'emo', that's it. All black and ugly. When I think of the care I took of her when she was a baby, worrying every little graze would leave a scar. And now look: all those ugly tattoos and pieces of metal stuck into her face. She looks like a bundle of wet newsprint. Why would such a lovely girl want to deface herself the way she has?

Then I see her expression as she watches David put his arm around Grace. Grace, our perfect daughter; the daughter who turned out so well, the daughter we can be proud of. Such a credit to her parents.

It never seems to have occurred to David that if we take the credit for Grace, we must take the blame for Susannah too.

'This is too weird,' Susannah says suddenly, pointing towards the bed. 'Look at her. You can tell. She's not even *there*.'

'Don't say that,' Grace snaps. 'Of course she's there.'

Typical Grace. Always believing that if she wants something badly enough, she can make it happen. That may be true of passing exams or getting into Oxford, but it's not true of life. She's still got a hard lesson to learn.

She pushes herself too hard. She's got so *thin*. She's not eating properly. I know she and Tom have been trying for a baby, but she needs to look after herself better if she wants to fall pregnant. She should take a leaf out of Susannah's book and try to relax more. I know how proud David is of the fact that she takes after him, but a career isn't everything. I managed fine without one.

Tom puts a supportive hand on his wife's shoulder. To look at them now, they seem like the perfect couple, though I've never been so sure. They have the perfect life, which isn't quite the same thing.

But still: Grace is flanked, supported, by her husband and her father. And Susannah has no one.

We only conceived Susannah because David, a lonely only child, wanted Grace to have someone to play with. Even before she was born, her existence was secondary to her sister's.

Unlike my first pregnancy, I had a very difficult time when I was expecting Susannah. They'd withdrawn the drug that'd given me Grace by then, and so I worried constantly that I'd lose the baby. I was tired all the time, had appalling morning sickness, couldn't sleep and my blood pressure fluctuated wildly. Grace had been born at home with just a midwife in attendance, but clearly that was never going to be possible with Susannah.

In the event, my waters broke five weeks early. After fourteen painful hours of labour, Susannah went into foetal distress, and had to be delivered by forceps. I bled very badly. They told me then there would be no more children. No son to carry on the family name.

Right from the start, David didn't bond with the new baby the way he had with Grace. He rarely picked her up if she was crying, and insisted she sleep in her own bed rather than share ours. The only time he photographed her was when Grace was holding her. My mother said it was only to be expected, that all men found small babies boring, but I remembered how besotted he'd been with Grace when she was born, and it hadn't just been the novelty of new fatherhood. He was *devoted*. Overly so, my mother said. He got up to see to Grace in the night, he soothed her when she was teething and rubbed her back when she had colic. He even took her into work when she was all of nine months old.

Grace, however, was thrilled with the new arrival; a month shy of her third birthday when Susannah was born, she was old enough to take her new duties as big sister very seriously. She loved helping me bathe or feed her, carefully spooning apple purée into Susannah's gummy smile, her own mouth opening and closing in the unconscious mimicry of mothers the world over.

But as David's indifference coalesced into cool detachment, Grace picked up on it, and, naturally, aligned herself with her father. She still loved her sister, but the feeling was tempered with a faint sense of disapproval; even before there was anything to disapprove of. I've found it very hard to forgive David for that.

I had hoped the divide that had opened up in my family, with David and Grace on one side, and Susannah and me on the other, would eventually heal of its own accord. But then, when Susannah was four, she suddenly got sick, and I realized things were never going to change.

David is looking straight at me; or would be, if he could see me. His eyes are dry, but I can tell from the tightness around his mouth that it's an effort. David cries often, in secret, something his daughters would never guess, but I can't remember the last time he cried in public. His mother's funeral, perhaps.

He squeezes Grace's shoulders, and, watching him, I exclaim with frustration. 'Why is it always Grace?' I demand, knowing he can't hear me, as tears sting my eyes. 'What has Susannah done that makes her so unlovable to her own father? She's your daughter too! Why can't you let the past go?'

His head turns sharply. I don't know if it was coincidence, or if, somehow, I'm reaching him.

The doctor coughs for our attention, and the moment is lost. 'Your mother can't respond, but she may be able to hear you,' he says. 'We need you to keep your tone upbeat. Encourage her. She needs to know you're here.'

'I'd like to spend some time alone with her,' David says.

'Dad—'

'Please, Grace. Just go back to the waiting room. I'll come and find you when I'm ready for you to come back in. I'd like to talk to your mother in private.'

Susannah and Grace bend over the bed, and I close my eyes and try to imagine the feel of their lips against my skin. I remember how they smelled when they were babies: that warm yeasty mix of milk and talcum powder. I can't leave just yet. Not while Susannah still needs me so much.

As the door closes, David pulls up a stark black plastic chair and collapses into it.

'I won't let them give up on you,' he says fiercely. 'No matter what, I won't let you go.'

'I know,' I sigh. *'That's* why I gave Susannah my power of attorney.'

He picks up my limp hand, mindful of the IV line, and strokes it gently. 'Don't leave me, Cathy. I know I don't tell you enough, but I love you so much. I have done since the moment I laid eyes on you at the end of the pier. You lit up the world.'

He chokes off a sob. I wrap my arms around him from behind, and lay my cheek against his. A shudder runs through him, and he touches his shoulder, almost as if he can feel me there.

'I love you too,' I whisper. 'More than you know. I don't want to leave you. If I can come back, I will. But there's something I have to do first.'

Through the glass door, I see the nurse returning. As it slides open, I straighten up and slip past her. Perhaps I can walk through walls, the way ghosts are supposed to, but I don't think I'm quite ready to try that yet.

I glance back at David. I wish with all my heart that I could stay with him, but I don't have a choice.

Sighing inwardly, I go in search of my daughters.

6

Grace

Music drifts over the garden wall as I park my low-slung BMW roadster – a thirty-fifth birthday present to myself; I'm not giving it up, even for Tom's green cause – behind the house. I climb out, shivering slightly in the crisp March air, and fight down an acid wash of resentment.

Three weeks. She's been here three weeks, and in that time, she's achieved what I couldn't in five years.

I let myself through the gate and walk towards the kitchen door as a roar of masculine laughter reverberates across the garden. I don't want to be that person, the girl who's jealous of her sister for daring to enjoy herself. I don't want to be petty and small-minded. But this is *my* house, in *my* village; these are *my* friends. I've lived here five years. In less than a month, Susannah has made me feel like the interloper, an extra in my own life.

Tom's thrown open the French doors and turned on the solar-powered patio heaters, so that the conservatory is open on to the back lawn. I stand for a moment in the shadows watching, unseen.

My sister is at the centre of both table and attention; as always. On one side of her is Tom, and on the other, Blake. Claudia is chatting earnestly to a neighbour, Paul, while his boyfriend, Ned, pours everyone another glass of wine. As I watch, Blake regales them with some witty, gossipy anecdote about the modelling world to which his cutting-edge photography gives him unquestioned entrée. His gaze is on my sister; I can tell that even from this distance. Even without being able to see his face. Perhaps that's why Paul is so conscientiously keeping Claudia entertained.

Blake's a natural flirt. Unlike Tom, he always notices if I've had my hair cut, or when I wear a new dress. His hand lingers on my back a fraction longer than it should when he guides me into one of the many dinners the four of us have enjoyed over the years. But his flirtation with me is a reflexive gesture, automatic, inbuilt. With my sister it's something else entirely. Something darker, more primitive. She brings out the worst in men.

She's your sister, Grace. She needs you. Why don't you try giving her a chance?

I can hear my mother as clearly as if she were standing next to me. With a sigh, I step into the light.

'Grace!' Tom exclaims, getting up from the table and kissing my cheek. 'We were beginning to give up on you.'

'Sorry. I should've called. The Baxter case I told you about – the judge turned down the continuance, so we've got less than four weeks to prepare. It's been a difficult day, as you can imagine.' I force a lighter note into my voice. 'Are you having a party?'

He shifts uncomfortably. 'Claudia and Blake dropped by, and then Susannah invited Ned and Paul over.'

'It's OK, Tom, you don't have to explain.'

'We ordered Chinese – there's still some left.'

'I'm not hungry.'

'Let me get you a glass of wine. We've got red and white open—'

'Actually, Tom, I'm pretty tired. I think I'll go up to bed.'

'C'mon, Grace!' Susannah calls suddenly. 'Don't wimp out. Come and join us.'

'I don't think so.'

'Oh, go on. Live a little.'

'Some of us have work in the morning,' I say, pointedly.

'*Some* of us know which day it is,' Susannah smirks.

'Tomorrow's Saturday, Grace,' Claudia says gently. 'Come on. Have a drink. It'll help you unwind.'

Try taking a leaf out of your sister's book once in a while, Grace. Smile. It'll suit you so much more than that sour expression.

I push my mother's voice out of my head. Claudia's right. I need to relax.

'Actually, I could do with a glass,' I say, pulling out a chair. 'This divorce case I'm working on is enough to drive anyone to drink. The wife is worth millions, but she's squirrelled it away God knows where so her husband can't get it.'

Blake reaches across me for the bottle of wine. 'Claudia's trying to talk your sister into giving her a tattoo. What d'you reckon she should have done?'

'Are you even allowed to get a tattoo when you're pregnant?' Ned asks.

Blake grins. 'Be good preparation for childbirth. You

should've seen her yelling when she had the twins. A bit of pain before she has to do it again will be good for her. Toughen her up a bit.'

Claudia thumps his arm. 'You try shitting a watermelon and see how you like it.'

I take a large gulp of wine.

'I'm thinking of giving up tattooing anyway,' Susannah says.

Blake looks surprised. 'Oh? What'll you do instead?'

My sister leans her elbows on the table, treating Blake to an unrestricted view of her breasts, and giving him the full benefit of her turquoise gaze, as warm and inviting as the Caribbean. He can't take his eyes off her.

'Lap-dancing,' she says, straight-faced.

It shouldn't sting, after all these years, and yet it does. Men have never looked at me the way Blake is now looking at Susannah. Not even Tom.

It's not just that she's beautiful, although, even with her tattoos and piercings and matted hair, she is. She has a dangerous, fearless charm that draws you in; there's a whiff of sulphur about her, Tom always says. She's funny and sexy and likeable; it's not just men who can't resist her, but women, too. They want to be near her, as if some of her allure will rub off on them.

I'm not beautiful. I'm not even pretty; I'd scrape to reach attractive. I know that. I know too that looks are not supposed to be important. But it's like being told that money isn't everything: the only people who really believe that are those who have it. Being plain, especially when you're young, is a misery you have to experience to understand. It's all very well to talk about beauty coming from within and being in the eye of the beholder, but the truth is that as a teenager – and actually, for most of our lives – looks do matter, are the *only* thing that matters, and without them, you're second rate, no matter what else you do.

My mother once admitted, under pressure, that my sister was prettier than me. She followed it with words like *striking* and *handsome* and *intelligent features*, but all I heard was that my younger sister outranked me in the only way that counted.

Of course, things change. I learned how to dress well, to perform a magician's sleight of hand and distract with witty conversation, chic accessories, smart friends. Success mends your looks, and so does money. Their scent makes you a different person. But when Susannah's around, it's as if I'm seventeen again, ungainly, unlovely, unloved.

'Susannah doesn't need a job,' I say suddenly. I knock back my glass of wine. 'She's not going to be staying much longer.'

It comes out more harshly than I intended, but I don't take it back. I've just come home after a gruelling fourteen-hour day, at the end of a week of fourteen-hour days, and I'm exhausted and stressed and worried, *so* worried, about my mother. And here is Susannah, relaxed, sleek, borrowing my clothes and returning them torn, dropping her damp towels on the bathroom floor, stealing from my wallet, losing my phone charger, smoking in the living room despite me asking her not to, burning the sofa with her cigarettes, drinking Tom's twenty-five-year-old malt, talking for hours on the phone to America, crashing my computer, denting Tom's car, seducing my best friend's husband, and—

—and yes, I know I sound like a teenager, *I do know*, but Susannah is behaving like one.

'Grace!' Tom exclaims.

'Well, she can't stay here forever. She has a life to go back to. A job. I'm sure she wants to get back to the sunshine as soon as she can.'

'Actually, Grace. About that. Me staying here, I mean.' Susannah hesitates. 'There's a bit of a problem with my visa. I'm sure I can sort it out, but it might take a bit of time—'

'What sort of problem?'

'Well. They'll deport me if I go back. But I'm sure I can fix it,' she adds hastily. 'It's just a question of filling in a few forms.'

She smiles, challenging me to call her bluff. *She knew about this*, I realize suddenly. She knew before she even left Florida. She let me beg her to come home, pay for her flight, and keep her once she arrived, knowing this. And she's telling me now, in front of my friends, because she knows I can't say anything.

I should have known. *I should have known*.

Tom's calming hand is on my arm. 'I'm sure it'll be sorted by the time Catherine's out of hospital, Grace. The doctors still don't know when she'll come round. Susannah can't leave before then, anyway.'

'We'll find her something to keep her busy,' Claudia smiles. 'Even if this village isn't ready for a tattoo parlour quite yet.'

'All these designs you do,' Paul asks. 'Did you train at art school, or was it something you picked up as you went along?'

'Susannah had a place at the Slade,' Tom says, seizing the conversational lifeline. 'I think you did a year or two, didn't you?'

'I left at the end of my first year,' Susannah shrugs.

'Oh, yes. You got pregnant with Davey, didn't you?' I say.

Ned picks up the wine bottle, and refills his glass. 'She should speak to Michael. Shouldn't she, Paul? He's an artist who lives in the village,' he explains, turning to Susannah, 'very talented. He's got a lot of contacts in Oxford. He might be able to get you work at one of the galleries or something if you do end up staying around for a while.'

My hand trembles as I raise my glass to my lips. Already she's weaving her web, inserting herself into other people's lives, whether they realize it or not. I paid for her to come home because I felt it was the right thing to do, because I'm her sister, because – despite everything – I love her and I couldn't bear the thought of her losing her mother without having had the chance to say goodbye. But now I wish I'd never picked up the phone.

'Will you be seeing Davey and Donny while you're here?' I ask over-loudly. 'Or will you be *too busy* with everything else to have time to drop in on your sons?'

'It's not about what I want, Grace,' Susannah says coolly. 'It's about what's best for them.'

I can't help a snort of derision. 'Since when?'

'I don't want to get into it now. If you had kids of your own, you'd understand.'

It surprises me every time. The pain. I've learned to avoid the obvious dangers – I cross the road so I don't have to walk past Mothercare, I time my journeys to avoid the school run – but I'm still ambushed a hundred, a thousand, times a day. A lost dummy in the street. A pregnant woman on the Tube. A child screaming at the supermarket checkout, a TV ad for Pampers, a leaflet through the door about family insurance. Every single time it's as raw and bitter and new as the day I walked out of Janus' surgery.

'If I had kids of my own,' I spit, 'they wouldn't have been living with complete strangers for the past five years while I spent my time screwing anything in trousers.'

This time, the silence is absolute.

'Grace—'

'Oh, come on, Tom!' I cry, rounding on him. 'Don't tell me you're defending what she did! She walked out on those boys! She left them; she dumped them in foster care, so she could run off to America with her new boyfriend. She's been here for weeks and hasn't even *tried* to see them!'

'Grace, we can discuss this later.'

Susannah is staring at the table, as if fascinated by the wood grain. Her face is pale, with two high spots of colour on her cheeks.

My anger leeches away as abruptly as it flared. I feel sick at heart.

I stand up and smile stiffly. 'I'm so sorry. Will you all excuse me? I think I'll make myself some tea and go to bed. I really do have a bit of a headache.'

In the kitchen, I lean against the counter and briefly close my eyes, hot with shame. *How could I say that?* Even if it's true, how could I say that, in front of everyone? What is it about my sister that brings out the worst in me?

It's not your fault. She'll understand, when you explain everything. She knows she's made mistakes. All she's looking for is a second chance.

'Oh, Mum,' I whisper. 'Why aren't you here when I need you?'

This isn't about Susannah, not really. I hate what she's done, but I love her, truly I do. She just reminds me fiercely of all I've lost; of all I can never have. To throw her motherhood away so carelessly – I can't bear it.

'What is it, Grace?' Claudia asks softly from the doorway.

I press the heels of my hands against my eyes. 'I'm just tired. I need to get some sleep.'

Claudia takes the kettle from my hands. 'Grace, I know what you're thinking. I'm exactly the same when my brother comes home. Susannah is interesting and different, but she isn't you.'

It's not a competition. Only you ever thought it was.

I laugh shortly. 'You sound like my mother.'

'I know how hard this has been on you. You and Catherine were so close—'

'*Are* so close. We *are* so close.'

She flushes. 'Of course, I didn't mean – I'm sorry.' She hesitates. 'Look, Grace, is there something else? Something you're not telling me? I don't want to pry, but you haven't seemed like yourself for weeks. If it's about Tom, you know you can tell me. I won't say a word to Blake.'

'It's not Tom.' I bite my lip. 'Well, not in the way you mean.'

Claudia waits. She has an extraordinary way of making you feel like you have all the time in the world, that you are the only person in her life at this moment who matters.

'I didn't tell you,' I say. 'I couldn't – I wanted to, but I couldn't. I was so sure I could fix it – and then I couldn't, but you were pregnant . . . how could I tell you then, how could I ruin it all for you?'

She wraps her arms around me, and finally it all spills out as I sob into her shoulder: the waiting, the tests, the hard, inescapable truth that I will never have a child of my own. After all these weeks of bottling it up, trying not to burden Tom with my grief when he is already dealing with his own, it's such a relief finally to tell someone.

'If only you'd said something,' Claudia sighs, when I've finally finished and have reached the ragged, hiccupping stage. 'I can't bear to think that you went through this alone.'

'I had Tom.'

She hands me a box of tissues. 'Yes. You had Tom. So, what will you do now? Adopt?'

'No. I'll get a cat. Lots of cats. I'll be the lady with the cats, I'll smell of pee and die alone, with my cats. Children will cross the road when they see me coming.'

'They already do! Grace,' she says, quietly, to be sure I'm listening, 'Grace, you know I'd have a baby for you if you asked. After the current tenant has vacated, of course,' she adds, glancing down at her belly. 'I mean it. You know that, don't you?'

For a moment, I'm too moved to speak.

I blow my nose noisily. 'Forget it. They'd never let an old crone like you be a surrogate. You'll be forty at Christmas. Your eggs are practically on Zimmer frames.'

'I make beautiful babies,' Claudia says, mock-indignantly.

'Yes. You do.'

She gives my hand a quick squeeze. 'And you make a beautiful godmother.'

I'm about to make a snappy reply, something witty involving coaches and horses and fairy godmothers, but my attention is caught by a movement in the darkened hallway. My sister has her back to me. She's standing on tiptoe, her short black skirt – *my* black skirt, I realize – riding up as she twines her arms around someone's neck. She tilts her head, kissing him.

And the man kissing her back is Tom.

7

Susannah

Grace is seriously pissed off with me. I can always tell. God knows why: these are all her bloody friends. You'd think she'd be pleased I've organized this party. If things were left to her, she'd have no social life at all.

She gulps back her wine, glaring at me over the rim of her glass. I ignore her, and turn my baby blues on Blake instead.

'I'm thinking of giving up tattooing anyway,' I say, treating him to an eyeful of cleavage.

He swallows. 'Oh? What'll you do instead?'

'Lap-dancing,' I deadpan.

I could pole-dance round Blake's cock, judging from the expression on his face. If I crook my little finger, he'll come running, gorgeous pregnant wife or not. Men. They're all the same.

Grace's eyes bore into me. God, she's so fucking *anal*. She looks like she's got a broom stuck up her arse, and if she grips that glass any tighter, it'll shatter. It's not my fault she's got the hots for Blake; not that she'll ever admit it. I don't want to rain on her parade, but he'd never give her a second glance in a million years. She's *so* not his type. Even if she did throw caution to the winds and open her legs, who'd want to have a fling with a goody-two-shoes like her? Blake must get enough of that missionary position, no-swallowing crap at home.

'Susannah doesn't need a job,' Grace blurts suddenly. 'She's not going to be staying much longer.'

Uhh-ohh.

'Grace!' Tom exclaims.

'Well, she can't stay here forever. She has a life to go back to. A job. I'm sure she wants to get back to the sunshine as soon as she can.'

'Actually, Grace,' I say, crossing my fingers and hoping she doesn't totally freak out. 'About that. Me staying here, I mean. There's a bit of a problem with my visa—'

I was right to tell her in front of everyone, I think. Grace always knows when I've pulled a fast one. She'd have chucked me out on the street if we'd been on our own. But because her friends are here, she keeps quiet. Poor, pathetic Grace. Always needing to be *liked*.

Tom and Claudia try heroically to steer the conversation back into calmer waters, but it's a lost cause. I brace myself. It takes a lot to make my uptight big sister lose her cool, but when she does, she flips big time.

'Susannah had a place at the Slade,' Tom is enthusing. 'I think you did a year or two, didn't you?'

I flick open my cigarettes. 'I left at the end of my first year.'

'Oh, yes. You got pregnant with Davey, didn't you?' Grace snaps.

Bitch. She didn't have to tell everyone. That baby cost me my career.

I'd never have got pregnant at all if Brady hadn't gone on and on about how much he wanted to be a father, what beautiful babies we'd make. OK, he didn't actually *tell* me to come off the Pill, but that's clearly what he meant. He was thirty-seven, nearly twice my age; I figured he was ready to settle down. Talk about naive. He kept saying how thrilled he was, until one day he stopped being quite so thrilled, and ran for the hills. He didn't even pack.

By then, I was seven months pregnant, too late for an abortion. So, there I was: nineteen, stuck in a crappy bedsit with a screaming baby on my own. Mum helped out with money, but Dad didn't even talk to me for a year.

'Will you be seeing Davey and Donny while you're over?' Grace demands now. 'Or will you be *too busy* with everything else to have time to drop in on your sons?'

Great. Rub it in that I fucked up *twice*, why don't you?

'It's not about what I want, Grace. It's about what's best for them.'

'Since when?' she sneers.

It's so goddamned easy for her, isn't it? Amazing Grace, mistress of all she surveys. Perfect life, perfect house, perfect husband, perfect job. She doesn't know what it's like to have everything you touch turn to shit. She's got no idea what it's like to be alone. She's always had Tom. She's never had to struggle for anything; it's all just been handed to her on a plate. No doubt when she decides she's got time in her perfect little life for a couple of perfect children, she'll have them on demand, a boy and a girl, born bang on their due dates so she can get right back to work.

I didn't *want* to give up my kids. I didn't have any

choice. My marriage to Donny's father had broken up before Donny was even born, and he didn't pay a fucking penny in child support. I'd like to see how Grace would've coped. Where was she when I was stuck in that crappy council flat with two screaming kids, no money, no job, and no bloody man? I couldn't sleep, I couldn't eat; I was down to less than six stone, and some days I couldn't even face getting out of bed. Grace never even came to visit me in hospital after I OD'd on my anti-depressants and had to have my stomach pumped. So, she paid for a private room. So what? I'd just lost my kids – Social Services stuck them into foster care before I'd even come round – and needed a bit of TLC from my sister, not a fucking open chequebook.

I stub out my cigarette, my hand shaking. 'I don't want to get into it now,' I say. 'If you had kids of your own, you'd understand.'

'If I had kids of my own,' Grace snaps, 'they wouldn't have been living with complete strangers for the past five years while I spent my time screwing anything in trousers.'

Nobody breathes. I bite my lip, unable to believe she just said that, in front of everyone. How *could* she?

Does she think I *wanted* to fuck up my life? That I used to lie in bed when I was a little girl and dream of reaching the age of thirty-four with three divorces under my belt, a father who hasn't spoken to me in ten years, and two boys by two different men who wouldn't recognize me if they passed me in the street? Some happy-ever-after. I haven't done a single worthwhile thing in my entire life except, perhaps, letting my sons go so they could have a chance of a better life without me.

'She didn't mean any of that,' Tom says, as Grace runs into the house.

'Yes, she did, Tom.'

Claudia stands up. 'Let me go and talk to her.'

'Grace isn't herself at the moment,' Tom sighs, as Claudia goes inside. 'She's been having a difficult time recently. She's just lashing out, and you're an easy target.'

I push back my chair. 'She's right. I can't stay here forever. The doctors have no idea when Mum's going to wake up, and you don't need a permanent houseguest. I'll go in the morning.'

'Don't be silly. It'll blow over. Anyway, where would you go?'

He has a point. But I don't want to stay, not if it's going to be like this. I'd rather take my chances with US Immigration. I thought Mum being sick might bring us closer together, but Grace is just a total bitch. To think I actually felt sorry for her at the hospital because she was so upset about Mum! I can't believe we're even related, never mind sisters. We're not friends. We're never going to be. The sooner I leave, the better for all concerned.

I go into the house, pausing only to get a new pack of smokes from my bag on the hall table. There's a low murmur of voices in the kitchen; and then I hear the sound of someone sobbing. *Grace*.

OK, I know I shouldn't listen. But Grace crying? Grace *never* cries. Not even when our marmalade kitten, Orlando, climbed into the wheel-arch of next-door's car for a nap and got turned into roadkill when Mr Tanner left for work. Buttoned-up, freaky-calm Grace doesn't do excessive displays of emotion. She'd spontaneously combust before she lost it over a man.

'. . . get a second opinion,' Claudia is saying. 'This is just one doctor, one test. He could be wrong—'

'He's not wrong. I saw the ultrasound. There's so much scarring on my ovaries, there's no chance of getting a decent egg, even with IVF.'

'What about using a donor egg?'

Grace laughs shortly. 'I'm that one-in-a-million woman who has also been blessed with a T-shaped uterus, apparently, which means I can't carry a baby to full term. There's no chance, Claudia. We can't even adopt, because of Tom's heart. I'll never be a mother. I'll never have a child.'

For a long moment, all I can hear is the muffled sound of my sister weeping into the shoulder of her best friend. *Grace can't have a baby?* The Golden Girl, the woman who has everything, the girl with the perfect life? She can't do the one thing I've always found too bloody easy?

I know it's mean, but I can't help a brief spurt of pleasure. It's about time she tried eating some of the shit I've been shovelling all my life. You've got to love the irony. Having a baby ruined my life. Now it seems *not* having one is going to ruin my sister's.

Claudia is talking again, and I edge closer towards the kitchen, straining to make out the words. 'Grace, you know I'd have a baby for you if you asked,' she says. 'After the current tenant has vacated, of course. I mean it. You know that, don't you?'

Christ. That's big of her. I wouldn't fucking volunteer, and I'm Grace's sister. I hated being pregnant. There's no way I'd go through it again.

A door opens behind me, and I jump, guiltily stubbing my cigarette into a depressed-looking cheese plant.

'Susannah?' Tom says. 'Is everything OK?'

Poor bastard. No wonder he looks so bloody miserable. He's stuck with Grace for the rest of his life, and now there won't be any kids to lighten the gloom. Impulsively, I throw my arms around his neck, and kiss him on the mouth. 'It will be, Tom,' I say.

I peer out of the lounge window again, impatient for Grace and Tom to get home from work. I hate being stuck here by myself all day. On the days when Tom can spare his hybrid, I can drive down to see Mum, but otherwise there's nothing much for me to do around here, apart from go on lots of walks. I've never been the country type.

I scoop another spoonful of Ben & Jerry's straight from the tub. Grace'd have a fit if she saw me. Grace has a fit over something I do most days. I'd forgotten what a pain my sister can be to live with. Even when we were kids, she'd freak if I left a damp towel on the bathroom floor, or spilled eyeshadow on her half of our dressing table. One summer, she put blue masking tape down the middle of our room to divide it in two. I wouldn't have minded so much, but the door was on *her* side. She made me pay a toll from my pocket money just to get into bed.

Crap. I stare in dismay at the lump of chocolate ice cream sliding down my shirt. Or, to be precise – and more to the point – down *Grace's* shirt. Her £295, never-been-worn, still-sporting-the-price-tag, black silk Dolce & Gabbana shirt.

Grabbing a linen tea towel, I mop ineffectually at the mess. Fuck. She'll have a total shit fit when she finds out. She's so anal about her clothes. Strike that. Grace is anal about *every*thing.

Oh, well. Maybe it'll come out in the wash.

Dumping the empty ice-cream tub in the bin, I pull out my cigarettes and light up in defiance of Grace's no-smoking-inside-the-house edict. It's bloody March, and she expects me to freeze my tits off outside every time I want a fag. Won't let me wear my shoes in the house. Won't let me eat in front of the TV in case I spill something. It's like living with the *Homes & Gardens* Taliban. Every time I crack open a beer, she's there with her bloody coasters. *Coasters!* Who the fuck under the age of ninety-five bothers with *coasters*?

OK, so this is *her* house. I get it. Her million-dollar, Grade II listed, Colefax & Fowler, turreted and moated fucking *castle*. But what happened to making guests feel welcome?

This place is gorgeous, but it feels more like a museum than a home. Even a peasant like me can tell how expensive it all is: antique grandfather clock in the hall, big fat leather sofas in Tom's 'den'. Matching Spode and Le Creuset in the kitchen. Wooden side tables, silver photo frames, original watercolours, books *every*where. My sister's rich. Seriously *rich*.

But I can do something she can't. For the first time in my life, I've got the upper hand. And it's time to use it to my advantage.

I jump at the sound of the back door opening, dropping my cigarette on the sofa. Frantically I brush it off, but there's already a neat brown hole in the centre of the pale aquamarine linen. I flip the cushion over, and realize I'd already done that last week when I spilled a glass of red wine. Shit! I turn it back, and cover the burn mark with a velvet throw. Maybe she won't notice.

'Tom? I've left the rotavator in the— Hey, Susannah.'

I grimace. 'Call me Zee. Grace is the only person who calls me Susannah, apart from my mother.'

Blake strolls into the sitting room, all six-pack and testosterone. Seriously, the guy is *hot*. Ashton Kutcher's better-looking, sexier older brother. Lean, ripped and boasting quite a package, if I'm not mistaken. And I'm usually not.

I reach for my smokes again. 'Tom's not back yet. Got held up in surgery. Want me to pass on a message?'

'He'll figure it out.' His gaze slides down my bare, tanned legs, then back up to my cleavage. 'You spilled something on your shirt.'

'Blame the boys from Vermont.' I exhale a cloud of cigarette smoke. 'Guess I should change,' I add, 'now I've got company.'

I hand him my cigarette and unbutton my blouse. Blake's smile is lazy, but I know the look in his eye. Rotavator my ass. He's been hanging around here like a dog on heat since day one.

I straighten the straps of my red lace bra, but make no effort to cover up.

'You want to watch you don't catch cold,' he says, passing me my cigarette back.

I shrug, and let him look.

'Nice tattoo,' he says, pointing to the vine twining from my left shoulder, down around my waist, and disappearing beneath the waistband of my skirt.

'You should see what's at the end of the rainbow.'

His smile doesn't falter. 'Don't flatter yourself, Zee.' He hands me my shirt. 'I'll see myself out.'

I storm upstairs to put on a new top before Tom and Grace get home. Arrogant bastard! Who the *fuck* does he think he is? Acting like he's God's fucking gift. Blake may be cute, but he's not all that. I've had better. And he's kidding himself if he thinks I don't know he's interested. I can tell. I can *always* tell.

I pull a faded black T-shirt over my head and stomp back down to the kitchen. Screw Blake. I've got more important things to think about right now: like keeping a roof over my head.

I've been here five weeks, and outstayed my welcome by at least four. Any day now Grace is going to give me my marching orders. Unless I come up with a really good reason for her to let me stay.

There's a crunch of tyres on gravel outside, and moments later the slam of car doors. I take a deep breath, and dig out my brightest smile. I've only got one shot at this, so I'd better make it a good one. I reckon I can convince Grace, but Tom's going to be a harder nut to crack. This is one of the few times I can't use sex to get what I want, which is something of a novelty. If I can just get Grace to go for it, I'll be home and dry.

I open the kitchen door as Grace runs towards it, her leather shopper held over her head to shelter her from the rain. Tom follows behind, looking tired. At a guess, I'd say she's been tearing him a new one again on the way home. Probably over me. It usually is.

'What's the matter?' my sister demands. She shakes her bag, scattering water droplets, and looks suspiciously around the kitchen. 'What have you broken now?'

Remember the big picture, I tell myself firmly.

'Nothing's broken,' I say. 'But I've had a *brilliant* idea.'

8

Grace

'I'm going to give you a baby,' Susannah announces.

For perhaps the first time in my life, my sister renders me speechless. I gape at Tom, sitting next to me on the sofa. He shrugs helplessly back at me. We both turn to Susannah, who's smiling delightedly and bouncing her knees up and down in the chair opposite us. She looks like a child who's found her mother the perfect Christmas present, bursting with pride and anticipation.

'I'm sorry, Grace, I didn't mean to spy on you or anything, but I heard you in the kitchen last night when you were talking to Claudia. You said you didn't have any eggs and you couldn't have a baby, and I just thought: what about me?'

'A baby,' I repeat weakly.

'It's the obvious answer!' she says excitedly. 'I can get pregnant just sitting on a loo seat a bloke has used. I'm only thirty-four, and my eggs are raring to go. You can't have a baby. So why don't I have one for you?'

'Absolutely not,' I snap.

'Grace, don't just dismiss the idea out of hand,' she says, a little crossly. 'I know I'm not good at much, but I can have babies. There's nothing wrong with my genes, they're the same as yours. I'm the one who's fucked up, not my eggs. They're pure and wholesome and they don't have a single tattoo.'

'Please, Susannah, this isn't a game. Don't joke about it.'

'Oh, for God's sake, Grace, lighten up. Look, it's no big deal. I'm not offering you my kidney, just the use of my womb for a few months. You've let me stay here for all this time without paying for anything. Think of it as my way of returning the favour.'

She gets up and goes into the kitchen, leaving us alone for a few moments to get used to the idea. Tom and I are still sitting there in shocked silence when she returns five minutes later with a sweating bottle of beer. Automatically, I push a coaster across the table towards her.

'Susannah, this isn't like watering the plants for us while we're away,' Tom says. 'This is a baby we're talking about.'

'Yes, Tom, I do realize that. I wasn't planning to give birth to a pit bull.' She puts the beer down. 'Look, I just want to help you. I can do this. Let me do this.'

'You're really offering to be our surrogate?' I ask.

'Do you have any idea what you're suggesting?' Tom demands, sounding almost angry. 'You'd have to carry this baby – our baby, Susannah, yours and mine – for nine months, go through labour, and then give it away. Forever. You won't be able to change your mind.'

'I get it, Tom. Jack Black No Take Backs.'

'Be serious, Susannah. You'd have to sign your baby over to us, to Grace and me. What on earth makes you think you could do something like that?'

'I've done it before,' Susannah says simply.

There's no answer to that. I'll never understand how my sister could have handed her own babies over to total strangers, apparently without a second thought; how she could have abandoned her own flesh and blood, the children she had nurtured inside her own body, kissed and hugged and taken care of, in her own haphazard fashion, for so many years, and just walk away. What was it that enabled her to just switch motherhood off when she decided she wanted to do something else?

An unexpected glimmer of hope flickers into life for the first time in weeks. Susannah may be the perfect surrogate precisely because she *can* switch off.

Almost immediately, I douse it. I can hear my mother's reaction as clearly as if she were in the room with us. *Don't even think about doing this! It's out of the question! Babies aren't handbags; you can't just swap them when you feel like it!*

'Look,' Susannah says, reaching for her beer. 'I know how much you want a baby, Grace. At least this way, you'd actually be related to it too, as well as Tom. It might not be completely yours, but it'd have the same grandparents and family as if it were. And you know I wouldn't suddenly change my mind and decide to keep it. What've you got to lose?'

'It's very good of you to offer,' Tom says stiffly, 'but we couldn't possibly—'

My voice cuts across him. 'Would you live with us while you were pregnant? Stay here?'

Tom looks at me sharply, but I squeeze his hand, signalling him to be quiet.

Susannah smiles sheepishly. 'I don't have anywhere else to go.'

'We'd support you during the pregnancy, of course,' I say. 'Take care of all your expenses. I don't know how much the going rate is for a surrogacy, but we can find out, and—'

'I only need enough to get by. Maybe a bit extra for things like clothes and cigarettes—'

'You can't smoke!' I exclaim. I point to the bottle in her hand. 'Or drink! You'd have to watch what you ate – no shellfish, or soft cheeses, or pâté – and nothing with caffeine in it, so no tea or coffee, and of course nothing raw, definitely no sushi—'

'Grace,' Tom says warningly.

'We'd pay for you to go private. I know the NHS is wonderful in a crisis, but I haven't got time to sit around in their waiting rooms for hours and hours, and of course I'd want to come with you to all the scans—'

Tom stands up. 'Grace! This is all very kind of Susannah, but you and I need to talk about it before we start discussing hospitals.' He grabs my hand, none too gently, and pulls me with him. 'In private.'

As soon as we get upstairs, I round on him, alive with excitement. 'Tom, this is the answer we've been looking for! Susannah's the perfect surrogate! She's had children before, so she knows what to expect. She's got nothing else to do right now, and as long as we keep a close eye on her, make sure she eats well and takes her vitamins and goes along to all the antenatal appointments—'

'Grace, you can't seriously be *considering* this?'

'Why not? It's perfect! The baby would almost be mine. Just think – a baby! *Our* baby!'

Tom takes both of my hands in his. 'Grace, Grace. Take a step back a moment. It's a nice idea, but your sister is hardly Miss Reliable. Who knows what she'll be thinking tomorrow morning? There's no point getting your hopes up.'

'Until today, I didn't have any hopes.' I follow him as he goes into the bathroom and splashes cold water on his face. 'Please, Tom. Think about it. This is as close as I'm ever going to get to having a child of my own. I know it's complicated, but we can do this. I know we can.'

'Just because you can do something, it doesn't mean you should.'

'You were prepared to consider adoption,' I press. 'What's so different about this? At least this way the baby would actually be yours.'

'And Susannah's.'

'So what? She's right: her bad habits can't rub off on an embryo. It's not as if she's going to want to keep the baby, either. Please, Tom. You'd think about it if was anyone but her.'

His head snaps up. 'Grace, I want a baby as much as you do, but you haven't thought this through. Susannah may legally sign the child over to us, but that's not going to be the end of it. There'll never be an end to it. She won't ever let you forget the baby is hers. I'm just not prepared to go down that path.'

My chest tightens. I want to argue with him, but I can't. Susannah's been jealous of me all her life. Who knows what games she'd start playing after the baby was born? I can only imagine the trouble she'd cause once we got to the teenage stage and the child was old enough to know the truth, playing us off against each other, acting the cool aunt and undermining Tom and me whenever she got the chance.

I turn away, my eyes filling with angry tears. I don't care. If she spent the next thirty years gloating and causing mayhem, it would be worth it.

'I'm sorry,' Tom says firmly. 'But the only person I want to have my baby is you. If that can't happen, then I'd rather not have a child at all.'

'Tom's agreed to give it a try,' I sing jubilantly, pushing a large mug of coffee across the kitchen table towards Claudia. 'It took me a week to talk him round, but in the end, he said yes.'

She wraps slim brown fingers around the warm china. 'Are you sure that's wise, Grace?' she says doubtfully. 'This is a huge decision. You don't want Tom going along with it just because you've worn him down and he's too tired to say no. Having a baby is tough enough on a marriage even when you both want it.'

'Oh, he really wants to go ahead,' I say blithely. 'He was just worried Susannah would change her mind and let me down. He's as keen as me now.'

'Really?'

'It was just cold feet. All men get nervous when they stare nappies in the face for the first time. You said yourself Blake wasn't keen on the idea of kids at first, but he's marvellous with the twins now. As soon as the baby's here, Tom will fall in love with it.'

'Of course he'll love it once it arrives. That's not the point,' Claudia argues. 'He's the one who's going to be sharing his DNA with your sister. This is a *lifetime* commitment. If you force him into something he doesn't really want to do, he'll never forgive you, especially if anything goes wrong.'

I read online that negativity is bad when you're trying to conceive. I don't want to think about all the things that could go wrong. I just want to focus on the positive.

'I thought you liked Susannah. I thought everybody did.'

'Come on, Grace. Don't be like that. Your sister can be good company, but this a totally different ball game. I don't want you getting caught up in something you'll come to regret.'

I get up from the table, and busy myself arranging a packet of Hobnobs in two neat semi-circles on a plate. All week, I've had to listen to my mother telling me the same thing in my head. I don't want to hear it. Why can nobody understand what this means to me?

'If the worst happened, and Blake left you,' I ask suddenly, 'would you regret that baby?'

Her hands flutter to her swollen belly. 'Of course not. But—'

'Or the twins?'

'Grace, you're talking apples and oranges. It's not the same thing.'

'It is to me.' I put the plate on the table. 'I know Susannah's not ideal mummy material, Claudia, you don't have to tell me. But she's not going to be this baby's mother. *I* am. I'm going to be the one to raise it. She's just babysitting it for me.'

'And afterwards? She's just going to go back to being its aunt?'

'Yes. Look, she hasn't even bothered to see her own children for five years. I don't suppose she'll even remember to send this one a birthday card. Even if she does try to interfere now and again, she can't be worse than most mothers-in-law. Look at yours. You said she drives you crazy over the twins. I can deal with Susannah, especially once she goes back to America. I probably won't hear from her from one year to the next.'

'So you're OK with the fact that your pretty, badly behaved little sister is going to be spending the next nine months living with you, and your husband, who will also happen to be the father of her child?'

The wind is suddenly taken out of my sails. I hadn't even thought of it like that.

Suddenly I picture Susannah swelling with pregnancy, ripe with Tom's baby. The baby I can't give him. The baby he'll share with my sister. My sexy, alley-cat-morals sister.

No. Even Susannah wouldn't stoop that low. And Tom would never – he doesn't even like her!

Claudia is twisting the bronze-and-turquoise bangle on her left wrist, a sure sign that she's nervous or upset. For a moment, I'm puzzled; and then understanding dawns.

'This isn't about Tom,' I say shrewdly. 'You don't want her near Blake.'

'Blake has nothing to do with this,' Claudia retorts guiltily. 'It's you and Tom I'm worried about. I like Susannah, you know I do, but she's trouble. She wants what you have; she always has. And if she can't get it, she'll wreck it for you. Remember what she was like when she came to stay with you in London? She nearly got you fired when she started sleeping with your boss. She stole your grandmother's cameo brooch from your bedroom and sold it. She nearly wrecked your wedding when she turned up stoned. It's like she can't help herself. She's had her eye on Tom for years. If you can't see that, you're blind.'

'That's ridiculous. She thinks he's middle-aged and boring, she's often said so.'

'It's not about Tom. It's about taking what's yours.'

'I think you're being paranoid,' I smile. 'She's going to be pregnant, Claudia. I think that'll cramp even Susannah's style.'

'So pregnant women aren't sexy?'

'You know that's not what I meant.'

'Blake loves me being pregnant,' Claudia says crossly. 'He finds it a total turn-on, he says it's like I'm walking around with a sign saying "I've been fucked" over my head. If he had his way, we'd be at it every night.'

'If that's the case, I'd definitely keep him away from Susannah.'

For a moment, Claudia looks disconcerted. She snatches a Hobnob from the plate, and munches it defiantly while she regroups.

'What about your mother?' she demands. 'What would she have to say about this?'

Grace knows fine well I wouldn't approve.

I straighten up. 'If it wasn't for her, I wouldn't be in this position in the first place.'

Every Wednesday afternoon for the past five weeks, I've left work early and made the four-hour round-trip to Surrey, where I've sat beside my mother's bed, listening to the rhythmic hiss and whoosh of the ventilator, counting down the minutes until I can leave. I always stay for an hour, timing it precisely. Sixty minutes that feel like a year.

I have nothing to say to her any more. I know it's child-ish and unfair, that I'm just looking for someone to blame, but I'm still so angry.

We both jump as the kitchen door slams open, and Susannah bounces across the threshold, her blue eyes shining, cheeks pinked by the chill. Wrapped in one of my classic black wool winter coats, her dreads hidden under a scarlet beret, she looks unexpectedly pretty and young and normal. I'm suddenly reminded of the sister I grew up with, the girl who shimmered with happiness whenever you looked at her, always ready with a warm hug and a generous smile. A golden girl: literally and figuratively. I so much wanted to be her then. To be the sister everyone loved, rather than respected.

'You'll never guess!' she cries.

'You got a job,' I say drily.

She looks surprised. 'Actually, I did. How did you know?' She flings her beret on the table, shaking out her dreads. 'So, that artist friend of Ned and Paul's, Michael? We met up for coffee in Oxford this morning. He's a really cool guy, we totally got on. He took me into the gallery to meet everyone, and they seemed to like some of my ideas, said I had a good eye or something, I don't know. Anyway, upshot is, they offered me some work – only a couple of afternoons a week, and it doesn't pay much, but they'll let me hang some of the shows, and Michael says I can use his studio when he's working at the gallery too.'

How does she do it? Make everyone want to help her. I work so hard at friendships, I'm conscientious and loyal, I've never betrayed a confidence; yet Susannah, careless and unreliable, never even has to try.

The Devil has all the best tunes, Dad always says.

My sister reaches past me for a Hobnob, and takes two. 'Anyway, that's not what I wanted to tell you about. Where's Tom?'

'It's Saturday afternoon,' Claudia sighs.

'Watching the rugby in the pub with Blake,' I translate.

'Well, you'd better call him and tell him to switch to orange juice. We don't want him falling down on the job.'

It takes me a moment or two to catch up.

'You got it,' Susannah grins, spraying a fine mist of biscuit crumbs. 'I just peed on the predictor stick, and got a big fat blue line. It's time to make a baby.'

9

Susannah

OK. So maybe I hadn't entirely thought the logistics of this bit through.

'Tell him to just do it into one of those Pyrex jugs,' I hiss to Grace. 'Then I can suck it into the turkey baster and squirt it up.'

'Susannah! Do you have to?'

'Give me a break. You think actual sex is any prettier?'

'When Tom and I make love,' Grace says pointedly, 'there's no squirting. Things just . . . flow.'

'Well, tell him to hurry up and flow into that jug. We haven't got all day.'

We both turn and regard her husband. Tom is perched on the end of their bed in an agony of embarrassment, looking like he's about to bolt any second. The tips of his ears and what little I can see of his face beneath that hedge of hair are bright red. Seriously, Grace needs to give him a haircut. He's starting to look like a hobbit.

She disappears downstairs for the supplies. Grace being

Grace, she didn't even have to buy a turkey baster specially: she actually has one she uses at Christmas. Well, she did. I bet she buys a new one after this.

I sit on the bed next to Tom. 'So,' I say conversationally, 'do you come here often?'

'Very funny.'

'Oh, come on, Tom. Lighten up. This is the worst bit. Once it's over, your job's done. I'm the one getting stretch marks, varicose veins, piles and uncontrollable sexual urges.'

Tom blanches.

'Just kidding about that last one,' I say, lighting a cigarette.

We wait in uncomfortable silence for Grace to return. Honestly. You'd think I was asking him to make an honest woman of me.

Grace finally comes back with the jug and baster, which is rather larger than I expected.

'Are you smoking?' she demands.

'No, they're packaging chocolate in a new and improved form,' I retort. 'Yes, Grace. It's my last cigarette. Even the condemned man gets a cigarette.'

She scowls, but shoves a china bowl towards me to use as an ashtray.

'Did you warm the baster?' I ask.

'What?'

'I don't want to get frostbite up my—'

'All right, all right,' Grace says, shuddering. 'Just run it under the hot water for a minute or two. Now can we please get on with it?'

'Over to you, Tom,' I grin.

He takes the jug and turns dejectedly towards the bathroom. Moments later, he opens the door again and sticks his head around the jamb.

'Look, can you two go downstairs? I can't do it with you listening.'

'For heaven's sake,' Grace sighs. 'It's not like I haven't heard it all before.'

'Me too,' I add. 'What? These walls are very thin.'

Grace rolls her eyes. 'Oh, come on, Zee, let's go. We're not going to get anywhere like this.'

I follow her downstairs. 'Any chance of a beer?'

'One. Have you been taking your vitamins?' she calls, going into the kitchen. 'And the fish oil supplements I gave you?'

'Sure,' I lie. I hate pills almost as much as needles.

She returns with a bottle of beer and a glass. I ignore the glass, and take a slug straight from the bottle, earning another disapproving look.

'Remember, you can't have sex with anyone until we're sure you're pregnant,' Grace says. 'We have to be absolutely sure it's Tom's.'

'Let's just wait and see if it has big hairy feet and worries about its preciousssssss.'

'What?'

'Never mind.' I put my feet on the coffee table just to annoy her. 'Look, Grace. Tom is into all this, right? I mean, he's OK with me being auntie-mom to the kid? Only he hasn't really talked about it much—'

'Auntie-mom? How long did you spend in LA?'

'Long enough to get my own shrink.'

'Not before time,' Grace snorts.

I'm about to point out that she's the one trying to impregnate her younger sister with her husband's sperm without telling either of the putative grandparents, but we both leap up at the sound of Tom's tread on the stairs.

'That was quick!' Grace exclaims tactlessly.

Tom looks dejected. 'Grace, if this doesn't work, I'm really not sure I can do it again.'

Tell me about it, I think, as I stare at the jug in the bathroom five minutes later and grimace with distaste. Jeez! How long has she kept the poor bastard bottled up? There must be a pint of the stuff in here!

Holding my breath, I suck up Tom's little swimmers into the end of the turkey baster. I'm starting to wish I hadn't offered to play rent-a-womb like this. Quite apart from the teeny matter of putting a roof over my head for at least the next nine months, I do actually feel quite sorry for Grace, somewhat to my surprise. Of course, I also get a bit of a kick out of rubbing her nose in the fact that I can do something she can't for once. But if it doesn't take soon, I'm pulling out of the deal, rent-free room or no rent-free room. It's bad enough being plied with vitamins the size of horse pills and having my sugar intake monitored, but I'm buggered if I'm going to ask my big sister for permission to have a shag.

I lie on my back, and shove the turkey baster up my va-jay-jay. This is so not my idea of a good time.

I squirt.

The first time Michael arrives at the art studio wearing a skirt, I'm a little taken aback. Given his addiction to Gap khakis and sensible brogues, I really didn't see this one coming.

'Sorry to disturb you when you're working,' he says. 'Mind if I come in?'

I put down my charcoal. He's got a great pair of legs, I'll

give him that. The hips in the navy pencil skirt are a little scrawny, and I'm not sure about the pussycat bow above his cardi – a bit too Maggie Thatcher – but overall, the dude pulls it off. I like the blonde wig: very natural. And he does his make-up better than Grace; not that that's difficult. Thinking about it, I reckon frocks actually suit him better.

He hitches his handbag onto his shoulder. 'If you're in the middle of something, I could come back—'

'Forget it. I was just going to take a fag break anyway.'

Michael follows me over to the small kitchenette in a corner of the studio, his high heels clicking on the mosaic-tiled floor. I root around for two mugs amid the jars of turpentine and paintbrushes, and give them a quick rinse.

'Coffee?'

I spoon grounds into the mugs and wait for the kettle to boil. Michael hovers next to me, fiddling with the clasp of his gold charm bracelet and clearly working himself up to say something.

I take pity on him. 'Michael, is something on your mind?'

'Michelle,' he murmurs.

'I like it.'

'Thank you. It's about Blake and Claudia,' he blurts suddenly. 'I know this really isn't my place, and I hate to interfere, but I have to talk to you. One woman to another.'

'One woman to another,' I echo.

'Blake's a lovely man, Susannah, but he's terribly easily led. Claudia manages him well most of the time, but she's got a lot on her plate right now, with the twins and the new baby coming. It must be *so* exhausting keeping him on such a tight leash.' He sighs. 'I'm sure he loves her, but really, the boy is a total man whore.'

I'm more thrown by the length of this speech than by the twinset and pearls. Michael usually restricts himself to monosyllables, uttered from the side of his mouth. Clearly his alter ego has no such inhibitions.

I flip open my Marlboros. 'All very interesting, but why are you telling me this?'

'Oh, darling,' he says reproachfully. 'I think you know.'

Of course I know. I'm just surprised Michael's cute enough to pick up on it. He's seemed a bit of a dud till now.

'How often do you do this?' I ask, waving my hand to take in his ensemble. 'Does Grace know?'

'Michelle visits when I need her,' he says. 'And yes, she and Grace have met. Don't change the subject. Blake is a weak-willed man, but he's not bad. He just needs to be saved from himself sometimes. You are an extremely beautiful and sexy woman, as you very well know. He'd have to be blind not to notice. You could have your choice of men, but Claudia could never love again. He's the one for her.'

I hum a few bars of 'Jolene'.

Michael – sorry, *Michelle* – smiles. 'Exactly. Please don't steal Blake just because you can.'

'I've never understood why she'd want him,' I muse, exhaling a long stream of smoke, 'if he's so hung up on bloody Jolene.'

'Susannah, be the better man for once. Let this one go.'

He puts down his untouched coffee, and straightens his skirt. His nails are neatly manicured and painted a sophisticated nude. Everything about Michelle is elegant and understated. Despite the scolding and the schoolmarm tone, I think I like her.

'You're not gay, are you?' I ask idly, as he goes to leave.

He pauses in the doorway and gives me a cool glance. 'I'd fuck you soon as look at you,' he says. 'Do give Grace my love.'

I snort. Scratch the above. I definitely like her.

I stay at the studio longer than usual, working on my charcoal sketch until nearly nine; not because I'm particularly inspired, but because I'm desperate to escape Grace's puppy-dog gaze. It's only been three days since I did the baby dance with a turkey baster, but that hasn't stopped her bringing half of Mothercare back home in plastic bags. Overkill as usual. She'll be knitting bootees next.

God knows what Mum would make of it all, I think, as I spritz the drawing with fixative. It's lucky she's in a coma, or we'd never hear the end of it. Tom lets me borrow his little hybrid, so I've been down to see her more or less every other day for the past month or so. It's not like I've got anything else to do. I quite like spending the afternoon chatting to her. At least she can't answer back.

I tidy my charcoals away, and turn off the lights, wishing I'd driven to the studio rather than walked as I bundle up in Grace's expensive black coat and step out into the bitter night. I'd sleep here on the sofa, only it's too bloody freezing. A converted dairy on the outskirts of the village, the studio is draughty and cold at the best of times, but the light is fantastic, and there's more than enough space for Michael and me to work. Best of all, it gets me out of the house and away from the Ubermother.

I've no idea if what I'm doing is any good, but it feels liberating to let myself go on a broad canvas. There's only so much you can fit on even the best-muscled bicep. Maybe I should think about going back to college, like Grace suggested. She's even offered to pay.

I pull my hat further down over my ears. Yeah, right. I can imagine what Dad would have to say about that. He thought I was a waste of space and resources the first time round, and that was before I caught with Davey.

I'm just reaching the corner of the main road when a dark shape materializes out of the darkness ahead of me and seizes my arm. Without thinking, I grab and twist, jerking his arm back behind his shoulder and driving my knee hard into his groin. He falls to the ground, and I stamp hard on his knee so he can't rise up and chase me like the baddie in some B-movie horror flick.

'Jesus Christ!' Blake yells, covering his head. 'Stop! It's me!'

He hauls himself onto his hands and knees, coughing and groaning. 'It's not fucking funny!' he exclaims, as I burst out laughing. 'Are you trying to kill me?'

I reach out to help him up, but he bats my hand away.

'Well, you shouldn't sneak up on people in the dark,' I retort. 'You could've been a rapist or an axe murderer. How was I to know it was you?'

'Any rapist who took you on would deserve a bloody medal.'

He does look a bit the worse for wear. Blood seeps from a nasty cut to his mouth, and there's another gash in his forehead, probably from a rock or stone he hit as he went down. He struggles to his feet, but his knee immediately gives way under him. If I wasn't there to catch him, he'd have gone down again. I guess those self-defence classes weren't such a waste of time after all.

'We'd better go back to the studio and clean you up a bit,' I giggle. 'If I send you home to Claudia looking like that, she'll think you've been up to no good.'

'I'm not sure it's safe to be alone with you. Where the hell did you learn to do that?'

'Chicago. I worked in a rough neighbourhood. I thought it best to be prepared.'

'Some Boy Scout you are.'

I slip my hand through his arm – 'Ow! Mind my shoulder!' – and lead the way back towards the darkened studio. 'What were you doing skulking around out here, anyway?'

'I wasn't skulking. I was going to ask you if you fancied coming to the pub for a drink. There's a band playing tonight, they're pretty good. Thought you might fancy it.'

'What about Claudia?'

'What about Claudia?'

We reach the studio, and I unlock the door and help him inside. He collapses onto the lumpy flowered sofa, and touches his swollen lip. 'Got any ice?'

'Sorry. I can do a cold beer?'

'Fine. And can you do anything to warm this place up? It's like a frigging ice box.'

I pass him a couple of chilled cans of Stella, one to drink and one to hold against his lip, and pour myself a generous slug of Jack Daniels in lieu of a decent beer. I light the oil stove, and settle in the semi-darkness on the floor, my back against the sofa.

'How's your shoulder?' I ask.

'Bloody painful, if you must know.'

'Want me to work on it?'

'You've done enough damage.'

I put down my drink. 'Get over yourself. It's not that bad. Give me ten minutes, and you'll feel fine. Come on, take your jacket off.' I move around the sofa behind him and start to massage his shoulder. 'Most inkers have neck and shoulder issues. I took a few classes. I used to work on the team after we closed.'

'You're pretty good,' Blake acknowledges, after a few moments.

'Shut up and keep still.'

I move over his shoulders and upper back, working the muscles in firm, rhythmic circles. He smells of soap and lemons and something I can't place, something sharp and spicy. His skin feels warm beneath the thin cotton of his shirt, and I feel a sudden pulse between my legs. Oh, be still my beating knickers. Remember poor Jolene.

'Why'd you stop?' Blake complains. 'That was just getting good.'

Tell me about it. 'Maybe we should think about getting you home.'

'Are you kidding? I can't walk on this knee yet. Come on, sit down, and stop being so damned twitchy. I'm hardly in a position to jump you.'

Reluctantly, I return to the sofa, careful to leave an ocean of flowery chintz between us. Bloody Michael and his 'be the better man'. It's like having a tub of Ben & Jerry's right next to me that I'm not allowed to touch. And if you want to extend the metaphor, I'm starving. Like, I haven't eaten in months. My stomach is growling in the worst way, and I'm practically dribbling. All I can think about is getting the lid off and plunging my spoon into—

'I said, can you get me another beer?'

'All right, keep your hair on,' I say crossly.

I grab another Stella out of the fridge. As I hand it to Blake, he wraps his hand around my wrist and pulls me onto the sofa. Before I can protest, his mouth is on mine, his tongue pushing forcefully between my lips. He tastes cool and yeasty from the beer. My nipples leap to attention, and my knickers twang. It's not often a man makes me hot, but I can feel this kiss from my earlobes to my toes. I wish I could get the lyrics of 'Jolene' out of my head. The guilt is distracting.

I wriggle free, and bolt to the other side of the room, still holding the unopened beer. 'What the hell did you do that for?'

'Just checking everything is in working order, after that knee to the balls.'

I throw the can at him. Blake deftly catches it, and then leaps up, his knee miraculously cured. His eyes are dark with hunger as he pulls me into his arms.

This time, when he kisses me, I don't give 'Jolene' a second thought. I kiss him back, hard, my hand on the back of his head. His arms snake around my waist, groping under my T-shirt, homing in on my nipples, which are now the size of walnuts. We shuffle backwards towards the sofa, and I'm unbuttoning his jeans as he pulls my skirt up around my waist. My skin sings as he skims his palms across it. It's like he's got a hotline to my pussy.

Blake kicks off his jeans, half-hopping, half-falling onto the sofa, and I rip my T-shirt over my head. He pulls off my knickers, and I press my pussy into his face, moaning with pleasure as his tongue flicks around my clit like quicksilver.

This is normally the point I fake an orgasm to move things along. But for once, there's no need. A surge of electricity zips up and down my thighs. I grip his shoulders so hard that he winces and pulls me down onto the sofa beside him.

Hooking my leg over his waist, I straddle him, my dreads brushing his chest as I bend over him so that he can take my tits in his mouth. I pinch his nipples hard enough to blur the line between pleasure and pain. His cock nudges against my pussy, and I tilt my hips, drawing him in. He fingers my clit, and I rotate my hips against him, feeling my orgasm start to build again.

His eyes half-close, and his body goes suddenly rigid, his cock swelling inside me. He comes moments before I do, our bodies slick and hot against each other.

Only as I tumble to his side, panting and sweating, do I remember Grace. *You can't have sex with anyone. We have to be absolutely sure it's Tom's.*

I'm sure it's going to be fine. Next month, I'll be more careful.

It'll be fine.

10

Catherine

I've heard some ridiculous things in my time, but this baby nonsense beats everything. I'd expect such foolhardiness from Susannah, but I'm disappointed in Grace. She should know better. Only Tom seems to grasp the implications of what these silly girls are planning, but I know from experience that on those rare occasions when my daughters stop bickering for five minutes and join forces, it's nigh on impossible to hold out against them. The poor man doesn't stand a chance.

Susannah hasn't told Grace what happened the last time she was pregnant. Grace has no idea how close we came to losing Susannah. How could she, since she was never there? Too busy making a roaring success of her life in London. Who knows what will happen this time? Even Grace would never let her go ahead with this if she knew the truth. It isn't worth the risk.

When I first left my body behind at the hospital and came home with Grace, I thought my mission was to make sure she took care of her younger sister. Now I see it's so much more important than that. Life or death, in fact.

I've tried reaching my elder daughter, but I can't get through to her. I'm quite sure she can hear me at some level, but she's blocking me. As she always has done.

So I must work through Susannah. There's no point appealing to her moral sense: as far as I can tell, she doesn't have one. Instead, I play by her rules.

I wait until she's about to step into the shower one morning before launching my first serve. 'Remember how hard it was to lose the weight last time,' I murmur in her ear. 'And Grace is looking so slender these days. Funny that you'll end up the fat one.'

Susannah drops her towel, and turns sideways to study herself in the mirror. 'I'm going to get *fat*,' she says, as if the thought has just occurred to her. 'Fat for *Grace*. I must be mad. I put on three stone with Davey, and I was twenty-two then. God knows how long it'll take me to get it off now.'

I feel like the Devil in *The Screwtape Letters*, tempting the Christian to sin.

'You lose a bra size every time you have a child,' I say. *The end justifies the means.*

Susannah frowns. 'Maybe I should let Grace pay me for doing this after all. I could afford to have implants and lipo then. Or a proper tummy tuck. Yeah. That'd work.'

No. *Wrong* direction.

'What about stretch marks?' I press. I play my ace. 'The baby will ruin your tattoos. They'll be so stretched you won't recognize them.'

'I should never have offered to do this,' Susannah says crossly. 'Who wants to fuck a pregnant cow? I won't get laid for months.'

I wince at the language, but applaud the general sentiment.

'Tell Grace you've changed your mind. She'll be upset, but Tom will take your side. He doesn't want to do this anyway. He won't let her throw you out. Maybe you can take her up on that college course idea instead—'

'Grace?' Susannah calls out suddenly. 'Is that you?'

She pulls on her red silk kimono and wrenches open the bathroom door. I follow her along the corridor to the round turret room Grace uses as a study. The door is shut, but I can still hear the muffled sound of sobbing from within.

Grace lifts her head from the desk as her sister enters the room, her face pale and tear-stained. Without hesitating, Susannah pulls her into a hug and strokes her hair and promises to make it better, and I know then that my cause is lost.

When Susannah was four years old, she collapsed with bronchial pneumonia. It was frightening, of course, but the doctors gave her antibiotics, and she soon got better.

Six weeks later, just before Christmas, she relapsed. This time, it took her longer to recover. A month after they'd sent her home from the hospital, she was still drooping around the house, exhausted and listless. The doctors recommended a break from the damp English winter to kick-start her immune system, so we flew to Greece for ten days. She seemed better; until we got her home again.

Since a permanent move to the Mediterranean wasn't practical, over the next eighteen months, we got to know the Royal Brompton Hospital in Chelsea like the back of our hands. Susannah contracted pneumonia no less than thirteen times. It took three Tube trains and an hour and ten minutes to reach the hospital from our home in Hampstead, and that was without delays or strikes. There were many nights when I simply slept in an armchair in her hospital room rather than make the journey home. I'm afraid Grace rather got lost in the shuffle.

She was very good about it, of course. During term time, I left her at home with David, but at weekends and in the school holidays I had no choice but to bring Grace to the hospital with me. She spent endless hours stuck in the children's waiting room, her nose buried in a book. I don't remember ever hearing her complain.

After the last time Susannah was hospitalized, just before she turned six, they decided to try treating her at home with antibiotics. By this time, she'd developed an allergy to oral penicillin, so a nurse came to the house each morning and evening to administer a deep, intramuscular shot in her bottom. Even I was awed by the size and length of the needle. The injections were obviously very painful, and poor Susannah was absolutely terrified of them. As soon as she saw the nurse coming up the garden path, she'd start screaming and cowering in a corner of the room.

Then she began having nightmares and wetting the bed. She often cried for no reason; we'd go into the kitchen to put on the kettle, and suddenly hear screams from the sitting room. We tried reasoning with her, bribing her with a new kitten, 'tough love', but nothing seemed to work. I'd actually made an appointment with a child psychologist when chance finally revealed the truth.

'It's not funny,' I told David fiercely that night. 'Grace has been sneaking outside and ringing the doorbell when she thinks no one's looking. I *saw* her. Susannah thinks it's the nurse with the needle. That's why she has hysterics.'

'Stop over-reacting,' David snapped. 'She's just teasing her sister. It's normal, Catherine. Maybe if you stopped treating Susannah like an invalid, she'd stop behaving like one. And while you're about it, it wouldn't do any harm to remember you have two daughters, not one.'

When it came to Grace, her father was blind. The polarization in my family had never been more clear. David took Grace cycling and sailing, and taught her to swim, play tennis, roller skate. They spent whole weekends fishing at the reservoir near my parents' home, or skimming stones at the beach. And meanwhile Susannah and I snuggled up on the sofa beneath the duvet and watched *The Sound of Music* for the umpteenth time.

I resigned myself to the fact that David would never bond with his younger daughter the way he had with her sister. It was Grace's relationship with Susannah I found really troubling. Like any mother, I wanted my children to be close. When David and I were gone, Grace would be the only family Susannah had.

The day after Grace's ninth birthday – which Susannah missed, hospitalized once again – she ran away. After I'd scoured the neighbourhood in panic, I called the police and then spent ten dreadful hours imagining Grace hurt somewhere, Grace dead in a ditch, Grace still and white on a table in the morgue, until at last we got a call from the matron on duty at the Brompton's paediatric ward.

'She's here,' she said. 'She brought Susannah some

birthday cake, she said she didn't want her sister to miss all the fun. She's asleep on Susannah's bed. Grace is safe, Mrs Latham. She's with her sister. She's safe.'

Time passes strangely for me these days. An hour can seem like a minute; a week goes by in the blink of an eye. I have no idea where I am when I'm not *here* – wherever here is.

I discover that I can travel simply by thinking where I want to be. I always make sure I'm at the hospital when anyone visits; it seems rude not to be there when they've gone to all the trouble of stopping by.

Susannah is here every other day, and stays for hours. David, too, though he rarely finds anything to say. It's difficult for him to see me like this, and my heart goes out to him. Men aren't made for sickrooms. But Grace's neglect I find hard to accept. She comes once a week, for an hour, no more, and no less. For the life of me I cannot fathom why she seems so *angry*.

Grace has also been avoiding her father, which is far more unusual. She hasn't told him what she and Susannah have done. David and I have rarely agreed about anything to do with raising the girls, but I know we'd be of one mind on this.

Accordingly, when David comes into my hospital room halfway through Grace's allotted hour, she starts, guiltily.

'Dad!' she exclaims, jumping out of her chair. 'I thought you came yesterday.'

He waves her back to her seat. 'I did. The doctor asked me to come back this afternoon; they're planning to run a few more tests. Needless to say, we're still no further forward. I don't need a test to tell me what I can see with my own eyes. Nothing's changed since the last set of tests. Nothing's changed in two months.'

'I haven't been here in a week,' Grace admits. 'I've been so busy—'

'Your mother would understand. She knows you have a career. You can't be expected to put your life on hold for her.'

'She'd do it for me.'

'She's your mother. That's her *job*. She was perfectly happy looking after you two girls. But we wanted more for you, Grace.' He squeezes her hand. 'I'm glad you didn't squander the opportunities you were given. If you'd had children, it would've been such a *waste*.'

She flinches, but David doesn't notice. 'I'm only thirty-seven, Dad. It's not too late.'

He laughs. 'Don't get broody and disappoint me now. I get quite enough of that from your sister.'

'Come on, Dad. That's not fair.'

'Would you call her a credit to her parents?'

Grace hesitates. 'She's made some mistakes, but she's trying to make up for it,' she says awkwardly. 'And she comes to visit Mum every other day. She's really good about it. She's started painting again, and she's even—'

'Why are you defending her?'

'I'm not. I just think she's trying, Dad. Maybe if you—'

'Your sister's behaviour has undermined every success you've ever had,' David says harshly. 'Your mother neglected you because she was always too busy worrying about your sister to give you a second thought. Now *you're* supporting Susannah and putting a roof over her head. It's about time that girl was left to stew in her own juice. She's made her bed. She should be left to lie in it.'

I did *not* neglect Grace. Susannah *needed* me. Grace is much stronger. She never required my attention the way Susannah did. In fact, she pushed me away.

Grace holds her ground. 'It's been nine years since you even spoke to Susannah, Dad. She's changed. Don't you think Mum would want the two of you to make up now?'

'Your mother has a blind spot when it comes to your sister. If she'd listened to me and been a bit tougher on her from the beginning, she wouldn't have turned out the way she has.'

I watch Grace struggle with herself. She worships the ground her father walks on; I don't think she's ever disagreed, much less argued, with him in her life. But she's nothing if not fair.

'I think you're being too hard on her,' she manages finally. 'I don't blame you, not after everything she's done; I felt the same way for ages. But don't you think she deserves a second chance now? She flew back to be with Mum. She obviously wants to be part of the family again. Why don't you come up and stay one weekend with Tom and me while she's here? We don't have to make a big deal of it. You could talk to Susannah, and—'

'If you don't mind, Grace,' David says coolly, 'I'd like a little time alone with your mother.'

'Dad—'

'Thank you, Grace.'

Grace sighs, and then gets up and kisses her father goodbye. He doesn't hug her the way he usually does, and she looks hurt. But I know David. Grace may not realize it, but her words have had more effect on her father than she imagines. He respects her opinion. When she takes a view on something, he treats it far more seriously than he would if it came from anyone else, especially from me. If Grace is taking her sister's side, he can't just brush it off.

It's about time Grace gave something back to Susannah. She's been Miss Superiority for far too long. I've been against this baby nonsense from the start, but if it swings the balance of power a little towards Susannah, maybe it's not all bad.

I watch my daughters closely the next evening, noticing the subtle changes already developing in their relationship. Grace bites her tongue several times when she would have rapped out a sharp comment, allowing Susannah to pour herself a glass of wine from the bottle in the fridge, and even to disappear outside several times for a cigarette without saying anything, regardless of the fact that she may already be pregnant. As she points out to Grace when she finally risks an objection the third time Susannah goes off to smoke, I suppose we should be grateful it isn't marijuana or something worse. Susannah is well aware of the liberties she's taking, and of Grace's unnatural restraint, the sly little besom. Heaven help us all if she does fall pregnant.

Susannah lounges against the kitchen island as Grace makes dinner, twisting her dreadful hair around her fingers. Even though she's a far better cook than Grace – my eldest daughter is domestically challenged: at ten, she made me tea without removing the teabag, and at sixteen, boiled an egg without putting any water in the saucepan – Susannah makes no effort to help. No doubt she's got too used to being rebuffed.

'What did Blake want?' Grace asks casually, as she melts a little butter in a pan on the stove.

Susannah stiffens. 'Blake?'

'Tom said he saw Blake's car in the driveway when he was walking back from the station, but Blake had gone by the time he got up the hill.'

'Oh. Yeah. He just stopped by to say hi to Tom. He couldn't wait. I'm sure he'll catch up with him next time.'

Susannah's up to something. Pound to a penny this man's at the bottom of it.

'Michael said you were at the studio all day yesterday,' Grace says, adding flour to the melted butter and stirring in the milk. It's not how *I'd* make béchamel, but Grace always thinks she knows best. 'He thinks you're doing some great work, Zee. He was even talking about you holding a show in the summer. Of course, that'll depend on how things go,' she adds hopefully. 'Have you—'

'It's a bit early yet, Grace,' Susannah says quickly.

'Sorry. Of course it is. I didn't mean to—'

'I'm not even due till Tuesday. It won't have worked the first time, anyway. We probably did it all wrong.'

'Maybe you should go and put your feet up,' Grace suggests brightly. 'Just in case. I can finish up here.'

'Well, if you're sure. I do feel a bit more tired than usual.'

Grace misses her smirk as she goes upstairs. I follow, wondering what the little witch is up to. I love Susannah, but I know her flaws better than anyone. I wouldn't put it past her to fake a pregnancy just to get her sister running after her and waiting on her hand and foot. One thing I know for certain: if Susannah ever does get pregnant, nine months is going to feel like nine years for all of us before we're through.

Susannah shuts her bedroom door behind her, and pulls her leather satchel out from beneath her bed. She riffles through it for a moment, then retrieves a pink-and-white box shoved towards the bottom. My heart sinks as I read it: 'First Response 6 Days Early Pregnancy Test'.

I pace impatiently as Susannah disappears into the bathroom. If the test is negative, there may still be time to save us all from disaster. The longer this takes, the more chance there is that Susannah will outstay her welcome, or Tom will refuse to take part in this charade. We can but hope.

The bathroom door suddenly opens, and Susannah flings herself onto her unmade bed, the little white stick still clutched in her hands.

'Crap!' she exclaims, her voice muffled by the duvet.

I peer at the stick.

I couldn't have put it better myself.

11

Grace

Susannah is violently sick, and I couldn't be happier.

'Why didn't you *tell* me?' I demand, holding her dreads out of the way as she bends over the toilet bowl. 'I'd never have let you drink so much coffee if I'd known.'

'I like coffee. I *need* coffee. It never made me barf before.'

'You shouldn't have caffeine when you're pregnant,' I scold. 'Even if it doesn't make you sick, it's bad for the baby.'

Susannah rocks back on her bare heels and wipes her mouth with the back of her hand. 'Bullshit. I drank buckets of Nescafé with the boys, and they were fine. I didn't have morning sickness with either of them. I bet this one's a girl. Everyone says they make you much sicker, something to do with the hormones.'

I hand her a flannel so she can clean her face properly, and quickly squirt Domestos around the rim of the toilet bowl. 'You have to start taking care of yourself properly, Susannah. These first few weeks are crucial. No alcohol, no caffeine, and *definitely* no smoking.'

'Give me a break. Christ, if alcohol was bad for babies, half the population would be gaga. How d'you think most of us are conceived?'

I decide to leave this argument for another day. 'How long have you known?'

'I only did the test last week. I knew you'd go off the deep end once I told you, and I didn't want you to get your hopes up if it was a false alarm.' She turns on the tap and cups her hands under the tap, splashing cold water on her face. 'I'm about five weeks gone, if you really want to know.'

'Of course I want to know! I want to know everything! Oh, Zee. You're pregnant! We're going to have a baby!'

'Grace, let go of me and calm down. You're making me feel sick again with all this dancing around.'

She does look a bit green. I release her and perch on the edge of the bath. 'Sorry. I'm just so excited! I can't believe the turkey baster actually worked! I never really thought it would. Wait till I tell Tom! He's going to be thrilled!'

'Don't,' she says quickly, 'not yet. It's still really early days. You shouldn't tell anyone for a while. Not even Claudia and Blake.'

'I have to tell Tom! I can't keep it secret from him. I promise I won't tell anyone else.'

'Just Tom, then.'

'Cross my heart.' I can't resist giving her another hug. 'Susannah, I can't tell you how much this means to me. You are the most wonderful sister anyone could ever—'

She wrenches herself free. 'Shit. I need to throw up again.'

She retches into the toilet until all she's bringing up is clear bile. Even though I know she's feeling dreadful, I can't help a fleeting twinge of envy that she's the one getting to experience this, however miserable it is. A new life, growing inside you! How amazing must that feel?

'When exactly are you due?' I ask, as she rinses her mouth with Listerine and ties back her dreads with a grotty elastic band.

'I don't know,' she says impatiently. 'I'm five weeks, I told you. You do the maths.'

'You're having a baby, Zee! Aren't you excited? Don't you want to know?'

'I'm having *your* baby,' she corrects. 'I've done this twice before, remember? For the next eight months, I'm going to greet each day from the inside of a toilet bowl. I'll get a great big hairy brown line running from my navel to my knickers. My tits will grow so huge they'll block light from the sun. I'll have piles, heartburn, stretch marks and varicose veins. My feet will swell up, I won't be able to smell coffee or curry without feeling sick, and my chances of getting laid will be roughly the same as the Pope's. Then, at the end of it, I'll have to shit a football out of an opening the size of my nostril. Yeah. I'm really looking forward to it.'

There's nothing she can say to dampen my euphoria. I dance back into her bedroom and throw open her wardrobe, flicking through the depressing racks of black – black T-shirts, black miniskirts, black jeans – until I find the charcoal wool tunic and cropped leggings she pinched from me last week. They're from Nicole Farhi and cost nearly nine hundred pounds, though I don't suppose Susannah knows that. Irritatingly, they look a thousand times better on her than they ever have on me.

I suppress a momentary surge of guilt as I pull the clothes off their hangers. Susannah probably doesn't earn in a year what I spend in a month at Harvey Nicks. OK, I can afford it, and I certainly work hard enough for my money, but still.

I toss the outfit on the bed. 'Come on. Get dressed.'

'What's the rush? Where are we going?'

'First, I'm going to call Dr Hagan at the Portland. If we're lucky, she'll have a cancellation today. You may not want to know when this baby's going to arrive, but I do.'

'The Portland? You mean where Posh Spice and Zoe Ball and Billie Piper had their babies? You're kidding me, right? That place must cost thousands!'

'Oh, *now* you're excited,' I smile.

'Maybe there'll be some hot footballer or rock star whose wife is having a baby at the same time as me,' Susannah breathes. 'We'll fall in love and elope, and I'll end up a WAG like Cheryl Cole.'

'Putting aside the husband-stealing bitch-from-hell aspect of that,' I point out, 'there's also the small matter of you being a little busy delivering that football through your nostril.'

'Spoilsport.' She reaches for her cigarettes on the dresser, but I snatch them away. 'Oh, for God's sake, Grace. No drinking, no smoking; I'm going to go mad. I suppose I can at least have sex now I'm thoroughly pregnant?

Something tells me this is going to be a very long nine months.

'Oh my God,' I say softly. 'Oh, Zee. Look. That's our baby!'

The sonographer moves the probe over Susannah's still-flat tanned belly. Such a shame it's covered with those ugly tattoos. She'd be so pretty if she just made a bit of an effort.

She twists her head and stares at the murky black-and-white images on the screen. 'What baby? I can't see anything.'

'There,' the sonographer says. 'That white bean. That's your baby.'

'Seriously? It looks like a squashed mosquito.'

'Didn't you ever have a scan with the boys?' I ask.

'By the time I got round to seeing a doctor, there wasn't much point,' Susannah shrugs. 'I was already so far along there was nothing anyone could do even if there'd been a problem.'

'You didn't have regular antenatal check-ups?'

'Motherhood wasn't exactly something I embraced,' she says sarcastically.

The sonographer clicks and measures, highlighting parts of the tiny image on the screen and entering the relevant data into her computer. 'I'd say your dates are fairly accurate,' she says. 'You're seven weeks along, give or take two or three days. That confirms your due date as 22 December.'

'A Christmas baby,' I breathe.

'Give or take two or three days?' Susannah says. 'You can't be any more accurate than that?'

'Why would you need to?' I ask. 'We know when you conceived.'

'This isn't an exact science,' the doctor points out. 'Normally the closest we can date with the ultrasound is within a few days of conception, which is pretty close. We usually use the date of your last period to estimate conception, and the ultrasound will simply confirm it.'

The sonographer finishes taking her measurements, then hangs up the probe on the side of the ultrasound machine, and wipes the gel from Susannah's stomach.

'It looks like the baby is developing normally so far,' she says. 'The heartbeat's nice and strong, and there's definitely only one baby, if you were concerned about twins. Everything checks out. I'll see you when you come back at around thirteen weeks for the nuchal scan.'

Susannah looks puzzled. 'What the hell is a nuke scan?'

'*Nuchal.* They'll measure the clear space at the back of the baby's neck, and check for an underdeveloped nasal bone,' I explain. 'They're looking for signs of Down's.'

'Is something wrong with the baby?' she says, alarmed.

'There's nothing wrong,' I soothe. 'It's just routine, to make sure.'

'But if there is? You'll still take it, right? You won't leave me with a—'

'Susannah, calm down. Nothing's wrong with the baby.'

'All these frigging scans and blood tests. It's all a lot more complicated than it used to be,' she grumbles, swinging her legs over the side of the bed and pulling down her T-shirt.

'Stop whining. You saw a rich footballer in the waiting room, didn't you?'

'Yeah. With his *wife.*'

She fidgets restlessly as we stand waiting in the accounts office, picking up and discarding magazines, fiddling with the water dispenser, rattling a charity box on the counter until it spills. Now that she's stopped smoking, my sister has the attention span of a goldfish. I'm already looking forward to the days when I only have a fractious toddler to entertain.

'I promised I'd take you shopping,' I say, as we walk out of the hospital. 'Where do you want to go?'

'Harrods,' she says promptly.

'Oh, Susannah, do we have to? It's a dreadful tourist trap. Harvey Nicks is much better. Or we can go to Bond Street – they have some gorgeous baby shops there.'

She looks mutinous. 'I've never been to Harrods. You said I could choose.'

I concede defeat with a sigh. Susannah steps into the street as a vacant taxi cruises towards us, flashing so much thigh I'm surprised the cabbie doesn't drive into the nearest lamp-post, and she instructs him to go to Knightsbridge 'via the scenic route'.

I study the scan pictures minutely as the cab driver takes full advantage of this licence to fleece. Maybe pregnancy is a bit old hat to her, but to me, it's the most miraculous thing in the world. I run my forefinger gently over the flimsy paper photograph. *This is real. It's actually happening. We're going to have a baby.*

Tom keeps saying it's too early to get excited, but I can't help it. For the past few weeks, ever since we did the 'baby dance', as Susannah put it, with the turkey baster, I haven't been able to think about anything else. At night, I dream of cradles; by day, I scour the internet, reading everything I can find on the subject of pregnancy. I know all the stages by heart. At seven weeks, webbed fingers and toes are poking out from your baby's hands and feet, his eyelids practically cover his eyes, and his 'tail' is almost gone. The external genitals still haven't developed enough to reveal whether you're having a boy or a girl. Your baby is about the size of a kidney bean, and constantly moving, though you still can't feel it.

I realize I've driven Susannah half-mad with my pestering and checking up, but it'll all be worth it when our baby arrives healthy. I just have to keep her on the straight and narrow for another thirty-three weeks. Surely even Susannah can manage that?

The cab finally deposits us in Knightsbridge, having taken us via Buckingham Palace, Hyde Park and the Royal Albert Hall, and I hand over a sum almost as outrageous as the one I just paid at the hospital. Susannah walks through the portals of the perfume department on the ground floor, and instantly lights up like a child in a sweetshop.

'This is awesome!' she exclaims. 'Can I have a makeover?'

'Do you have any idea how many chemicals are in all these scents?' I demand, dragging her towards the lifts. 'You really shouldn't even be using deodorant when you're pregnant.'

'Are you kidding me?'

'I can get you a herbal one,' I say earnestly, 'or you can just use baking soda. It works really well, according to an article I read recently in *Vegan Views*.'

I suspect Susannah is about to deliver anatomically impossible instructions when the lift doors open on the fourth floor.

'The toy department?' she says scathingly.

'The *Harrods* toy department,' I correct.

Even she is silenced when she glimpses the carousel in the centre of the floor. Pandas and polar bears seven feet tall tower over us. Model trains skirt a miniature painted landscape the length of a swimming pool. On one side, rows and rows of dolls are lined up like a pink tulle regiment preparing to go over the top. On the other, Lamborghinis and Ferraris vie to be first off the grid. Gauze butterflies and model planes hang from the ceiling, while in an alcove a young man demonstrates some magical coloured substance that expands into a series of bright balloons. A walkie-talkie doll the size of a three-year-old picks up a china teacup and offers Susannah tea. It's Aladdin's Cave, Father Christmas' Grotto, a glittering, seductive, tawdry Arab souk.

'Hello?' I tease. 'Calling Planet Zee. Are you still with me?'

'Can we buy something?' Susannah demands breathlessly. She looks like a small child.

'What did you have in mind?'

'I don't know! Anything! A cuddly toy?'

I smile. 'Pick one out.'

She disappears into a mountain of improbably coloured plush fur and glass eyes, but returns with an old-fashioned dark blond teddy bear. 'Look! It's Big Ted!'

'Big Ted?'

'From *Play School*. Remember? There were five toys: Big Ted, Little Ted, Jemima, Humpty and – shit, what was the last one?'

'Hamble.'

'Hamble! God, I hated that doll. She looked like Elizabeth Taylor on cocaine. I was convinced she was going to sneak into my room in the middle of the night and cut off my ears or something.'

'Susannah!'

'Admit it. She could've given Chucky a run for his money.' She dances the bear in front of me. 'Can I have him? Please, pretty please?'

My sister could charm Eskimos into buying ice. I reach for the bear, and my indulgent expression petrifies as I catch sight of the triple-digit price tag. Good Lord, has she picked up a Steiff?

'It's OK,' Susannah says quickly. 'It's too expensive. I'll put it back.'

I summon my brightest smile. 'Don't be silly. It's yours. Now, are you ready for the nursery?'

Unexpectedly, she slips her arm through mine. I'm surprised by a sudden, protective rush of love: not for the baby, but for Susannah herself. She's had a tough time for the past few years, and regardless of the fact that many of her problems have been of her own making, I still want her to be happy. No matter what she's done in the past, she's my little sister, and I love her.

The nursery floor is as spectacular as the toy kingdom. Susannah flits from one rack of tiny delicate dresses and romper suits to the next, oohing and aahing like Charlie Bucket on arrival at the chocolate factory.

I finger a pair of minute white bootees threaded with satin ribbon. They're so tiny! I can't imagine the little foot that will fit them.

I'm going to have a baby. I'm going to have a baby!

'You've got to see this,' Susannah gasps, pulling me towards the nursery furniture. 'This crib is just amazing. It looks like something out of a fairy tale.'

She stops before a pale blond wood cot, tented in pale pink gauze and muslin like a miniature four-poster bed.

'It's beautiful,' I say. 'But what if it's a boy?'

In the end, we decide on a traditional cherrywood cot that converts into a child's sleigh bed, with apple-green 400-thread pure cotton baby sheets. It's far more expensive than I'd planned, but it's fun to spoil Susannah. I find I can't say no to her: not to the armfuls of smocked Victorian night-dresses, or to the cream cashmere receiving blanket – three hundred pounds for twenty-four square inches! – or even to the ridiculous Silver Cross pram and Bugaboo pushchair that Susannah seems to think essential additions to any well-appointed nursery. We pick out tiny yellow socks, muslin mittens, lace shawls, Ralph Lauren romper suits, satin-edged matinée jackets. Even as the cashier is ringing it up, I know it's all hopelessly extravagant and impractical: everything must be hand washed, and since when did an infant appreciate Dior tailoring? But it makes Susannah so happy, and so I say yes: yes to the designer bibs, yes to the silk bootees; yes to it all.

I spend over five thousand pounds in a little over two hours, and tell myself firmly that I can afford it, and that it's worth it; that Susannah's smile is worth it.

When she drags me with childlike guile towards the jewellery department on our way out of the store, I follow. She sighs dreamily over the Tiffany counter, and I can't resist her. She doesn't have anyone to spoil her. And when I direct the sales assistant towards the solid silver bracelet from the 1837 collection that Susannah has picked out, the same bracelet Tom gave me for my last birthday, her pleasure is mine.

I'm so lucky, I think, as we jump in another taxi back to the station and home. No matter how much I spend on her, I can never repay Susannah. I'm so lucky to have her, to have this chance. I have the perfect life.

I don't think I've ever been happier.

12

Susannah

I can't tell anyone else I'm pregnant. Not now the pathetic, whiny bastard's backed out of the deal.

I can't fucking believe it. I'd never have got up the duff if I thought for one second I'd end up stuck on my own with this kid. I don't want a fucking baby! Why did I have to go and spoil a good thing? Once again, I've snatched defeat from the jaws of victory, as Dad would say. He'll disown me for life after this.

Only Grace knows. And naturally I haven't seen her for dust since the whole thing went belly up.

Shit, I am so screwed. I've got nowhere to go, and no job. I don't have a thing for the baby, apart from what Grace and I bought on our last shopping spree, most of which is pretty but useless. And I have precisely seven pounds fifty-two to my name. Grace opened her first savings account when she was eight, but I've never been a rainy-day sort of girl. My credit cards are maxed out, I'm overdrawn at the bank, and I owe nearly four grand to a loan shark at forty-two per cent interest. Without Grace, my choices are a council flat and benefits, or starve on the street.

I've called her, like, about ten times, I've left messages telling her where I am, and she hasn't bothered once to come and find me. She knows the trouble I'm in. She could afford to bail me out if she wanted to. She's my sister; she owes me!

A skanky shop assistant hovers behind me as I finger the thin, cheap babygros on the rack. 'Can I help you?'

'No, it's OK. I'm just looking.'

'How nice. For you.'

The bitch doesn't move, making it abundantly clear she thinks I'm about to stuff her crappy tat in my backpack. In fairness, if she turned her back, I would.

This is *so* not what I'd planned for this baby. She was supposed to have the best of everything. One of those fancy three-wheeled strollers. Designer outfits. Not a second-hand cot with teeth-marks in the rails and scratchy nylon dresses from a market stall.

Seven pounds fifty-two. I can buy the baby some clothes, or I can eat tonight.

I slink out of the seconds shop, my cheeks burning. I've fucked up my life before, but never like this.

It takes me two hours to walk the mile back home to the crappy bedsit I'm sharing with two other art students, who seem to spend most of their time fucking each other and getting high. The place is a total shit hole, but beggars can't be choosers. It's twenty-five quid a week, and frankly, if I wasn't a dab hand at the old teenage shoplifting, I'd be hard-pushed to stretch to that.

But the bedsit's not going to work when the baby comes. It's worse than a Victorian slum. The kid would never survive. I've already picked up a lousy cough from the mildew and damp; it'd kill a baby. The sink is backed up with grease and rotting food, the sofa and stained mattress on the floor are alive with fleas – I'm covered in bites – and fast-food wrappers and mouldy take-away boxes cover the floor. The only bathroom in the entire building is a vomit-encrusted toilet one floor down, shared by at least twenty people. When I want a shower, I sneak through the fire exit of the local swimming pool. I'll have to hope the council gives me something better when I sign on, though I'm not going to hold my breath.

Gil and Bryony have left their works all over the mattress. I step over them, glad I'm wearing DMs. Last thing I need is to get HIV jabbing my foot on a dirty needle. If I stay here much longer, I'm going to give in and start using again, and I promised myself I wouldn't while I was pregnant. But, Christ, even Grace would be tempted if she was stuck in this dump.

Fucking Grace. I know she and Tom make enough to set me up in a half-decent place, at least till I'm back on my feet. How come, no matter what happens, she ends up smelling of roses, and I'm the one covered – literally – in shit?

It's always been the frigging same. If we got caught talking after lights out, I was the one who got a wallop from Dad. We both bunked off Guides to go to the Youth Club disco, but when Mum found out, Miss Goody-Two-Shoes played her favourite 'I was just looking out for Susannah' card: I got grounded for a month, and she was Big Sister of the fucking Year. I spent six months interning for free in a magazine art department, desperate for a break, and at the end of it they just let me go and signed up a cheap new sucker. Grace got a column on the financial pages of the *Mail* simply by going to college with the right people. Guess who renewed her car insurance and twelve hours later wrote her car off and got a huge pay-out? And guess who forgot to renew it and smashed into the side of a Mercedes and is still paying off the debt?

Grace married a solvent, faithful, decent man. I shacked up with a spineless loser. She has a career. I have a record.

There's never been any point trying to compete. So, guess what? I haven't. My life has been one long might-as-well-be-hung-for-a-sheep fuck-up. It's her fault I'm up the duff, but guess who's going to pay for it? It's not fair. I want her life—

'Hello? Calling Planet Zee. Are you still with me?'

I jump about a foot, knocking a tower of fluffy red hippos to the floor. The memory of my first pregnancy is so vivid, it takes me a moment to realize where I am. *Harrods*. The most expensive fucking toy department in the world. The contrast between then and now is so surreal, I feel like I'm in some kind of weird Dallas-style dream.

Grace laughs and picks up some of the fallen hippos. I watch, but don't offer to help. Any one of these stupid stuffed animals probably costs more than I spent on Davey in his entire first year.

For a dizzying second, I hate my sister so much I can't breathe. If she'd looked after me when I really needed her, maybe my life wouldn't have ended up in such a huge fucking mess. Maybe Davey's dad wouldn't have walked out when I was seven months pregnant. Maybe I'd still have my kids. Maybe *she'd* be the one desperate for a few crumbs of happiness from *my* table.

The feeling dissolves into shame. I don't hate Grace, of

course I don't, but that doesn't mean I'm filled with sisterly peace and love right now either.

'Can we buy something?' I demand abruptly.

She laughs again. She's really loving this Lady Bountiful bullshit. 'What did you have in mind?'

'I don't know! Anything! A cuddly toy?'

'Pick one out.'

Pick one out. Price is no object, blah blah. Yeah. I get it. It must be just *peachy* to be able to buy stuff without having to look at the price. I know she's trying to be nice, but she's so fucking patronizing I want to spit. She's got no idea how the other half live.

I suddenly spot some ugly old-fashioned teddy bears like the ones they used to have on *Play School*. I look at the price tag, and nearly shit myself.

OK. Let's see what happens when I pick one of *these* out.

I go back with it and give her my best Little Sis routine. Everything's sweet till she sees how much it costs, and then I think she's literally going to have a cow.

'It's OK,' I say innocently. 'It's too expensive. I'll put it back.'

'Don't be silly. It's yours. Now, are you ready for the nursery?'

Got to hand it to her: she took that on the chin. Grace is a lot of things, but she's not a coward. She never quits. Most women would curl up under the duvet after a doctor told them they'd never be able to have kids, but not Grace. Even if I hadn't come along, she'd have sorted it somehow. Once she sets her mind on something, you can't stop her.

I suddenly remember the time she brought me a piece of her birthday cake when I was in hospital. She was only, like, eight or nine. She made it all the way across London on her own, changing trains and walking miles in the dark, just for me. I'd have been terrified, but not Grace. That night, I'd cried myself to sleep because I'd missed the party. I woke up to find her asleep on my hospital bed, the cake squished in a paper bag in her hands.

Impulsively, I slip my arm through hers as she leads us towards the nursery floor. For the first time since this whole baby thing started, I'm glad I'm doing it: for *her* sake.

We've got nothing in common, really. She doesn't understand the way I live my life, never has. She's got no idea how broke I really was when I was pregnant with Davey: the loan shark banging on the door, the threat of losing my kid because I simply had nowhere safe to live. Grace has never had to buy anything second-hand in her entire life. Her idea of hard up is having to shop at Asda instead of Waitrose. She was born to Prada and Osborne & Little wallpaper. I'm more your Top Shop and Argos sort of girl. But it's not her fault. I want to blame her, but I can't. It's just the way it is.

We spend the next two hours stripping the nursery bare, and even though I'm totally playing her, it's also the most fun I've had in years.

Grace seems happy, too. She spends the entire return journey back to Oxford happily poring over those scan photos like they're Van Goghs. I don't get it. You can't even see anything. It's just a bunch of cells.

Mind you, it's already worth more than I am. I can't believe how stupid rich people are. Silk sheets, cashmere blankets, white linen dresses? For a baby? For fuck's sake, have the people who market this shit ever *had* a kid? Babies aren't all cute Gerber ads and soap bubbles. They puke. They drool. They shit, pee, vomit, posset, dribble and leak from every frigging orifice. Frankly, if you have a child under the age of three, you'd be better off covering everything, including yourself, in plastic for the duration. That fancy crap might look nice in a photo shoot for *Hello!*, but it won't last five minutes in real life. I suppose that's the point. *I'm so rich it doesn't matter if my kid only wears this once.*

I tilt my new bangle this way and that on my wrist, sending a scatter of light around the carriage. I picked out the exact same one Tom gave Grace for her last birthday. I don't really like it, to be honest: it's boring, and I prefer a bit of good honest gold bling to this oh-aren't-I-tasteful silver thing Grace goes in for. But if it's good enough for her, it's good enough for me.

By the time we get home, I'm knackered. And the constant need to pee is driving me nuts. I feel like some incontinent old cow as I leap out of the car and race upstairs to the bathroom. I might as well put a blue rinse through my dreads and have done with it.

As soon as my arse hits the loo seat, I pee like a racehorse, wincing as a familiar pain shoots through my kidney. Cystitis again. Happens every time I have good sex. Yesterday with Blake was great, but four times in one afternoon is pushing it a bit, even for me.

I shower and change into a clingy black T-shirt and a pair of grey sweats with the words 'Tits' and 'Ass' picked out in diamante, and go back downstairs. Grace is curled up in an armchair in the sitting room, reading one of those skinny books that win prizes and sell about four copies (and two of those are to the author's mum). Personally, I like fat glossy paperbacks that give you carpal tunnel and have pictures of stilettos and juicy single cherries on the front. Grace probably thinks chick lit is something to do with Tom's hens.

When I go into the kitchen to make some tea, I find Tom flat on his back on the floor, head and torso out of sight beneath the sink. Slimy grey water is puddled all over the terracotta floor.

I poke suspiciously at the lamb stew Grace has left bubbling in a pot on the Aga. 'What happened to the sink?'

'Bacon fat,' Tom grunts. 'Blocked solid.'

Oops. Can I help it if I crave BLTs at 3 a.m.?

I duck my head beneath the sink. 'Need a hand?'

'Please. Been trying to get this U-bend unscrewed for twenty minutes. If you can hold the other end of the – great, thanks.' He bangs around for a few moments, then swears. 'Bugger. The thread's gone, and it just keeps twisting. I need someone to hold the tap steady up top while I try to loosen this nut.'

'You want me to get it?'

'Wait, don't let go of the pipe you've got, or we'll have water everywhere. Shit. We need another pair of hands.'

'I could go and get Grace—'

'No, no, don't disturb her. She's reading.'

She's reading. If I had a fucking dime for every time I've heard that, I'd be able to buy out Simon Cowell.

Susannah, can you set the table, your sister's reading. Susannah, put the laundry away, we don't want to interrupt Grace when she's reading. Catherine, ask Susannah to finish the washing up, Grace is trying to study. I need you to peel the potatoes, walk the dog, stand on your head and spit fucking quarters: your sister's reading.

I was the family skivvy because Grace was too 'intellectual' and 'academic' to get her hands dirty. Not for Grace the shitty jobs like sorting dirty underwear and cleaning the loo or even making Dad a cup of coffee. No, Grace was reserving herself for Better Things. Like degrees from Oxford and brilliant jobs and adoring, handsome – well, OK, adoring – husbands. *Susannah can do the ironing. She can chop onions and grate cheese. After all, she's got nothing better to do.*

I kneel down and reach past Tom, gripping the tap and the overflow drain and somehow holding them both steady, my boobs about half an inch from his face. OK, so Grace got the degree and the success and the house and the nice, kind husband. But I've landed the two things she really wants, so yah boo sucks.

The baby, of course. And Blake.

I can't believe Tom doesn't notice. It's so *obvious*. Every time he walks into a room, she lights up like a Christmas tree. She gets all smiley and over-excited, and then starts asking these super-interested questions about Stella McCartney's latest collection and who's on the cover of *Tatler*. She was just the same when she got her first crush on Gareth Lonergan when she was sixteen and discovered a sudden fascination for Dungeons and Dragons.

'Thanks, Zee. Nice job,' Tom says, emerging from beneath the sink, and brushing himself down. 'OK. It should be fine, as long as no one dumps hot fat down it again.'

I knuckle the small of my back as I straighten up. 'Sorry about that. My bad.'

'Are you all right?' Tom asks, concerned. 'I shouldn't have had you bending like that. Grace would have my balls in a sling if she knew.'

'Forget it. I'm fine. What did you think of the scan pictures?'

'Not much, if I'm honest.'

I smile. 'I thought you'd be a bit more excited to see the fruit of your loins.'

Tom turns on the tap, nods in satisfaction as water drains swiftly from the sink, and starts to rinse his hands. 'Judging by that scan, you're having a fruit fly.'

'Don't tell Grace that. She's very attached.'

'The word you're looking for is *obsessed*.'

'Come on, Tom. Aren't you the least bit excited?'

'I'll wait till things are a bit further along to get excited, thanks.' Briskly, he towels his forearms dry. 'I suppose I'd better shower and get cleaned up properly. Grace has invited Blake and Claudia over tonight for a celebration dinner.'

'She's told them already?' I exclaim, annoyed. I'd wanted to get a couple more shags out of Blake before he found out and I acquired all the allure of a flannel nightie.

'No, thank God. I'm not in the mood for more baby hysteria – no offence.'

''S OK. None taken.'

'This party's for some big contract Blake landed last week with one of the glossies. Grace's idea.'

I knew it. Seriously, has the girl no shame? I mean, Claudia's her best friend! Even I feel a bit bad about shagging Blake, and I don't even *like* Claudia.

Pregnancy must be turning me soft. I'm usually more of a you-snooze-you-lose girl when it comes to husbands. My philosophy: if you can't keep your man happy, you deserve to lose him to someone who can. All wives have to do is follow one simple rule: lots of sex and no nagging. Get it the other way round, and he'll be off. I refuse to feel guilty about Claudia. She's got nothing to do with me. *I'm* not the one being unfaithful. I didn't make any vows.

I scrutinize Grace as she flits around the dining room later that evening making sure everyone has a drink or another helping of potatoes Dauphinoise. It's weird: when we were kids, she was useless in the kitchen. Couldn't boil an egg without forgetting to add water. Now she's knocking out fancy four-course meals like she's Nigella Lawson. *I'm* supposed to be the domestic one. *She's* the clever one. Can't she throw me a bone and just be bad at something for once?

Grace practically climbs over me to give Blake the biggest piece of homemade pecan pie, and goes on and on about the stupid *Vogue* contract for about an hour. I was right. She's got the hots for him big time. But the *really* hysterical thing? She has no idea how she feels! It's not an act. This love is so unrequited, she hasn't even told herself about it!

I don't know if it's my hormones or the unlikely prospect of prim and proper Grace wetting her sensible M&S knickers for her best friend's husband, but suddenly, I'm *gagging* for it. I squirm beneath the table, trying unsuccessfully to catch Blake's eye.

'I'm going outside for a fag,' I say finally, shoving back my chair and hoping he gets the hint.

I'm on my second cigarette by the time Blake joins me behind the greenhouse.

'What kept you?' I demand crossly.

'I couldn't run out after you. I had to fake an important text just to get away. I can't be long. Grace has been giving me odd looks all evening as it is.'

'She probably wanted to get you behind the bike sheds herself.'

'What are you talking about?'

'Creams her jeans every time she looks at you.'

'The Ice Queen? You're kidding me.'

I unzip his flies. 'She'd give it to you on a plate if you asked.'

'You dirty bitch,' Blake pants, his hand already inside my sweat pants. His fingers probe between my legs, and I back up against the greenhouse door, Grace forgotten. 'My wife's right here, and you still can't get enough.'

His free hand tangles in my dreads, pushing me down until I'm kneeling at his feet. I take his cock in my mouth, expertly whirling my tongue around its length as I run my fingernails over his balls. He tastes of sweat and salt, and even though I'm Queen of the BJ, I struggle not to gag. Fucking pregnancy hormones.

He curses as his fancy watch snags in my hair, and snaps it free.

'Fuck!' I yelp.

'Not my fault. Ever thought of ditching the ghetto look?'

I'm tempted to bite down. Hard.

Instead, I scramble to my feet and pull him by his dick towards me. Blake laughs, cupping my ass with both hands and lifting me onto him. I'm so wet, I practically slide off again. I don't know what it is about this man, but the sex is really fucking hot. Gotta to be careful, or I'm going to get burned.

He stumbles slightly beneath my weight, and I grab the doorjamb for balance. As I turn, the moon comes out from behind a cloud, bathing Blake and me and the figure on the garden path in brilliant yellow light.

Ooops.

13

Grace

'She doesn't *act* very pregnant,' Claudia says doubtfully.

I watch my sister. She is currently perched halfway up the apple tree at the bottom of the garden like a ten-year-old boy, reading a celebrity magazine. Unlike most ten-year-old boys, however, she has a cigarette in one hand and bottle of Budweiser gripped between her knees. Her skirt barely covers her bottom, and the holey black leggings reveal at least three of her tattoos. Her flip-flops are silver, her toe-nails purple. She didn't stagger home till two this morning; I suspect her 'morning sickness' at breakfast-time owed more to her hangover than her hormones. As Claudia points out, Susannah neither acts – nor looks – pregnant at all.

'You are sure she actually *is*?' Claudia adds. 'I don't want to be mean, but you know what she's like.'

I want to defend Susannah, but there's not much I can say. My sister is actually *proud* of the fact that she faked pregnancy to gull her first and third husbands into mar-riage, as if it's a credit to her ingenuity. Claudia's scepticism over a pregnancy that conveniently puts a roof over her head is not unreasonable.

I pour us both a cup of green tea. 'I went with her to her scan. And, yes, before you ask, it's Tom's. The first thing I did was check the calendar and make sure the dates matched.'

Susannah tucks her beer into a convenient crook in the tree above her head, and stretches her endless legs along the length of the sun-dappled branch. She flips the pages of her magazine, tapping ash mid-air and nodding in time to her iPod. She looks young and carefree.

I wish I was her. And not just because of the baby. Susannah may be hard up, but she's done what she wanted all her life. She's never had to be responsible for anything. I think I envy her that most of all.

When we were children, Susannah was the baby of the family, and I was the Big Sister, which meant that I fretted and worried about her, and she let me, knowing I'd pick up her slack. Thanks in no small part to my mother's contagious paranoia, I was terrified she'd get sick and die, and somehow it'd be my fault. So I followed her around school with a spare jumper so she wouldn't get cold. I got up early and walked the dog – *her* dog – so she could have an extra half-hour in bed. I did her paper round in winter because she was scared of the dark. Even though I hated the Youth Club because everyone laughed at me for being square, I tagged after her when she insisted on going so I could make sure she was OK.

Growing up changed nothing. I bailed her out when she got arrested for shoplifting, and kept it secret from Mum and Dad. I sent her money when she was about to get evicted. I paid off a loan shark who was threatening to beat her up. In return for all of this, Susannah mocked me and called me Goody-Two-Shoes.

My sister has never planned for anything. She didn't save money for a rainy day, or worry about exams. And yet somehow she's the one who always falls on her feet and comes up smelling of roses.

I wanted to be fun and carefree like her, but Mum and Dad had to be able to rely on one of us. We couldn't both drift along assuming someone else would take care of tomorrow.

My hand tightens on the teacup. I thought I'd got past this petty jealousy years ago. Susannah's paid for her freedom. She's lost her children and three husbands, and she doesn't have a penny to her name. Maybe my life hasn't been quite as impulsive or exciting as hers, but I have a wonderful husband, a satisfying job, a beautiful home. I made the right choices. The one thing I truly envy Susannah – motherhood – would have been denied me no matter how carefree my lifestyle.

'She really shouldn't be smoking,' Claudia says crossly. 'Can't you stop her?'

'She's cutting down. The doctor said the baby was the right size for thirteen weeks, and it seems healthy. And the quad test came back clear.'

'I admire your patience. I'd want to strangle her if it were me.'

I smile serenely, when the truth is that I want to take my sister by the throat and force-feed her vitamins. I want to lock her in her room and make sure she drinks nothing but fresh orange juice and eats lean protein and lots of fruit and vegetables and doesn't go near a mussel or a piece of chèvre, but I've signed a deal with the Devil. I have to console myself with the thought that it probably won't affect the baby at all. Davey and Donny are fine, and she behaved much worse when she was expecting them. Thousands of children are born to irresponsible teenagers every day and are perfectly all right.

But this baby is different. This baby is mine.

Mum always says having a child is like spending the rest of your life with your heart walking around outside your body. I suppose I'm just getting used to that feeling ahead of time.

Claudia shifts uncomfortably in her chair, shading her eyes from the bright June sunshine. She's thirty weeks now, and looks enormous; surely double the size she was when she was expecting the twins.

'You didn't have to ask Susannah, you know. I'd have had a baby for you. I told you that.'

'I know you would, and I love you for it.' I get up and tilt the umbrella so that it shades her from the sun. 'But you have your own family to think about. Susannah's on her own, and besides, she's my sister. I'm grateful to her, of course, but she *is* family. I feel less beholden this way. After all, I'd have done the same for her.'

Would you? Would you really?

I can hear my mother's voice now. *Selfish*, she called me. Every time I wanted to study or read instead of taking Susannah swimming or returning Dad's library books. *You won't put yourself out for anyone! Susannah has her faults, but she'll be the one who takes care of me in my old age. The only person you ever think of is yourself.*

Perhaps she's right. Susannah willingly drives down to the hospital to see her every other day. I go once a week, and even then, my heart's not in it.

Tom emerges from the greenhouse, and stands beneath the apple tree, chatting to Susannah. I watch them. Last night, he said I was selfish too, for putting Susannah through this, even though it was her idea. He said it was too much to ask, after she'd had to give up her own children. He and Susannah are getting on much better than they did when she first came to stay with us. Quite often when I come home late these days, the two of them are chatting at the kitchen table over a half-empty bottle of wine. If he was anyone but Tom, I'd be worried.

'I think Blake is seeing someone,' Claudia says abruptly.

I pivot towards her, shocked out of my self-absorption.

'Her name's Layla. He forgot to log out the other day when he used the computer in the kitchen to check his emails. Layla! What kind of a name is that?'

'Claudia, are you quite sure there isn't an innocent explanation—'

'For the way he described how he'd like to fuck her? Hard to misunderstand that. He'd deleted most of his emails, but it wasn't difficult to recover them from the hard drive once I knew what to look for. As far as I can find out, it's been going on for about six months. Probably since the day after I found out I was pregnant.'

Her gaze is resolutely trained on the horizon, but I notice her hands are trembling.

I finally find my voice. 'I thought you said he likes it when you're pregnant—'

'This isn't about *sex*! It's about attention. He's jealous of the baby.'

'Oh, Claudia. I don't know what to say.'

Her eyes flash at the pity in my tone. 'None of us get all the pie, Grace. You have a wonderful husband, and I have wonderful children. We cope with the bits of our lives that aren't perfect as best we can. I love Blake. And despite everything, he loves me. I *know* he loves me,' she repeats, uncertainly.

'Have you said anything to him?'

'I don't want to give it too much notice and turn it into something it's not. I just have to wait for it to blow itself out. It always does.' She laughs shortly. 'Blake has a very short attention span.'

'He's done this before?'

'Don't be naive, Grace. Did you really think a man like Blake was faithful?'

I suppose, like Claudia, I've always known. I liked to tell myself he wasn't interested in other women, when the unflattering truth is, he was just never interested in me.

Later that night, when Tom reaches for me, I struggle to respond. Normally, it doesn't take me long to get in the mood if Tom is persistent, but tonight, I'm dry and closed. He thumbs my nipples with waning optimism for another five minutes, and then rolls over in bed with a gentle sigh and reaches for his book.

'Did you know Blake was having an affair?' I demand.

He doesn't answer; which is answer enough.

'Tom! Why didn't you tell me?'

'Because *he* didn't tell *me*. Not in so many words. Anyway, even if he had, what difference would it have made? You know you couldn't have said anything to Claudia, not unless she came to you first. You'd have been in an impossible position.'

'But she's pregnant!' I exclaim. 'How *could* he?'

Tom closes his book. 'Look, Grace. I know they're our oldest friends, but even we don't know what happens behind closed doors. Who knows what's going on in their marriage? Affairs don't usually happen in a vacuum.'

'Are you *defending* him?'

'I'm simply saying there are two sides to every story.'

I sit up in the bed, punching the pillows behind me with unnecessary force. 'There's no excuse for—'

'Grace, it really isn't any of our business. Blake and Claudia have been together a long time. Whatever we think, it clearly works for them.'

'Claudia told me, so that makes it my business,' I argue.

'Claudia told you because she needs a friend. Be one. Listen to her, and be there for her. That's what she needs, not for you to pick up a flaming sword of justice on her behalf.'

'Claudia wouldn't have told me if she didn't want my help,' I say stubbornly. 'And before you start taking his side, she says this isn't the first time, did you know that? He's been having affairs for years! I can't believe she hasn't thrown him out. If I found out you were having an affair—'

'You'd what?'

'You'd never have an affair,' I amend quickly. 'You're not like Blake. I trust you.'

'Trust me? Or take me for granted?'

I'm taken aback by the unexpected steel in his tone. He doesn't sound like my comfortable, familiar old Tom. All of a sudden, a dark undercurrent of fear has seeped into the room.

'You're so busy worrying about Claudia and Blake's marriage,' Tom says evenly. 'When was the last time you even gave ours a second thought?'

His expression as he waits for me to speak is interested but strangely detached. His composure chills me in a way his anger wouldn't. I realize his question isn't an idle one, born of the moment. He's been waiting a long time to ask me this.

The sick, cold feeling spreads. At some point, when I was worrying about IVF treatments and putting in fourteen-hour days to raise the money we'd need to leapfrog the NHS, my sweet, easy-going husband was calmly appraising my performance as a wife. And, judging from the look on his face, finding me wanting.

I wait for him to fill the silence, to bridge the gap between us as he always does, but still he says nothing. My fear intensifies. The safe, known landscape of our marriage is suddenly unfamiliar, and I'm struggling to find my bearings.

'Of course I think about you,' I manage finally. 'I think about us. Why would you even ask that?'

'Because this marriage has felt very one-sided recently,' Tom says. 'I know how much you want a child, Grace. I understand how much it means to you. But sometimes the only thing that seems to matter to you, at all, is having a baby. There have been times, both in bed and out of it, when it's like you don't even see me, I matter to you so little.'

'That's not true! Of course you *matter*—'

'Do you', Tom says suddenly, 'have *any* idea how high-maintenance you are?'

Fear is replaced by anger. How *dare* he? The *last* thing anyone could say about me is that I'm high-maintenance! I've never asked for, or expected, to be showered with gifts; the most extravagant thing Tom's ever given me was that Tiffany bangle for my birthday last year. I don't buy into the self-obsessed because-you're-worth-it mentality. The last time I had a pedicure was my wedding day. I get my highlights done at a small salon in Oxford. I've always paid my way, earned my own living. How can he call *me* high-maintenance?

Because it's not about money. You're a difficult person to love, Grace. You give nothing back. It makes it so hard for anyone to know you.

'I thought you wanted this baby as much as I do,' I snap. 'You helped to make it. You could have said no.'

'Don't put this on me, Grace. You knew how I felt. I agreed, yes, but only for *you*. Because I love you, and I couldn't say no to you.'

'You should have said—'

'Grace, I did. You just didn't listen.'

'It's not like I forced you at gunpoint! Why couldn't you have been man enough to say no if that's how you felt? You can't just throw it back in my lap! We *both* did this!'

'Why couldn't I have been *man enough*?'

I throw back the covers. 'Forget it. I'm going to sleep in the spare room.'

Tom grabs my arm. 'No! This is something we need to talk about!'

Angrily I yank myself free. 'I don't *want* to talk about it.'

'Go on then,' Tom says bitterly. 'Yell and walk away from it. It's what you always do.'

Do you see, Grace? Do you see?

In one of those rare moments of clarity, I *do* see. Tom is the one who nurtures our relationship. He asks me how I feel, what I'm thinking. I throw up defensive walls, and he batters them down. I hang up the phone, and he calls me back. I storm out of room, and he follows me. He's never worried about losing face; only about losing me. We rarely argue, because Tom never lets it get that far. If we can't agree, he finds a compromise I can live with. In fifteen years together, he's never raised his voice to me. He's never backed me into a corner like this. I look at him now, at this stranger sharing my bed, and it's as if the ground itself is shifting beneath my feet.

'Tom, Susannah's pregnant,' I whisper.

'And when this baby arrives, I'm going to love it. Don't be in any doubt about that.' He pinches the bridge of his nose wearily. 'I'm not really talking about the baby, Grace. That's just part of it. I'm talking about *us*. I'm talking about the fact that I need you, and you're not here for me.'

I sit stiffly on the edge of the bed, my back towards him. My chest is tight with misery. How can this be happening? Just as I thought everything was finally coming right with the baby, how can it all be falling apart?

'Grace, please,' Tom begs. '*Talk* to me. Ever since we started trying for a baby, it's as if I've lost you. You're my best friend, my lover, my wife. I *miss* you.'

I knuckle my eyes. 'It doesn't mean I don't love you,' I say thickly. 'It doesn't mean you don't matter. I love you more than anything in the world, I couldn't manage with-out you—'

Suddenly he's gathering me into his arms. The relief at his touch is so strong, I twist and bury my face in his bare shoulder – his familiar, comforting shoulder – and sob like a child, even though a part of me is still coldly furious with both him and myself.

'That's all I needed to hear,' he whispers into my hair. 'That's all I needed to hear.'

'I'm sorry,' I mumble. 'I'm so sorry.'

'Ssssh,' he soothes. 'Come on now. It's OK. Don't cry. It's going to be OK.'

He holds me tight until the crying jag has passed, and I stop hiccupping. Gently, he lifts my chin with his finger, and kisses me sweetly on the lips. I kiss him back, tasting salt from my own tears. His hands circle my waist, pulling me towards him. I reach beneath the covers, searching for his penis, but he shifts away. I try again, and this time, he takes hold of my hand, and firmly guides it back above the bedclothes.

'Not now,' he says.

Tom turns out the bedside light and settles me in the crook of his arm. I lie there awkwardly, listening as his breathing grows steady and regular. I feel hollowed out and drained. Claudia warned me not to push Tom into something he didn't really want. The baby isn't even born yet, and already it's coming between us. I can almost hear my mother saying *I told you so*.

For the first time, the realization hits home: *I've changed everything*. And right now I have no way of knowing if it's for better or worse.

14

Susannah

Now I'm actually here, I can't get out of the fucking car. Seriously. I'm shitting bricks. My knuckles are actually white on the steering wheel.

I take a deep breath, unclench my hands, and reach for my cigarettes. The huge surge of adrenalin that propelled me here has bloody vanished like morning mist. I was mad to come without at least calling in advance. They might not even *be* here.

I exhale, calmed by the nicotine, and look up at the house. It's not as posh as I'd expected. I had this image of a huge detached mansion, with maybe an outdoor pool and a couple of fancy cars parked in the drive. But this looks pretty much the same as the house me and Grace grew up in: bog-standard red-brick three-bed Seventies semi, bay windows, sad-looking rose bushes either side of the covered porch. Identical to every other house in the road. A skateboard lies on its back in the middle of the concrete front path. Upstairs, the curtains are closed.

Well, of course they're fucking closed, you moron! It's six o'clock on a Sunday morning! Only burglars and hormonal pregnant women go running around the country at such an insane hour!

Suddenly, the spell is broken. I stub out my cigarette and throw the car into gear, reversing quickly out of the driveway. Thank Christ nobody in the house woke up and saw me. Fingers crossed I get back home before Grace realizes I've gone. I really don't need her pointing out what a dumb idea this was.

That, I've figured out already.

Michael ignores me as I follow him round the studio, helpfully straightening pots and brushes as he scatters them in his search for a particular paintbrush or pigment. Apart from Dad, I've never met anyone who could sulk as thoroughly as this. It's been weeks since Michelle caught me mid-shag in the garden with Blake, and he still hasn't spoken a single word to me.

'Please, Michael,' I beg. 'Grace is doing my head in. I thought she'd be chuffed my boys have got in touch, but she's being really weird. She point-blank refuses to come down to Surrey with me, and I can't go back on my own. Not after I made a right tit of myself driving over there in the middle of the night the other week.'

I dodge as he flips a huge half-finished canvas out of the rack and carries it over towards the window. Michael fancies himself a landscape painter on a large scale, but actually, his small pencil portraits are by far his best work.

'I've tried asking Tom to talk to her,' I persist, shadowing him across the studio, 'but he's in a weird mood too.

And he's got enough problems of his own, what with what's happening at the hospital and everything.'

I pause significantly. Not even a flicker of curiosity. Men. What *is* the point of them?

Michael positions his canvas to get the best light, deliberately blocking me out. I move round it and stand so I'm right in his way. 'Look, I don't mean you. It's *Michelle* I need. I can't talk to Claudia for obvious reasons. Anyway, she's as bad as Grace on the baby front. Michelle's the only person left Grace will listen to. Can't you – you know. Ask her to come back?'

'I'm not a schizophrenic, Susannah! That isn't how it works, I've told you that—'

'Oh, thank God. *Finally.*'

'You don't deserve another word from me,' Michael says crossly.

'I know, I know, but please don't freeze me out again. You know I'm sorry. I told you so enough times.'

He picks up his palette knife. 'I can't talk to you about this. It's not me you need to apologize to.'

'How can I apologize to Michelle if she's not here?'

Without looking up, he squeezes a startling yellow pigment onto his palette. For a moment, I think he's going to go back into strop mode again, but then he nods tersely. 'Fine. But I'm making no promises when.'

I'd hug him, but I know he'd hate it. Instead, I content myself with blowing him a kiss, and skip out of the studio. It's been bloody miserable this last few weeks without Michelle to talk to. Tom's a sweet guy, and I'm glad he's come round to the whole baby thing, but it's not the same, talking to a bloke. They don't ask the right questions. I need a girl to talk to. Someone who gets how I feel.

I spend the next three days on tenterhooks waiting for Michelle to show. She finally turns up when I'm sunbathing topless in the back garden, making the most of the brief summer heat wave. She looks as cool and chic as a Fifties housewife in her stylish black-and-white sleeveless shirt-waister and oversized flat black straw hat, though she sticks out like a sore thumb around here. Outside of *Desperate Housewives*, real women never look this good.

'The first thing out of your mouth better be an apology,' she says crisply, as I fumble for my bikini top. 'And the second better be a promise never, *ever* to go there again.'

'I'm very, very sorry,' I recite obediently. 'And I really appreciate you not telling Grace. She'd have gone ape shit.'

'Grace doesn't need to know how badly you've let her down. You are carrying her baby, after all. She's got worries enough.'

I could take offence at this, except it's true. I sit up, stubbing out my cigarette and scrabbling under the sunlounger for my flip-flops.

'I'm disappointed in you, Susannah,' Michelle says. 'I thought you were a little better than this. Blake is a player. Worthless. I'd expect nothing more from him. But I had hoped *you* had a little more class.'

Suddenly, I feel about twelve years old. It's dumb, but for some reason I actually care what Michelle thinks of me. She tells it like it is, she doesn't judge, and she doesn't put up with any bullshit. It makes her respect worth having.

'I'm still waiting for that promise,' Michelle says.

I indicate my swelling belly. 'I'm nearly seventeen weeks pregnant, Michelle. How much mileage do you think I have?'

'Don't be smart. You're a very beautiful girl, and we both

know Blake likes his women blooming. Pregnant is his thing.'

I laugh nervously. 'Oh, come on! It's just a fling! It doesn't mean anything—'

'In that case, it won't be much loss.'

I hesitate. Blake's hot, and he's brightened things up around here, but the truth is, I don't actually like him all that much. I don't get why he and Tom are even friends. He's too cocky by half; he reminds me of too many men I've screwed, and been screwed by, in the past. I don't trust a man who looks in the mirror more than he looks at me. Michelle's right: he won't be much loss.

'Susannah,' Michelle threatens.

'Fine. Fine. Whatever.'

Grace is just walking around the side of the house towards the garage, briefcase in hand, as we reach the top of the garden. She looks up at us in surprise. 'Michelle! Were you looking for me? I'm just on my way into work.'

'On a Saturday? Darling, how *is* that going to work when the baby's here?'

'The baby', says Grace tightly, 'is why I'm trying to get ahead of the game now.'

'Oh, don't worry. This won't take long,' Michelle says breezily, pushing past Grace into the house.

Grace looks annoyed, but she's too polite to argue. I hide a grin as we all troop into the kitchen. Props to Michelle: not many people can tackle my sister head on and win.

She doesn't beat about the bush, either. 'I've heard about Susannah's letter from the boys' social worker,' she says briskly. 'I think she should meet them. And I think you should go with her.'

I witness the unthinkable: my sister lost for words.

'Michelle, I really don't have time to discuss this now,' Grace says finally, throwing a quick glare my way. 'I know Susannah has visions of a fairytale ending, but the truth is rather more complicated.'

'Donny and Davey want to see their mother again,' Michelle says sweetly. 'How complicated is that?'

'It's not that simple, and Susannah knows it. No doubt she'll be heading back to America before long, and the boys will lose touch with her again. It's not fair to give them hope that she's going to be a proper part of their lives. She should never have contacted them—'

'I didn't,' I say indignantly. '*They* asked to see *me*.'

Grace turns her back on the two of us to fill up the kettle. Her hands are shaking. I really don't get why this is such a big deal. She was the one bawling me out for not going to see the boys a couple of months ago. What's suddenly changed?

I skip smartly out of the way as Grace slams the kettle on the Aga hotplate, and then picks up a sponge and starts to wipe down the kitchen counter so aggressively she's in danger of taking the colour off the granite.

'Gracie, the baby's going to show soon,' I plead. 'I've got enough bridges to build with the boys without laying this on them—'

'Which is why I don't think it's a good idea,' Grace says, rubbing furiously at a non-existent spot of grease. 'Not yet.'

I throw an imploring glance Michelle's way. She puts her hand on Grace's sleeve, stilling her frantic scrubbing. Her French manicure is perfect, I notice; no sign of paint or charcoal beneath those polished nails.

Grace looks from Michelle to me, and then puts down the sponge. 'Zee, it's not that I don't want you to see your children,' she sighs. 'They're wonderful boys, and you should be proud of them. Of course I want you to meet them, and you know I'll come with you. After everything you've done for me, it's the least I can do. All I'm saying is, why not wait until after the baby's born? It's just a few more months. It'll be so much easier for all of you—'

'No!' I yell suddenly. 'I haven't seen my sons for nearly *six years*, Grace! I don't want to wait! The boys want to see me *now*. If I don't go, they might think I don't want to see them. They might change their minds. If it were you, would you take that risk? Would *you* wait?'

'If it were me—' Grace snaps.

I brace myself for another blast of abuse. Grace took it personally when I left the boys, and she's never got over it. You'd think *she* was the one I'd abandoned.

'Grace?' prompts Michelle.

'If it were me,' Grace says quietly, 'I wouldn't want to wait either.'

'You'll come? You'll take me?'

Her face softens, and she nods. I fling myself into her arms – and then gasp and clutch my stomach.

'What?' Grace cries, alarmed. 'Susannah, what is it? Is it the baby?'

I grin delightedly. 'Yes,' I say, grabbing her hand and placing it on my belly. 'I just felt it move!'

'Keep still,' Michelle scolds. 'This is hard enough without you wriggling.'

'Well, it hurts! You're pulling my hair out at the roots!'

She pushes me back down on the stool. 'Don't be such a baby. You're the one who let it get into this state. Unless you want to chop the whole lot off, you're just going to have to sit still and be patient.'

I grit my teeth as she goes at my hair again with the proverbial fine-tooth comb. For the last three days, I've slathered my dreads twice a day with a special heavy-duty conditioner the texture of tar that's supposed to help with take-down; I smell like a chum bucket, and my hair looks like I've been slimed. Worse, it still feels like she's ripping my hair from my scalp. But as she points out, I either sit it out, or shave my head and start practising my Nazi salute.

For the next four hours, Michelle patiently teases the knots and tangles from my hair, one dread at a time. My eyes water from the pain, and several times I'm tempted to just grab the scissors and razor and do the job properly, but I don't want the boys to think their mother looks like a freak. It's them I'm doing this for. Nothing else would have persuaded me to go through this grief.

Finally, Michelle throws the comb down, knuckling her hands in the small of her back. 'Well, that's the best I can do.' She checks me out, and frowns. 'Hmm. Let's hope it looks better when you've washed it.'

No kidding. I grimace at my reflection in the bathroom mirror after Michelle leaves. My hair has been dulled to a sludgy brown by the whale gloop, and hangs in slimy ropes around my face. I look like a lentil-eating, Birkenstock-wearing, week-dead hippy.

It takes five shampoos to get my hair to squeak clean. I leave it to dry naturally, and set about removing the metal from my face. The nipple rings I can leave in, but the tongue-stud, multiple earrings and lip piercing all have to come out. My tattoos are mostly covered by the ash-coloured tunic and jeans Grace and I picked out – she tried unsuccessfully to get me out of black and into what she called a 'real colour', but in the end we compromised on grey – and it also hides the slight baby bump. I stick my tongue out at my image as I leave the bedroom. I look like fucking Suzy Homemaker. Still, at least the kids shouldn't be too embarrassed when I turn up now.

Grace literally does a double take when I reluctantly present myself downstairs. 'Susannah! I can't believe it! You look so like Mum!'

I resist the temptation to hurl myself over the banisters. She's right: I do look like Mum; at least, when she was younger. It's the boring housewife get-up. No wonder I've spent all my life trying to be different.

The boys' foster family lives less than fifteen minutes from Mum's hospital, so at my suggestion, we pay her a quick visit first. I notice Grace spends hardly any time actually *with* Mum; most of the time, she's talking earnestly to the nurses about her. She's never been very good with sick people. I think the lack of control freaks her out. When she's ill herself, she shuts herself in her room and won't let anyone see her till she's better, like an animal hiding in a cave.

I stand at the end of Mum's bed while Grace and the doctors talk gravely in the corridor. She looks so pale and still, like she's made of plaster or something. I talk to her, but I might as well be talking to a statue. There's no sign she's even there.

I know Grace doesn't want to accept it, but it's been more than five months now. Mum isn't getting better. She isn't *going* to get better. She keeps getting infections, and her organs are gradually shutting down, one by one. The doctors keep pumping her full of drugs, putting out fires, but another one just breaks out somewhere else. How long are we going to keep pretending? I'm sure Mum wouldn't want it. Anyway, what makes Mum *Mum* has already gone.

I'll go when I'm good and ready, and not before. I can't leave you and Grace. Not until we get this mess sorted out.

'Zee? It's time to go,' Grace says from the doorway, making me jump. 'We said we'd be with the Mayses by three.'

By the time we get to the Mayses' house, I'm practically hyperventilating from nerves. Even with Grace here, I'm petrified. The boys were nine and six when I last saw them, children. They're teenagers now. What if they don't recognize me? What if they blame me for abandoning them? What if they *hate* me?

'I can't do this,' I say, my teeth chattering with fear. 'I shouldn't have come.'

'It's going to be fine,' Grace says. 'They want to see you. They asked to, remember? You're going to be fine.'

She takes my hand as we start to walk up the path, and doesn't let go. My big sister, looking after me as usual. I don't mind. I've never really minded.

The front door opens, and suddenly a skinny blond boy comes rushing out. My heart lurches. *Donny.* I'd know him anywhere. When I last saw him, his hair was cut short and neat behind his ears, and now it's brushing his shoulders, a cool, skateboarder shag, but otherwise, he hasn't changed. My Donny. *My baby.*

I hang back, hiding behind my sister.

'Auntie Grace!' he cries, launching himself at her.

She laughs, and hugs him, then turns as his older brother slouches out of the door. I gasp. Davey must be over six feet tall! He looks like a man. For a second, I feel a pang of loss for the little boy I left behind, now gone forever.

Davey nods at his aunt, but doesn't come forward. He was always more reserved than his exuberant younger brother. Donny wears his heart on his sleeve, but Davey always held something back, even as a small child. He reminds me of Grace sometimes.

'Aren't you going to say hello to your mum?' Grace asks them.

For a terrifying second, I think they're going to say no, and then Donny throws himself at me, wrapping his arms around my waist and burying his head in my chest. I pull him into me, not caring that I can hardly breathe. How could I leave them? How did I?

'Mum,' Davey says hesitantly.

I free up an arm and hold it out to him. He doesn't take it. Instead, he wraps his own around me, pulling the three of us into a fierce embrace. I don't realize I'm crying until I taste salt.

Reluctantly, I release my boys as their foster parents come out onto the doorstep, their smiles polite but stiff. I'm more grateful than ever for Grace as we're shown into a neat sitting room with royal souvenirs on every sparkling, dust-free surface. Thank God I took out the dreads and covered up my tattoos. I wouldn't have been allowed in the house otherwise.

The Mayses serve tea and digestive biscuits – plain, not chocolate – while the boys rush back and forth from their bedrooms with treasures and photos and pictures they've drawn for me. Eventually, Mr Mays tells them to go out and play in the garden while we 'get to know each other'.

'Your sister tells me you plan to return to America soon,' Mrs Mays says, as soon as the boys have left.

'Actually,' I say, with a quick glance at Grace, 'I'm thinking about staying now. For a bit, anyway. I'd like to get to know the boys properly. If that's OK with you, of course.'

'It's not up to us,' Mr Mays says tightly. 'If the boys want to see you, I'm sure the social workers will arrange it. Maybe we can make it once a month to start with. We don't want to rush things until we know for sure how it's going.'

Until we know you're going to stick around.

'I'd like to see them a bit more often than that,' I say firmly. 'I want to be a proper part of their – ohhh!'

'Zee?' Grace says excitedly. 'Was that the baby again? Did it move?'

'Baby?' Mrs Mays says sharply.

I'm too stunned to even speak. My belly feels as if it's being crushed in a vice. A thousand red-hot knives are stabbing my lower back. Black spots dance in front of my eyes. I can't breathe for the pain.

'Grace,' I whisper, 'I think . . . *ambulance* . . .'

And then I pass out.

15

Catherine

I can't put my finger on what tips me off. Call it a mother's intuition, but when Tom comes home just a little too early three times in the same week, I know instinctively something's wrong.

Grace is too wrapped up in her baby obsession to spare a thought for the child's father. No doubt her single-mindedness is what's helped her achieve such success in life. But when applied to family and relationships, the reverse is true. She always was a selfish child.

I tell her as much, when the worm turns and Tom finally dares to stand up to her one night. Obviously I don't make a habit of invading the privacy of their marital bedroom – it goes without saying I absent myself when they have relations – but I'm her *mother*. I have a right to know what's happening in her life. Lord knows, if I waited for Grace to confide in me, hell would freeze over.

I don't mean to intervene, but Tom is absolutely right when he calls Grace high-maintenance, and I'm sorry, but I just can't keep quiet. Grace is a difficult person to love, as I make no bones about telling her. She gives nothing back. It makes it so hard for anyone to *know* her.

I watch her pull the shutters down on Tom, just as she always has on me. Even as a small child, Grace was a closed book. If you chastised or rebuked her, she wouldn't cry or throw a tantrum the way Susannah did. Instead, her eyes would go blank and opaque, and I'd know she was simply shutting me out. Trying to reach her was like hitting a sponge for all the lasting impact I made. There were times when her self-control and composure almost made me fearful. I told David: it wasn't *natural*.

The summer Grace was sixteen, when she was right in the middle of her O levels, I nearly died. It started with a bad headache that simply wouldn't go away, and when I awoke with my temples pounding for the third morning running, I took rather more aspirin than usual on an empty stomach, and suddenly started vomiting. The spasms were so violent they tore a hole in my oesophagus, and I began to haemorrhage, passing out on the bathroom floor before I could even call for help. I was literally choking on my own blood. If David hadn't come home from work to collect a forgotten briefcase, I would have died. The doctors said later that another fifteen minutes and it would have been too late.

Naturally David kept the details from the girls, fobbing them off with stories of tummy bugs and flu, but the mere fact that I was in hospital was enough to shock Susannah to the core. There were tears, angry outbursts at school, and nightmares that persisted long after I came home.

Grace got straight As in all thirteen of her exams.

No child should be that detached. Her mother was hovering between life and death, and all she could think of were ox-bow lakes and French verbs. As usual, David defended her. He said Grace had learned to shut down to protect herself; he even blamed *me*. As if it was *my* fault Susannah needed so much of my time and attention!

David sees self-sufficiency as a strength, which I suppose it can be. But no man – or woman – is an island, as Grace is discovering now. She's having to rely on Susannah, which can't be easy for someone as controlling as she is. She's learning a very important lesson. I was very much against this baby enterprise at first, but the Lord works in mysterious ways.

A much-chastened Grace fusses around Tom the morning after their row, and I expect him to glow with triumph and lap up the attention. However, he's just as preoccupied and distracted as ever. Regardless of whatever the two of them resolved last night, clearly Grace isn't the source of Tom's malaise after all.

My son-in-law is a straightforward, uncomplicated man. If the problem isn't his wife, it must be his work. Which means that's where I need to go next.

It's not that I'm nosy. I've never been the type to interfere in anyone's business. But clearly I'm here for a reason. It might seem there's not much I can do to help, given I'm little more than a ghost – and one lacking in the traditional ghostly gifts, such as rattling chains – but I've learned over the past few months that I can make myself heard and nudge things along rather effectively at times. Lord knows where Susannah and Grace would be now without me to pour oil on troubled waters.

But I can't read minds. I need Tom to articulate his problem aloud. Since he's little given to talking to himself – unlike Susannah, who is revelatory in the shower – I have to hope he's a little more forthcoming with his colleagues. If he doesn't unburden himself to someone, I may be condemned to follow him around for a very long time.

The Monday after his run-in with Grace, I trail him to the railway station, feeling like a sleuth in a penny dreadful. I wish I could feel the cool morning sun on my skin as he does. Living *in* the world, but not *of* it, is the hardest aspect of my strange situation. I can neither touch nor be touched. When I bend to my favourite sweetpeas, their scent is lost to me. The nights I spend with David, in our bed, unable to comfort him or be comforted, are by far the hardest I have ever known.

I'm not comfortable travelling without a ticket, but console myself with the fact that at least I'm not occupying a seat. Tom spends the journey staring out of the window, his newspaper unread. Fortunately, the train terminates at Paddington, or I think he'd miss his stop altogether.

His mood grows more morose as we take the Tube to Fulham Broadway and then walk down the Fulham Road to the Princess Eugenie Hospital. I knew it. Wife or work.

Tom swipes his ID at the hospital entrance, and slopes – there's no other word for it – inside. Instead of leading us to a grim, cramped office somewhere, as I expect, he takes the lift up to the fifth floor, and turns right, towards the Neonatal Intensive Care Unit.

Once more, he stops and runs his ID through the security pad, then squirts antiseptic gel on his hands from the dispenser on the wall and pushes the Plexiglas doors open. I follow him as he strides down the corridor, nodding curtly at nurses and doctors as he passes. No one questions him, or offers assistance. Clearly this visit is not just unremarkable, but routine. I wonder why this should be, given that as chief of paediatric anaesthesiology, his job must rarely bring him up to the NICU.

At the end of the corridor is a viewing gallery, on the other side of which are about eight or ten perspex incubators, each surrounded by monitors and heat lamps and whatnot. All but two or three are occupied by tiny babies barely visible beneath the wires snaking in and over their little bodies. I wonder where their souls are while they lie trapped and unconscious like this. I can't bear to think of them wandering alone and lost, as I am.

Tom taps smartly on the glass. A doctor seated next to one of the incubators looks up. She has wild Titian curls like rusty bedsprings pinned haphazardly on top of her head with a pencil, and extraordinary eyes.

The woman mouths 'Five minutes!' to Tom before returning her attention to the little mite in the incubator. Tom smiles and relaxes against the window, his arms folded, not taking his eyes off the woman.

So that's how it is. I can taste my disappointment. I didn't expect this of Tom; Tom, of all people. Safe, comforting, predictable Tom.

The door opens, and the red-headed doctor gives Tom a warm hug. I don't want to witness this sordid little scene any longer. I would rather think myself anywhere than here. I don't know what I expected to discover when I followed Tom, but I'm hard put to think of anything worse than this.

I turn to leave, and then, for a fraction of a second, I hesitate.

When I hear what Tom says next, I'm glad I stayed.

*

'Grace is right,' Susannah muses, lolling against the end of my hospital bed. 'I *do* bloody look like you.'

Actually, she doesn't. I haven't seen my daughter look as pretty as this since she was about fourteen. The piercings have gone, the tattoos are covered and her lovely strawberry-blonde hair hangs to her waist in a smooth loose sheet. She doesn't look at all like me. She looks like a princess.

She comes around the foot of the bed and perches on the edge next to my still body. 'We're on our way to see Davey and Donny,' she says. 'I'm fucking terrified, Mum.'

I stroke her cheek, though of course she can't feel me. 'Oh, darling. There's no need. It'll be fine.'

'Grace didn't want me to go,' she says. 'I think she's a bit ashamed about the boys being in care. It must kill her that I'm even going to be related to her kid.'

She tucks my cold hand beneath the covers, and smoothes my hair back from my face, as gentle as if she were the parent and I the child. They've cut my hair short, to help with my care, I suppose. Hard for the nurses to wash it, given that I'm trapped in my bed, tethered to machines. It's gone very grey since I've been in here. I look very old.

'She thinks I'm scared the boys won't like me,' she adds, picking fretfully at her nails. 'She's right, but that's not the worst bit. I figure I can take it if they get mad. I'd flip out, if I were them. I mean, I *left*. I don't mind if they yell. I think it might make it a bit easier, actually.'

I ache to put my arms around her. Susannah could have made a good mother if she hadn't been born in Grace's shadow. Of the two of them, she's the one I thought would have the happy marriage, the nice home, the car full of children. Grace was the most undomesticated child imaginable. She hasn't *earned* a family life.

Susannah gets up and paces restlessly towards the window. 'What if I don't like *them*, Mum?' she says hoarsely. 'What if I see my boys again and nothing happens? I don't feel anything? What do I do then?'

Her hand shakes as she pulls out a cigarette and lights it, in contravention of every rule. I wish I could tell her there's no need to worry. I wish I could tell her the real irony: that Grace's biggest fear, the dread that has her tossing and turning all night, and waking before dawn drenched in sweat, the real reason she didn't want Susannah to see Davey and Donny is precisely the reverse of what Susannah fears. Grace is deathly afraid Susannah *will* love her sons. She's frightened her sister will want to reclaim her boys, and put her family back together.

I wish I could tell her that Grace is too terrified even to ask herself the question that must come next, the one that's been consuming her for weeks: *what if Susannah wants this baby back too?*

Less than three hours later, I'm with her when she collapses at her sons' house. I don't leave her side as the ambulance races her to the nearest A&E department, which just happens to be at the same hospital where my useless body is lying. We are only one floor apart.

I can't even bear to look at my other daughter as she harangues the triage nurse and demands that Susannah is seen *now*!

This is Grace's fault. She was the one so insistent on having it all, the one who dragged Susannah into this nonsense, this *stupidity*. Another baby, after all we went through last time! But Grace doesn't know how sick Susannah's previous pregnancies made her, because she wasn't there to see it. She was too busy being the successful high-flying career girl who made Daddy proud. Susannah didn't tell her, because she doesn't want to admit that having babies isn't quite as easy for her as she pretends. She chooses not to remember that after Donny was born the doctors told her that another child might kill her.

Grace creates so much furore that Susannah is taken straight into an exam room, but I don't fool myself that she's doing it for her sister. Her anxiety is all for the baby. Susannah is conscious now, but her skin is the colour of sour milk and her lips are blue. She won't let go of Grace's hand.

A nurse comes in to set up an IV, because Susannah is dehydrated and they're worried about the baby. As soon as she sees the needle, Susannah recoils, shaking so much the nurse can't begin to find a vein.

'Come on, Zee,' Grace says. She takes her sister's jaw lightly between her thumb and forefinger, and turns her face away from the nurse. 'Never mind her. Look at me. Do you remember when I used to ring the doorbell to make you think the shot nurse had arrived?' she says cheerfully. 'You screamed the place down. I couldn't believe you got so upset.'

Susannah grimaces as the nurse finally finds a vein, but doesn't flinch. 'Mum made such a fuss when she found out it was you. God, she was over-protective. I was fucking *glad* you teased me. It made me feel a bit more bloody *normal*.'

That's not how I remember it.

'I still feel a bit bad about it,' Grace says.

'Well, there's no need. You must have got really sick of me being ill all the time. Do you remember when Mum forgot your birthday? And you never said a word, you just got on the train and came and brought me a piece of cake the next day?'

Grace sighs. 'Mum made a fuss about that too.'

The nurse moves the IV pole to the head of the bed, and then whisks the curtain shut around us. Susannah closes her eyes again. Her face is swollen and filmed with sweat. I'm so angry with Grace, I could scream.

'How are you feeling?' Grace asks, after a few moments.

'Like shit,' Susannah mumbles, without opening her eyes.

Grace snatches the curtain back open. 'Where's the damn doctor? I told them you're pregnant. They should be prioritizing you! You need an ultrasound. There might be a problem with your placenta, it could be pre-eclampsia, early labour, you could bleed out or—'

'Stop panicking, Grace. My waters haven't broken, and I'm not bleeding. I'm sure the baby's fine.'

'Don't be ridiculous. Look at you! Your skin is yellow! You *collapsed*, Zee. How can I not panic?'

'I told you, the baby—'

'Never mind the baby for a minute,' Grace says fiercely. 'I'm talking about you. I don't want anything to happen to *you*.'

She waits another ten minutes, and then marches back out to the front desk. Within another twenty, a doctor has been to tell us what Susannah and I already knew, but is news to Grace: Susannah's kidneys are failing. She was born with only one functioning kidney; the other was shrivelled and useless, a dried prune instead of a full, ripe plum. The good kidney wasn't even that good: only one half was properly healthy, and instead of one tube draining into the bladder, she had two, both of them too narrow to do the job properly. It worked well enough until she got pregnant the first time, and then the growing baby pressed on the tube and blocked it, forcing toxins to back up in her body. Davey was born six weeks early, and Donny was nearly eight weeks premature. Each time, it gets worse. Susannah isn't even halfway through this pregnancy. If the antibiotics don't work, if the doctors can't jump-start her kidney into working, they'll have no choice but to put her on dialysis until the baby is born.

'Why didn't you *tell* me?' Grace demands, when the doctor has gone. 'How could you offer to do this when it was going to make you so ill?'

'I *wanted* to,' Susannah says thickly. 'It's not that bad. I wanted to give you a baby.'

Grace picks up her bag. 'I'm getting you a private room, I don't care what it costs. You're not going on some Crimean mixed ward. I'll be back in a while.'

Susannah nods wearily. She waits until Grace has left and she is all alone, and then turns her face into her pillow. Her shoulders shudder, and I realize she's crying. 'Oh, fuck. What the hell have I done?' she groans, her voice muffled by the pillow.

Even though I know it's pointless, I sit on the bed next to her and smooth her hair back from her forehead, reversing our roles from just a few hours ago. 'Please don't cry, sweetheart,' I soothe. 'It's going to be OK.'

Suddenly she twists away from me and flings herself violently onto her back, nearly pulling out her IV. Her eyes are unexpectedly dry and hard. 'I have to keep this baby,' she says furiously, her fists clenched by her sides. 'I'm going to keep it. I *have* to keep it.'

'It's OK, darling,' I repeat. 'You're not going to lose it. You got to the hospital in plenty of time. They've got you hydrated again and the doctor said the baby's heartbeat was strong. They'll do an ultrasound tomorrow to make sure. You mustn't worry. The baby will be fine. You're going to keep it—'

And then I realize what she meant.

16

Grace

Tom begins, as he so often does, by kissing my face and stroking my breasts. It's not that it isn't nice, or that I don't enjoy it. It's just that it's how he always begins these days.

Without exception.

He strokes my legs, from my ankles, up my calves, to my knees, and then back down again. It's Saturday night, so I shaved my legs this morning in readiness. Because we always have sex on Saturdays.

After a short while, Tom eases the straps of my cream négligé off my shoulders and gently sucks my nipples. Cursorily, I stroke his back and twist my fingers in his hair – when did he get it cut? I rather miss the boyish curls – but the truth is I'm not really concentrating. I have to get up early tomorrow to collect Susannah from the hospital, and I want to finish off the nursery first. It's freshly painted a pale primrose, and the oak floor has been newly sanded and varnished, but I still haven't unpacked the boxes that arrived from Harrods this morning. I want to have it all ready so I can surprise her when she gets home.

I'm jolted back to my own bedroom when Tom puts his hand between my legs, opens my lower lips and inserts his middle finger to check if I'm wet. Clearly he thinks I'm ready, since he pushes himself up on his forearms, but I wince at the thought. Quickly, I find his penis with my hand and start to squeeze, partly to see how ready he is, but also so that he doesn't push inside me just yet. Tom moans softly, and half-heartedly tries to return the favour, missing my clitoris by at least an inch. We used to be so much better at this.

Susannah talks about sex all the time. In detail. I didn't think some of the things she's described were even possible, never mind legal. I've only ever slept with one man, with Tom, but I used to think our sex life was quite adventurous. Not recently – not since we were married, really – but certainly in the beginning. We did it in all sorts of positions, and not always in bed. There was one time, years ago, at a friend's summer wedding, when we did it in full view of everyone on the front lawn. No one actually knew, of course; I was sitting astride Tom's lap on the grass, my long formal gown hiding the fact that his trousers were unzipped and he was inside me, but still. It makes me excited just thinking about it, even now.

Tom feels the sudden wetness between my thighs, and takes it as a green light. He stops manhandling my genitals and shifts his body into the tried-and-tested missionary position. I imagine the closest Susannah has ever come to missionary is seducing a Jesuit priest when she was backpacking around South America.

I don't let go of his penis, to stop him entering too hard

and too soon, but I can only keep him at bay for so long. He pushes inside me, and I realize I'm still not really moist enough. He thrusts for several minutes before I'm wet enough for him to get going properly.

Once he finds his rhythm, my mind drifts again. I'm so relieved Susannah's coming home. For the past two weeks, while she's been in hospital, I haven't slept. Worrying about her, about the baby; and of course about Mum.

I've seen Mum every day, at Susannah's insistence – 'Give me a break, Grace, you can't come and see me and not bother to walk ten feet down the corridor to her?' – and it's made everything a hundred times worse. When I was only visiting her for an hour a week, I was able to compartmentalize it. It was almost as if she was still at home, still running her committees, still doing her Meals on Wheels, still dead-heading roses and composting tomatoes. But now, after a fortnight of making the same small talk with myself while the machines breathe for her and feed her and collect her urine, I can't ignore the truth. Mum's not getting better. She doesn't even look like herself any more: in fewer than six months, she's aged ten years. Sooner or later, Susannah's going to suggest we tell them to switch off the life-support machines. And I can't let her do that. I can't lose Mum. Not with everything still unresolved between us.

For the past five years, since Susannah ran away to America, Mum and I have dutifully played the same game. She's taken a conscientious interest in my career, and enquired after Tom. In return, I've gone home every third weekend, and for birthdays and holidays, to admire her camellias and pretend to remember neighbours I last saw when I was six. We have perfected our roles – proud mother, loving daughter – so well that we could almost believe them ourselves.

But Susannah left a hole I couldn't fill. I was the daughter who'd stuck around, the daughter she could talk about with friends without needing to change the subject. But we both knew I wasn't the one she wanted. A ten-minute phone call from Susannah to ask for more money meant far more to her than the dutiful, joyless weekends she and I shared.

I don't know why she's never felt about me the way she does about Susannah. I don't know if it was because I was hard to love, or simply because Susannah's need was so overwhelming that it left no room for me. But I want the chance to ask her. She can't die yet. She can't die until I know.

A spasm of pain as Tom thrusts awkwardly refocuses my attention. His rhythm suddenly increases in speed and intensity, and I realize we're close to the finish. Years of practice enable me to time my moans with his movements, and I allow my breathing to quicken with his. There are occasions in bed when one knows an orgasm isn't going to happen, and it's far easier on a man's ego to gloss over those times – only a few, admittedly – rather than ruin it for him with a sense of failure. As Michelle would say, you can't get a coconut every time.

Although there was a time Tom would have noticed.

Susannah is in the middle of another ultrasound when I arrive on her ward the next morning. As soon as I see the sonographer at the side of her bed, my pulse and step quicken nervously, but even before I reach my sister the sonographer has hung up her wand and unplugged the portable machine, and Susannah is wiping off the last of the gel and pulling down her T-shirt.

'Is everything OK?' I ask anxiously.

Susannah climbs off the bed and slides her feet into a pair of crippling black stilettos. 'The baby's fine. They just wanted to check everything before they let me out.'

I've known my sister her entire life. I can always tell when she's hiding something.

'*Susannah*,' I warn.

She rolls her eyes. 'All right. The doctor wasn't supposed to say anything. Stupid rules. I don't know why it matters. She told me the sex of the baby,' she explains, as I'm about to launch into full-blown panic mode. 'She said she was about ninety-nine per cent sure it's a girl. They're not allowed to tell you these days in case you freak out and have an abortion because it's not the sex you wanted.'

'A girl? We're having a girl?'

'Yes. Can we go now?' my sister says impatiently. 'I've been flat on my back for the last fortnight and I'm going to go mental if you don't get me out of here soon.'

She stalks down the ward, her heels ricocheting like gunfire on the hard linoleum. I pick up her holdall and trail after her, grinning like a fool.

In the car park, I throw Susannah's bag into the boot of my BMW and lower the roof while she struggles to get into the low-slung roadster. At nearly nineteen weeks, she's suddenly started to show, and I'm surprised how protective of her – not just the baby – I feel.

The traffic is light. My heart sings with happiness as we speed back towards Oxford. It's a beautiful morning, one of those rare perfect English summer days: all vivid blue sky, warm breeze, lawnmowers and church bells. Very

Midsomer Murders. I'm going to have a daughter! Pink dresses. Ballet lessons. Ponytails. A daddy's girl.

The wind whips Susannah's long blonde hair around her face as we reach the motorway, and she pulls up the hood of her sleeveless T-shirt. She's very quiet, but then the lowered roof makes conversation difficult. I select Bach on the CD system, and turn it up, anticipating her excitement when she sees the surprise I have for her.

'Do we have to listen to this?' she says irritably.

Without argument, I switch to the radio instead, and find a pop station she likes. She says nothing more until we reach the outskirts of Oxford, and then only to point out that I've missed the exit.

'We're not going home just yet,' I say. 'I've got something to show you first.'

'I'm really not in the mood,' she mutters.

It's no wonder she's out of sorts, what with her hormones and all she's been through in the past couple of weeks. There's no point taking it personally. Anyway, nothing can wipe the smile off my face today.

I reach into the side pocket for her pack of Marlboros and hand them to her. 'It's OK. The roof's down, I don't mind.'

'You might not, but what about the baby?' she says indignantly. 'Have you any idea how bad those things are for her?'

I drive through the centre of Oxford, and out past Headington. A few minutes later, I turn right down a side street perpendicular to the river, and pull up in front of a pair of tall iron gates. Behind them is an elegant Georgian apartment building. Susannah doesn't even look up as I punch numbers into the security panel and the gates swing open.

'Come on, then,' I say, slotting the roadster neatly into one of the parking bays in front of the building.

'Look, Grace. I'm tired. I just want to go home.'

'You *are* home,' I say. 'Well, it's not home yet. But it will be.'

Susannah throws me a look, then sighs heavily and climbs out of the car. I lead the way up to a bright, airy first-floor apartment overlooking the river. The kitchen and bathroom are lurid orange and avocado Seventies horrors, but the bones of the flat are good. High ceilings, well-proportioned rooms. It'll be gorgeous once it's had a bit of work done.

'What are we doing here?' Susannah says pettishly.

'I'm showing you your new flat,' I say.

'What are you talking about?'

'It's yours, for after the baby. I've leased it for a year, but there's an option to buy if you decide you want to stay longer. The kitchen and bathroom need updating, but the management company is fine with letting us do that.' I cross the living room and throw open French windows leading onto a tiny wrought-iron balcony just big enough for a couple of café chairs. 'It's only about fifteen minutes' drive from Tom and me, and you can get to the boys in just over an hour. It's perfect.'

'Grace, are you *nuts*? I can't afford something like this! It's way out of my league!'

'No one's asking you to,' I say quickly. 'It's my way of thanking you. I'm paying for it.'

No need to let on that leasing this flat for Susannah is a bit of a stretch, even for me. Money is a bit tight at home these days. My company is doing better than ever, and yet I never quite seem to catch up with the bills. I even had a credit card declined last week when I tried to buy a walnut dresser for Susannah's room at home, since she'd ruined the last one with her cigarettes. Tom forgot to transfer his salary from his account to our joint one last month, too, so there wasn't enough to cover the household bills. I must speak to him about that.

Susannah shuts the French windows again with a sharp click. 'What makes you think I even want to stay in Oxford?' she demands. 'I'm not a child, Grace. You can't just go round taking charge and making decisions for me.'

'I'm not trying to,' I say, hurt. 'I thought you'd be pleased.'

'You're trying to take over, Grace. Like you always do.'

'That's not fair! I'm just trying to help—'

'No, you're trying to get rid of me and salve your conscience at the same time. I hand the baby over to you, and you pension me off with your fancy apartment like I'm some kind of old slapper you don't want to fuck any more.'

I wince. She's a little too close to the mark for comfort. 'You know that's not true. But you can't stay with me and Tom forever,' I cajole. 'You need your own space, and so do I. We can go shopping for furniture and you can pick anything you like. I won't say a word. You can even paint the place black if you want and put mirrors on the ceiling.'

She turns back towards the window, wrapping her arms around herself. 'Look. I'm not trying to piss on your parade. Maybe we can talk about it tomorrow. I just need to get home now. If that's OK.'

Trying not to feel too offended, I quietly lock the front door and we go back to the car. Maybe I *did* railroad her a bit. Mum always says I'm too bossy. And Susannah's right: I'm not doing this just for her. In the nicest possible way, I *do* want her gone after the baby's born. I don't want there to be any doubt at all as to who this child's mother is. Having Susannah there in the house would be too strange. But I don't want her to go back to the US either. I'm surprised how much I've got used to having her around. I'd actually miss her if she left now.

I'm fishing for my car keys when Susannah makes a strangled sound. 'Look,' she hisses. 'Over there!'

I glance up. A tall, familiar figure is just coming out of a peeling Victorian semi a couple of houses down. Behind him, a thin blonde woman hovers on the doorstep, holding the fluttering edges of her pale green silk dressing gown together with one hand. In the driveway is a new silver Audi bearing the vanity plate B1AKE.

'The fucking *bastard*,' Susannah spits, as Blake turns and gives the woman a kiss that, even at fifty yards, clearly involves tongues.

I look away, ignoring the sudden beat between my legs. 'That must be Layla.'

'Layla? Who the fuck is *Layla*?'

'Claudia said Blake had been seeing another woman, some model he met through work. She found some emails a few weeks ago. She thinks it's been going on for about six months.'

'Six *months*?'

'Since Blake found out Claudia was pregnant.'

'Who the fuck does he think he is?' Susannah demands angrily. 'He thinks he can screw anyone he likes and just get *away* with it?'

'It's Claudia's choice. She knows what's going on. This isn't the first time it's happened, Zee. I don't know why she puts up with it, but she does.'

I reach across the passenger seat to open the door for my sister. Still she doesn't move. 'Come on, Zee. Leave it. It's none of our business.'

'No,' she says vehemently. '*No.*'

Her blue eyes are like chips of ice in her pale face. For a moment, I'm touched she cares so much about Claudia, and then the penny drops.

I want to slap her – *He's married! His wife is pregnant! What were you* thinking? – but more than that, I want to *kill* him. Susannah isn't nearly as tough as she makes out. She wears her heart on her sleeve like her tattoos; she falls in love far too easily, and with the wrong men. She was never any match for a player like him. She's not even *second* in line for his affections. She's my baby sister. He should have left her alone.

Oh, Zee.

'Let her have him,' I say bitterly. 'He's not worth it.'

She rounds on me. 'You fucking hypocrite!' she hisses. 'You're just jealous! You'd think he was fucking worth it if it was *your* bed he was in!'

'Susannah!' I gasp, taken aback. 'That's not true!'

She leans over the car, eyes blazing, a cat about to spring. And then suddenly the fight goes out of her. Without another word, she opens the door and climbs awkwardly into the car, then slumps back against her seat and closes her eyes. She doesn't even open them when I reach gently around her and fasten the seatbelt below her swelling belly. I start the car and ease out of the gated courtyard, keeping my gaze firmly on the road when we drive past Blake's car.

When we get home, I help her out of the car, and she thanks me, both of us carefully polite. I take her bag upstairs, and she sits on the edge of her bed, her arms dangling at her sides, as if the life has been sucked out of her.

'Can I get you anything?'

She shakes her head. 'I think I'll just sleep.'

Tom is outside, messing about in the vegetable garden. I put the kettle on the Aga, and sit down, my anger building. That bastard has hurt the two women I care most about. What kind of man cheats on his wife because she's pregnant, and then starts an affair with another pregnant girl? Was it a one-night stand, or something more?

I realize I haven't even asked Susannah if it's still going on. Is she in love with him? Did she think he was going to leave Claudia for her?

Claudia. How can I tell her? How can I *not*?

'This is why I didn't tell you,' Tom sighs later. 'Whatever you do now is wrong. And if you do nothing, you become part of the lie.'

'She's my best friend, Tom. It's bad enough that she thinks Blake is screwing around because she's pregnant. What will it to do her when she discovers the baby has nothing to do with it and he's just a lying, cheating bastard?'

He plunks down on the kitchen sofa and pulls off his muddy work boots. 'I give up. I don't care any more. If you think she needs to know, tell her.'

'But what about Susannah?'

'What *about* Susannah?'

'Everyone loves Claudia. If they know Susannah's been sleeping with her husband, Susannah'll be *persona non grata*. She's just getting settled here. I don't want her to spend the next four or five months miserable. It's not good for her or the baby.'

'So *don't* tell Claudia.'

I throw a tea towel at him. He ducks, and it flies over the back of the sofa, catching Susannah on the chest as she suddenly appears at the foot of the stairs.

'I'm sorry,' I laugh, 'that was meant for Tom.'

She doesn't smile back. 'Grace, can I talk to you?'

Tom stands. 'I'd better have a shower before Grace throws me in the pig pen—'

'Please stay, Tom,' Susannah says clearly. 'This concerns you too.'

She looks tense, but calm. I remember her having the same expression the day she told us she was putting the boys into care. As if she's finally found the courage to face the truth and take whatever is coming her way.

She doesn't sit down with us. Instead, she stands defensively behind a kitchen chair, gripping the back for support. 'I'm sorry,' she says. 'I didn't mean for this to happen. I didn't want to feel like this. I've spent the last two weeks trying to feel different, but I can't help it.'

'It's not your fault,' I say quickly, thinking she's talking about Blake. 'We all make mistakes—'

She cuts me off. 'You don't understand.'

Tom and I glance warily at each other, waiting for her to continue. She opens her mouth several times, and then closes it again, as if unable to find the right words.

'Susannah, it's OK,' I say softly. 'Blake's the one who's married. He should—'

'I'm not talking about Blake.' Her eyes fill unexpectedly, and suddenly she looks about twelve years old again. 'I'm so sorry, Grace. I was just trying to help. I didn't know this would happen. I never meant to hurt you.'

'Hurt *me*?'

'I wanted to do the right thing. I was going to, I swear.'

I want to go to her, but a terrible foreboding settles on my shoulders, pinning me to my chair. I know what she's going to say. I've known ever since she decided to see her sons. Deep down, I think I've known it would end this way since the whole thing started.

'It's a girl,' Susannah pleads. 'A girl. *My little girl.* I can't give her away, Grace. You must see that. I'm her *mother*. I can't give her away.'

'I do see,' I say calmly. 'I understand.'

Her head jerks up. 'You do?'

'Oh, yes. Perfectly. There's just one thing, Susannah. That baby isn't your little girl. She's *mine*.'

17

Susannah

Complete fucking bed rest. They won't even let me out of bed to pee in case it sends me into labour. For thirteen frigging days, I've done nothing but lie on my back and stare at the ceiling. It's like being a tart but without the cash benefits.

I'd be crap at doing solitary. I've never been much for reading books, and there's only so long you can spend flicking through *Heat* and *Closer* without wondering if the entire world is out screwing their extended families. Grace made a big song and dance about private rooms, but it turned out they were all full, and so far everyone's refused to snuff it and free up a bed. So I've been stuck in this crappy ward with no TV and no internet and too much bloody time to think.

At first I thought it was my hormones making me all dumb and broody. But I didn't get like this with the boys, and, trust me, my hormones were in overdrive then. It was really bad with Davey; I'd burst into tears if Princess Di so much as changed her hairstyle. One memorable morning, I sobbed for two hours when I found out the bin men didn't recycle latex. I ate chocolate ice cream with cheese Quavers, and started a refuge for sugar ants. But maternal urges? I had about as much nesting instinct as Myra Hindley. What I'm feeling now has nothing to do with my hormones.

I never wanted another baby. Not once since I gave up the kids have I even thought about having another one. I was crap at it last time round! I hated every Napisan-soaked minute of it. Why the fuck would I want to do it again?

I agreed to play rent-a-womb for Grace because I wanted to keep a roof over my head and maybe prove to her and everyone else I could do something cool for once. I never considered what might happen if I changed my mind, because that *so* wasn't going to happen.

Something weird happened to me when I saw my boys again, all grown up. For the first time in my life I realized what I'd been missing. But I knew, even then, I wasn't going to get a second chance with them, not really. I can see them every week or two, and maybe even get to know them a bit, but Social Services won't let me take them home, not now they're settled with their foster parents. I can't argue with that. Let's face it, how could I turn round and become a mum to two teenagers I barely know? It's never going to happen. It's too late.

This baby is different. It's not too late for this baby.

When the thought first popped into my head, as I was sitting on the sofa looking at Donny's drawing of his mum and dad and brother, a picture that had nothing to do with me, of course I didn't take it seriously. This baby wasn't mine! I was having it for Grace. Yeah, sure, it would've been nice to have a bloke in tow and a baby and a family of my own, but it'd be nice to win the lottery too. It was never going to happen. I'm just not mother material.

Once I'd let the genie out the bottle, the thought wouldn't go away. It kept on buzzing round my head. *I want to keep my baby. I want to keep my baby.* I told myself it was just my hormones running haywire. I almost managed to laugh at the idea of me going back to nappies and pushchairs and puke. As if!

But love isn't logical. And so for two weeks, I've lain on my back and the idea has gone round and round in my head and I've gone back and forth, back and forth. I know it's stupid. I know I'm the last person who should even contemplate motherhood again. I know I'll break my sister's heart, and she'll probably never speak to me for the rest of my life. But I can't give my baby away. Not this time.

And then I hear Mum's voice in my head, reminding me how much I hated being tied down by the boys. How the responsibility freaked me out. *This notion to keep the baby is pure selfishness, Susannah. You're no more ready now than you were then.*

Grace comes to see me every day, and she's so excited, so full of plans, glowing with happiness. She talks about the rocking horse she's having restored for the nursery and the wonderful kindergarten in the village and ponies and bedtime stories, and I realize how much better a mum she'd make than me. How can I deny my baby all the things she can offer it, a stable home with two parents, and a good education and all that stuff, just because I'm feeling broody? How can I smash up her life and tell her I've changed my mind?

Because this is my baby, I think passionately now. Not Grace's baby. Mine. My DNA, my flesh and blood. I can feel it kick inside me! I know Grace will be heartbroken, but she *will* get over it. If I let this baby go, it'll kill me. It's as simple as that.

I pick my nails nervously, glancing along the ward every couple of minutes. Grace is coming to collect me any moment now, and I still haven't told her. I keep meaning to, but every time I think I've finally screwed up my courage, I bottle it.

Maybe . . . maybe we can still find a way round this. Somehow. Perhaps we can – I don't know – share the baby? I could keep living at Tom and Grace's and she could keep working, and I could be a kind of nanny, or something. It *could* work.

A girl in a white lab coat pushes a portable ultrasound towards me. 'Susannah? We just want to check the baby before you leave? Make sure it's OK?'

'What, again?'

'Better safe than sorry?' she sing-songs. 'Won't take long?'

I scowl, but slide back on the bed and lift up my T-shirt. She squirts cold gel on my belly, and slides her probe thing over it. She looks about a year older than Davey.

'She looks like she's doing fine?' the girl says, clicking and pointing.

I glance at the monitor, but it still looks more like a fish fossil than a baby, if you ask me. 'Wait,' I say suddenly. 'Did you say *she*?'

She whips her probe off my belly. 'I shouldn't've said anything.'

'I'm having a girl?'

She nods nervously. 'Like, I'm ninety-nine per cent certain? You won't let on I told you, will you?'

'Told me what?'

'About the baby being a— Oh. Right. Yeah, thanks.'

Seriously: *she's a doctor?*

She quickly wheels her machine off before she puts her foot in it any further, almost colliding with Grace. I'm having a girl. *I'm having a girl!*

There's no way I'll let my daughter end up like me, I vow suddenly. I'll make sure she knows better than to let a man fuck up her life. I won't let her diet, and get obsessed by the pictures of skinny models in stupid magazines. I won't let anyone ever make her feel the way my father and every other man in my life have always made me feel.

In that moment, I know there's no way I'll ever let her go.

I can't even look Grace in the eye as she leads the way out to her fancy sports car. She puts down the roof, and sings along with the radio as she drives us home precisely five miles an hour under the speed limit. She's so fucking *happy*. I pull up my hoodie and scrunch down in the seat. All I want to do is get to my room and hide under the duvet until I figure out how the hell I'm going to tell her I'm about to ruin her life.

I'm in such a funk I can't even talk to her. Only when she goes sailing past our exit off the motorway do I open my mouth. I really don't have the energy for her games today. I just want to go home.

She drags me halfway across Oxford, and then makes me look round some stupid posh flat. I don't even want to get out of the car, but Grace doesn't give me much choice.

'What are we doing here?' I demand, as I follow her into the empty apartment.

Grace waves her arm around the room. 'I'm showing you your new flat.'

'What are you talking about?'

'It's yours, for after the baby,' she says, flinging open the doors onto a tiny balcony overlooking the river. 'I've leased it for a year, but there's an option to buy if you decide you want to stay longer . . .'

I don't know whether to laugh or cry. Grace is exclaiming over cupboards and pointing out period features, and any minute now I'm going to blow up her world.

I won't be staying in Oxford. I won't be staying within a hundred miles of my sister. Once she finds out I'm not going to give her my baby, she isn't going to be renting me expensive flats or lending me Donna Karan. I'll be lucky if she doesn't kill me. I plan to get the fuck out of Dodge as soon as I've told her. Manchester, maybe. It's as cool as London, but not so frigging expensive. And it'll be easy for Blake to find work if he comes with me—

Don't be a little fool. Married men never leave their wives. If you do this terrible thing to Grace, you'll be on your own.

I can just hear Mum's voice, but she's wrong. I'm not being stupid. Why shouldn't he leave Claudia? We get on really well. If the baby's his, which it's got to be, he'll have just as much reason to come with me as stay with her. More, even. There's no way he gets the kind of sex from her that he gets with me.

My knickers go into meltdown at the thought. It's been *weeks*. Blake couldn't visit me in hospital, obviously, so I haven't even seen him since Grace told the bloody world I was pregnant. I wanted to break it to him myself, but maybe he'll have guessed anyway that the baby's really his. He'll probably suggest he leaves Claudia himself. Perhaps we can even break the news to Grace together. It'd be easier for her if she hears from him that the baby isn't Tom's.

Behind me, Grace is just going on and on about the apartment, doing my head in. I round on her, and then feel like a complete bitch.

I apologize, but I can tell she's hurt. We trail out to the car, and I'm too tired and stressed to make it all right. I just want to get this over with. I wish Blake would return my calls. I've rung him about five times this morning, and texted him, like, every ten minutes. He must have his phone switched off because of his stupid wife.

For a moment, when I see him coming out of the house across the street, I think I'm imagining it because he's on my mind. And then I realize I'm not hallucinating. The bastard really is here.

When we get home, Grace leaves me to stew in my room while she fusses around downstairs. I sit on the edge of the bed, too sick and raw even to cry. I shouldn't have been such a cow to her. I wish I could take back what I said. She does fancy Blake, but unlike me, she's not stupid enough to do something about it. I'm the fucking idiot who homes in on assholes like a heat-seeking missile and invites them to walk all over me. Why am I always so fucking *stupid*?

Blake isn't going to leave Claudia. Why would he, when he can have his cake and eat it? The only way they'll split is if she kicks him out, and if she hasn't done that by now, she's not going to.

I'm not even second in line. He's been shagging that blonde bitch since way before I was on the scene. What am I, a bit on the side of his bit on the side?

I've put off telling Grace for lots of reasons: mainly because I'm a fucking coward. But also because I didn't want to have to leave Blake. I guess I always knew he wasn't going to come with me.

I get up and go into the bathroom, where I splash cold water on my face. I'm running out of excuses. There's no reason for me to stay here now. I won't end up on the street. I'm pregnant, so the Social will have to give me somewhere to live. It'll be a shit hole, but I've survived worse. I climbed out of the hole before. I'll manage.

In the kitchen, Grace and Tom are laughing and for a second, I nearly bottle it again. They've been my family for nearly six months, and they're going to hate me. As soon as I open my mouth, it'll all be over.

'Grace,' I say, 'can I talk to you?'

I think afterwards that if Tom hadn't been there, Grace might actually have killed me.

There's only one person who can make it better, but she's not here. Instead, when Tom drops me off at the studio, his normally cheery hobbit face grey and drawn, it's Michael who opens the door.

He does his best. He makes tea and sits me down on the sofa and listens while I sob hysterically, even though I can tell he's desperate to be anywhere but here.

'I've never seen her like this before,' I hiccup, when I've finally stopped crying and reached the snivelling, shuddering stage. 'She *hates* me.'

Silently, Michael passes me another tissue.

'You should've seen the way she looked at the kitchen knife,' I say pitifully. 'If it wasn't for the baby, I think she'd have killed me there and then.'

'I'm sure that's not true,' Michael mumbles.

I grab another tissue from the box, and blow my nose loudly. 'It is. She's been mad at me loads of times – after I left the boys in care she didn't speak to me for five years – but she's never been like this. The way she just kept saying the baby was hers, like some kind of zombie. It was totally weird. And then she *smiled*. Like, this cold, hard smile as if she hated me so much it actually turned her on.'

Michael flushes to the tips of his ears. If I wasn't so upset, it'd be sweet.

'She's never going to forgive me, is she?' I say miserably. 'There's no going back now. She's never going to get over this.'

He looks at me helplessly, saying nothing, because there is nothing to say. Even I can see that what I've done is unforgivable. Grace didn't need to tell me: as far as she's concerned, she no longer has a sister. And this time, she means it.

Michael offers me dinner, but I can't eat. Instead, I follow him upstairs to his spare room, a tiny box room under the eaves over the studio. It's a bit cold, but after two weeks in a hospital bed, I'm just glad to be sleeping on my own without the constant noise and disturbance of patients moaning and coughing, and nurses waking you up to give you your medication. I change into an oversize T-shirt that used to be Tom's, and scramble into the narrow single bed. It's actually made up with blankets and sheets and one of those candlewick bedspreads like we used to have when we were kids. It's strangely comforting. I don't expect to fall asleep easily, but I'm out almost as soon as my head hits the pillow.

The next morning, Michael has already disappeared, no doubt terrified of more girly tears and confidences. I hope Michelle comes back. I really need to talk to her.

I make myself a cup of sweet tea, and search the studio galley kitchen for something quick and easy to eat. On Michael's side of the fridge are probiotic yoghurts and tofu and prune juice. Thankfully, on Michelle's there are chocolate mousses and Camembert.

I'm hanging on the fridge door and debating whether I can be arsed to make an omelette when I hear Michael come back in. 'D'you have any eggs?' I ask, without turning round. 'I thought I'd whip up a quick—'

'If I had any eggs, we wouldn't be in this mess,' Grace says.

I nearly drop the carton of milk in my hand as I spin round. My sister hovers in the doorway, as if afraid to cross some invisible line. She looks totally different from yesterday: tired and red-eyed, but calm. That scary look in her eye has gone.

I nod warily, and she takes a couple of steps forward. I don't move from the fridge. For all I know, she's got a Smith & Wesson tucked in her expensive handbag.

'We need to talk,' she blurts finally. 'We can't leave it the way we did yesterday. This isn't just about us. A child is involved.'

'I'm not going to change my mind,' I warn.

Grace glances around, taking in the half-finished canvases and tubes of paint and cans of brushes and turpentine on the floor. Seen through her eyes, it does look a bit of a pigsty.

She pulls a plastic garden chair over to the chipped Formica table, and then looks around fruitlessly for a second, before clearing a heap of small canvases from a wooden stool. She sits down, and after a long moment, I unfold my arms and join her at the table, kicking my chair further away from it, just to make the point.

'I've never had a child,' she says, so quietly I have to strain to hear. 'I'm not a mother. I can't begin to imagine how it must feel to have a baby grow inside you.'

For several minutes, she doesn't say anything more. When I finally glance up, I'm shocked to see she's crying.

'Grace, please,' I say awkwardly, 'don't do this. It's just going to make it worse.'

'When you offered to have a baby for me,' she continues, as if I haven't spoken, 'it was like a dream come true. I'd given up on having a family. Tom and I couldn't adopt, and I was too terrified of surrogacy, in case it went wrong.'

I flinch. I didn't think it was possible until now for me to feel any lower.

'But then you came home,' she says, her voice suddenly filled with wonder. 'You offered to do this amazing thing for us. Maybe I should have stopped to think about it more. Tom wanted to, but I wouldn't listen. It seemed like the answer to my prayers, and I didn't stop to question it. I see now that I never even thought about what it would be like for you. You offered something I wanted, and I just took it.'

'I'm so sorry, Grace,' I say, and now I'm in tears too. 'I never meant to hurt you. I thought I could do it, I really did.'

'The thing is,' Grace says painfully, 'it's not about you *or* me now. It's about this baby. What's best for *her*.'

The silence between us stretches. I realize my sister, the selfish, controlling career woman who has no experience of motherhood or children, is right. It *isn't* about us. It is about a little girl who has no say in what's going to happen to her, and is relying on us to make the right choice.

Think of the baby, Susannah. Can you really give her the best start in life? Grace will love this child with every ounce of her being. She'll want for nothing.

For the first time since I left the hospital, I waver. What can I offer this baby? I don't have a home, a job or a husband. If she stays with me, she'll grow up in a crappy council flat with drug dealers hanging around her school playground. There'll be a parade of sleazy stepdads in and out of her life – let's face it, my track record at picking men is hardly stellar. I had the benefit of two nice middle-class parents and a private school, and look how I turned out. What chance will my daughter have without even those advantages? Chances are she'll be pregnant herself before she's sixteen.

'I know it's not about fancy pushchairs and designer clothes,' Grace says quietly. 'I can give her all the toys, all the *things*, she could possibly want, but that's not what really matters, is it? What matters is that she'll have two parents, a mother and a father, who'll love her and protect her no matter what happens. Please, Zee. Let us be her family. Not for my sake, but for hers.'

Maybe, if my daughter hadn't kicked, *right then*, I'd have said yes.

'I'm sorry, Grace. I'm her mother. She's meant to be with me.'

'What about Tom?' she says tearfully. 'He's her father. Doesn't he get a say in this?'

I shake my head. 'Tom isn't her father.'

She jerks back. 'Not Tom? Then who— Wait. Not *Blake*?'

'It just happened,' I mumble. 'A day or two after – you know, with Tom. And the jug.'

'How do you know? How do you *know* it's Blake's, and not Tom's?'

'Tom did it in a jug! It's bound to be Blake's, it just is. I'm sorry, I never meant—'

'It could be either of them,' she insists.

I get up from the table and pace towards the window. 'It doesn't make any difference, Grace. Even if it is Tom's, she's still meant to be with me.'

'It makes all the difference in the world,' Grace says.

She stands up. 'Please, Susannah. Think about what's best for *her*.'

'I am,' I say stubbornly.

Moments later, I hear the click of the door as she shuts it carefully behind her. I'm not sure which is more terrifying: her anger or this strange, eerie calm. I wonder what happens next. I know Grace. She isn't going to just give up. She'll be planning her next move already.

I don't have to wait long to find out what it is.

18

Grace

'If you go ahead with this,' Nicholas Lyon warns, 'it's going to get very messy.'

Nicholas Lyon is clearly a decent man. He has a silver-framed photograph of his wife on his desk – I recognize her from her cookery show on television – and, next to it, another of his children, three pretty girls and two boys, the youngest a gummy-smiled baby. The wall behind him is covered with primary-coloured artwork, and his pencils are propped in a lumped, misshapen clay pot with 'hapY faTheRs Day' engraved in wobbly letters on the side.

If Nicholas says it's going to get messy, I believe him. He's known as the best family lawyer in London precisely because he doesn't embark on litigation unless it's absolutely necessary. As, in this case, it is.

'I didn't want it to come to this, but Susannah hasn't given me much choice,' I say grimly. 'I've tried to talk to her at least three times in the past two weeks. She won't even open the door to me now.'

Nicholas uncaps an old-fashioned fountain pen, and pulls a pad of foolscap towards him. 'In that case, let's discuss your options. The current law on surrogacy is rather convoluted, as science outpaces the judiciary, I'm afraid. Under the Surrogacy Arrangements Act, a surrogate mother is defined as a woman who carries a child in pursuance of an arrangement made before she began to carry the child, and made with a view to any child being handed over to, and the parental responsibility being met by, another person.' He looks up. 'Under these terms, your sister fits the bill as a surrogate, even though there was never a written contract.'

'It didn't seem necessary,' I say helplessly. 'She's my *sister*.'

'Indeed.' He nods briefly. 'The law differentiates between total surrogates, who carry a child to whom they are not related, a host womb, as it were, and partial surrogates. Your sister is a partial surrogate, in that she is the genetic mother of the child.'

'Does it make a difference?'

'I'm afraid it does. Under the law as it stands now, where the surrogate mother is also the genetic mother, she is legally the child's mother and has parental responsibility.'

'Susannah has parental responsibility?' I demand furiously. 'She couldn't even spell it! She put her sons into care! If it wasn't for me, she wouldn't even *be* pregnant!'

Nicholas holds up a hand. 'Please, Grace. This isn't about what's fair. This is about the law and, ultimately, what the law considers best for this baby.'

'What's best for her is to be with *us*, with Tom and me. Susannah doesn't have a place to live, or a proper job, she's got no money—'

'If the court determines the child should be with her, she will be entitled to benefits and housing,' Nicholas points out. 'But naturally, her ability to provide a decent home for the child will form part of our case against her, should it come to that.'

'But I do *have* a case?'

'If we pursue the transfer of parental responsibility from Susannah to you,' he says, not answering the question, 'there are two legal routes open to us. One is to ask the court to make a Parental Order under the Human Fertilization and Embryology Act in your favour, so that you and Tom are treated in law as the parents of Susannah's baby, which is the most straightforward option in this case. The other would be to adopt the child. Even if the court doesn't agree to transfer parental responsibility to you, it can still make a Residence Order in your favour. That would mean you would have custody of the child, even though Susannah would still share parental responsibility with you, rather as a divorced parent might with the custodial parent.'

'So we apply for the Parental Order,' I say briskly.

Nicholas hesitates. 'It's not that simple, I'm afraid. You said that Susannah has stated your husband might *not* be the baby's father. If this does indeed prove to be the case, I'm afraid we won't be eligible for a Parental Order.'

'But what difference does it make? If the baby is better off with me, what does it matter who her father is? I'm still her aunt. I'm her nearest relative. I thought you said the court looked at what's best for the baby.'

'It does. But one of the conditions for granting a Parental Order is that at least one of those applying is the child's biological parent. If Tom *is* the baby's father, he can in turn extend parental responsibility to you on the slightly strange premise that you, as his wife, are the baby's legal step-parent. Otherwise, I'm afraid we don't have a leg to stand on.'

'But Susannah has *proved* she's a bad mother,' I plead. 'She gave her two boys away! She can't give a baby a stable home! Some of the people she mixes with aren't even *safe*. She—'

'Grace. Even if what you say is true,' he says gently, 'if Tom isn't the father, you have no legal right to the baby. The State may deem her an unfit mother and remove her from Susannah's care, but they still wouldn't give her to you.'

Nicholas' kind features blur. I look down, tears splashing on my hands as I twist them together in my lap. How can this be right? How can some faceless judge who has never even met me decide I don't deserve this baby? I may not be carrying her in my own body, but I've loved her since before she was conceived. I've traced her outline on the scan photographs so many times with my fingers that I've worn her image away. She is mine in every meaningful sense of the word.

Nicholas comes around his desk and presses a box of tissues into my hands, waiting patiently for me to bring my emotions under control, as if women burst into tears in his office on a regular basis; I suppose they do. He must see this all the time. Perhaps not in these exact circumstances, but how many parents – estranged fathers, tug-of-love mothers – has he had to console as they come to terms with the fact that they will no longer be a part of their child's daily life? How many times has he broken the news to a father that he will only be allowed to see the child he loved and protected for one day every other weekend? Or tell a mother whose babies have been whisked to the other side of the world that there's nothing she can do? My tragedy is overwhelming, but commonplace.

'The most important thing to determine is whether Tom is the father,' Nicholas says evenly, when I finally look up and nod for him to continue. I'm grateful that he doesn't attempt sympathy or kindness.

'A DNA test?'

He nods. 'Unfortunately, we have to wait until the child is born before we can request a paternity test and discover if it's appropriate to apply for a Parental Order.'

'But she's only twenty-two weeks pregnant. The baby isn't due until Christmas. She could leave the country long before then and go back to America. I might never find her again!'

'I'm sorry, Grace, but our hands are tied.'

'What about amniocentesis?' I demand. 'Susannah insisted on having the test, even though she's not high-risk. She's terrified of Down's. Can't you determine paternity from the amnio test?'

'Even assuming the sample is still available for testing—'

'She only had it done a few days ago. I paid for her to have it done privately,' I admit, correctly interpreting his look of surprise. 'I know it's stupid, but I kept thinking, if I could show her I'd be a good mother, if I can prove how much I care . . .'

Nicholas returns to his side of the desk, and scribbles a note on his legal pad. 'We would need Susannah's written agreement,' he warns. 'We have no legal right to insist on a DNA test at this stage.'

'She'll agree. She's positive the baby is Blake's. She wants to prove that just as much as I want to prove it's Tom's.'

I know my sister. She's living in cloud cuckoo land. No doubt she's convinced herself Blake will leave Claudia – and Layla, and anyone else he's screwing – and run off into the sunset with her once he's sure the baby is his. Just as she's convinced herself she can be a good mother this time round.

'If she does agree to a DNA test, we may be able to set things in motion before the baby is born,' Nicholas says thoughtfully. 'I would suggest an intermediary – perhaps your husband? – put it to her sooner rather than later. Once we have the results, we can take a view as to the next best step.'

I stand up and hand him a cheque for five thousand pounds, as his secretary requested. I just hope it doesn't bounce. 'Your retainer,' I say.

He escorts me to the door, and then pauses. His grey eyes are filled with concern as he looks at me, and I wonder at the phenomenon: a lawyer who actually cares.

'Grace,' he says kindly, 'I'm not going to bank this cheque yet. I want you to take some time to think about this. If we go into battle against your sister, it will get very dirty. Others will get dragged into the fight. People you care about will get hurt. If the baby *is* Tom's, we still face an uphill battle to take her from her mother. Even if you eventually win, there will be scars. You need to be very sure you want to go ahead before we press the button.'

Nicholas is a nice man, a decent man, but he has five children. He cannot possibly know what I have gone through just to get to this point.

It took me six months of trying even to acknowledge that a baby wasn't going to come as effortlessly to me as everything else in my life had done. And when I was finally, resentfully, forced to face the fact that I was going to have to *work* at it, I was determined to leave no stone unturned.

The moment I went online and stepped into the first trying-to-conceive – TTC – chatroom, I entered a different world. When you are trying to conceive, I mean *really* trying – when you have moved past the excited, nervous stage when you stopped trying to prevent it, when you have started to count the days in your cycle and make notes on the calendar, when you are beginning to feel a little more nervous, a little less excited, with every month that passes – you join an elite, obsessive club that feeds off itself. There is even a special website devoted to home ovulation and pregnancy tests: www.peeonastick.com. Like so many of the sad, desperate clubs we know exist but hope never to join – the rape victims, the cancer survivors, those who have lost a child – the TTC community has a language and a culture all its own, flowing beneath the surface of ordinary life like a river.

I learned to converse in the acronymic shorthand of the experts. I discovered the all-important 'Day 3 FSH': the follicle-stimulating hormone whose levels need to be in single digits when your blood is drawn and tested on the third day of your period, or no fertility clinic that values its IVF success rate will touch you. I bought a special OvuWatch to wear at night the week before I ovulated, to analyse my sweat so that I'd know the exact hour my egg was released into my fallopian tubes, ready to be fertilized. Every new vitamin or supplement or snake-oil someone somewhere recommended, I added to the growing fist of pills I choked down every morning: black cohosh to boost oestrogen, ginseng to lower my FSH, kelp to tone my pituitary gland so that it produced the right levels of the right hormones at the right times . . .

All of it pointless.

Rendered an outcast from the TTC club by my apocalyptic *no chance* diagnosis, I'd simply joined another: those desperate to adopt a child from anywhere, by any means. The day before Susannah had offered to be our surrogate, I'd actually emailed a girl in Tennessee who'd advertised her unborn child online. For less than the price of three Vuitton handbags, I could have bought her son.

I can't go back to that life. If I step back into that obsessive, cloistered world, I'll never find my way out. Susannah's baby needs me, and I need her. We were meant for each other.

I look Nicholas Lyon in the eye. 'Bank the cheque,' I tell him.

'No,' Tom says again.

We've been having this same argument for ten days. Nothing I've said has made Tom see reason. I'm running out of time. Susannah still won't even speak to me, and Tom stubbornly refuses to help. I don't want to take legal action against my own sister, but they're leaving me little choice.

'I'm just asking you to *talk* to her,' I plead, near to tears. 'I just want you to see if she'll agree to the test. She doesn't even need to do anything; they already have the sample they need. Please, Tom. Just *ask* her.'

'Why won't you get it into your head?' Tom shouts. 'I'm not going to agree, not to this, not to any of it! I don't give a damn *who* the father is! Susannah is this child's *mother*. That's all that counts!'

'But look at the kind of mother she is!' I cry. 'You can't *possibly*—'

'Grace,' he bellows, 'I am not going to wrench that child out of its mother's arms!'

The contempt in his face brings me up short. I don't think I've ever seen Tom look like that: not at me, not at anyone. My heart folds over with fear. In the fifteen years we have been together, I have never once doubted that Tom and I will survive anything life throws at us. He is my constant. But before this baby is even born, she's created a gulf between us that's already wider than I'd ever have thought possible. For the first time, I'm beginning to realize that my solid, impregnable marriage is just as vulnerable as anyone else's.

I want to tell him I'm sorry and beg him to forgive me. I open my mouth, and choke on the words.

This baby has no one but me. Susannah doesn't really want her. If she did, she wouldn't be living the life she is, risking her child's health with her drinking and partying. If I thought it could be different . . . if I knew this little girl would be loved and looked after and cared for, that Susannah wouldn't change her mind one day and run back to America without her . . . maybe I wouldn't feel so strongly.

Tom's never wanted her. He's not going to lift a finger to save her. I'm going to have to do it on my own.

Grace, forget the baby for five minutes, and think about your husband. Please, think about Tom—

'What am I supposed to do now?' I demand. 'You can't expect me to just *abandon* her!'

'You do what you have to,' Tom says coldly.

He picks up his jacket. 'Where are you going?' I cry, running after him.

'In case you'd forgotten, your best friend has just given birth to our godson,' he snaps, 'and we have promised to go and see him. We are going to tell her how beautiful her son is, and how wonderful she looks, and we are going to congratulate them and mean it.'

I take a step backwards, as if he's about to force me into the car. 'I can't! Not after what's happened!'

'She is your *best friend*,' Tom says fiercely. He takes my linen summer coat and literally throws it at me. 'If you insist on going ahead with this nonsense, you'll be throwing a hand grenade into Claudia's life as well as ours. You can't expect Blake's affair with your sister to stay a secret once you bring the lawyers in. Claudia may have turned a blind eye to Blake's other women, but another child will be a different matter.'

'But we have to *know!*'

Tom looks at me for a long moment. 'Does everything have to be a battle with you, Grace?' he says tiredly. 'Can't you just forget about what *you* want for once and think about someone else?'

I'm shamed into silence. Tom is right. I've been so blinded by what's happening with Susannah, I'm missing things that matter. My best friend has just had a baby, and she needs me; even if she doesn't yet know it.

Chastened, I put our gifts for the baby in the boot of Tom's car. He doesn't even glance at me as he starts the engine. When we arrive at Blake and Claudia's smart Georgian house, he parks the car, climbs out, and walks briskly ahead of me as if I'm not even there.

Blake opens the door to us full of pride and bonhomie. I'm hard-pressed to smile back. He couldn't keep it in his trousers for five minutes. Because of him, I may lose my only chance at a child of my own. Susannah would never have reneged on the deal if she was certain the baby was Tom's. It's only because she thinks it might be Blake's that she's doing this. Doesn't she realize this selfish, overgrown schoolboy is never going to leave his comfortable, secure domestic set-up for a peripatetic life with a flaky druggie?

Every time Blake puts his arm round Claudia's shoulders and says how proud he is, I want to vomit. I'm scarcely able to contain my relief when, after five minutes watching us coo dutifully over the new arrival, Blake invites Tom to wet the baby's head in his den.

'What's going on?' Claudia demands, as soon as Tom leaves the room. 'Are you two not speaking?'

I shrug.

'Want to talk about it?'

'Nothing to talk about.' I lean over the Moses basket on the floor between us, teasing the baby's fingers with my index finger until he grasps them with surprising strength. 'We had a bit of a row before we left, but it'll sort itself out.'

'About Susannah,' Claudia sighs.

'We've never argued like this before. It frightens me, Claud. Sometimes he looks at me like he almost hates me. I'm scared I'll lose him.'

'Do you want a baby that much?'

'It's not just about what I want,' I say, 'not any more. If I thought Susannah had changed, it'd be different. But I can't let this baby end up in foster care, lost in the system, which is what'll happen, sooner or later. I can't do it, not even for Tom. Anyway.' I shake myself and change the subject. 'You look wonderful. No one would ever guess you'd just had a baby.'

She smiles. 'He was a walk in the park compared to the twins. Four hours, start to finish. Maybe it's because he was a couple of weeks early. I was in labour for thirty-six hours with the girls. I thought I was going to die. You have *no* idea how lucky you— Oh, God.' She covers her mouth, aghast. 'Oh, Grace. I'm so sorry, I didn't mean—'

'Forget it.'

'I didn't think. I'm a complete idiot.'

'I think you're amazing,' I say honestly.

Claudia hesitates. 'Would you like to hold him?'

My arms are reaching out for the baby before she's even finished speaking. Claudia scoops him out of his basket and hands him to me, and I cradle his tiny head in the cup of my hand, nestling him in the crook of my arm. I can feel the ache in my empty womb, as physical as a punch to the stomach. The baby turns his head into my chest, snuffling for a nipple, and I want to howl with misery. I look at Claudia, unable to speak. Holding this child is simply too overwhelming.

'Maybe Susannah will change her mind,' Claudia says softly. 'Just give her a little time.'

'Tom says I should stop asking her,' I whisper thickly. I stroke the baby's dark quiff of hair against my cheek. 'He never really wanted a baby. Not this way. I shouldn't have pushed him into it. He's not prepared to fight for her. He thinks she belongs with Susannah.'

'But she's his baby too!' Claudia cries indignantly. 'Sorry, Grace. I know it's none of my business, but he can't just wipe the slate clean and pretend she doesn't exist!'

I feel like the worst kind of Judas. If Claudia knew the

truth: that Blake has not just cheated on her, but fathered my sister's child – and worse, that I knew about it and didn't tell her – would she still be so quick to defend me?

Her baby stirs in my arms. I gaze at him, breasts and heart aching with longing. Claudia is my dearest friend, but she has her son. She has her girls. I have to fight for my child, just as she would do for hers if it came to it. She's a mother; surely she can understand that? Wouldn't any mother do the same?

Later, as Tom and I make our awkward, separate good-byes on the doorstep, I suddenly remember the presents I brought for the baby and Claudia's girls, still in the boot of Tom's car. He's parked a little way down the lane, since there isn't room for a third car in their narrow driveway, so I go outside to get them. As I open the boot, Blake materializes behind me in the dark.

'Need a hand?'

'It's OK,' I say, reaching into the car for the wrapped presents. 'They're not heavy.'

'You should learn to accept help,' Blake smiles, 'or people will stop offering.'

I hesitate, charmed despite myself by that movie-star smile. Whatever I think of him, it's nice of him to lend a hand, even if I don't really need it. Tom pointedly didn't offer. Blake hasn't actually done me any harm, not directly. Making a scene now will hardly help matters.

I stand back as he pulls a second large waxed-paper bag out of the boot. A huge plush cocker spaniel peeps out, ears flopping waggishly over his glass eyes. 'Jesus. This is ten times bigger than the baby.'

'Susannah picked it out,' I say, 'months ago, when we were shopping at Harrods.'

Our eyes meet. I'm the first to look away.

'You know,' Blake accuses.

'She told me. About you and – the baby.'

'The baby? Christ, she's not pinning that on me. There's no way that kid's mine.'

He's very close to me now. I can see the pulse beating at the hollow of his throat. He smells of whisky and smoke and something else, something I can't name but which causes a sudden heat between my legs.

He reaches up and tucks a strand of hair behind my ear. 'Susannah was a mistake. You've always been the sister I wanted.'

Heat and pleasure flood my cheeks. *You've always been the sister I wanted.* Not Susannah, glorious, golden, sexy Susannah, with her long tanned legs and dancing blue eyes. Grace. Dull, ordinary Grace. Me.

'The Ice Queen,' Blake whispers, so close now that I can feel the warmth of his skin. 'What does it take to melt her, I wonder?'

I should move, but I can't. I should protest, but I don't. This is what it's like to be Susannah, I think giddily. Handsome men falling all over you, propositioning you at every turn, risking all for a single kiss.

He dips his head to mine. My lips open beneath his, lust racing across my skin. My nipples ache to be touched, and a flood of moisture seeps between my thighs. I press my body against his, yearning to be naked. If he pinned me against the car now and lifted my skirt, I'd welcome him without a second thought.

But he lets me go.

'Your phone's ringing,' he says, and I can see in his eyes that he knows precisely the effect he's had on me, knows that the bells of Notre Dame could have been ringing and I wouldn't have heard them. 'You might want to answer it.'

He saunters back to the house with the plush spaniel tucked under his arm. I watch him go, hating him for kissing me, hating him more for stopping.

Belatedly, I remember my phone.

19

Susannah

I'm woken by the sound of banging at the front door. I scramble off the sofa, where I've been dozing in front of *Loose Women*, and peer through the frosted porthole to the left of the studio door.

Grace. Shit. Quickly I duck out of sight and hide beneath the kitchen counter, hoping she doesn't go round to the back door. I'm not sure I locked that.

My calves start to cramp as I hear Grace clipping round the outside of the studio, knocking on the full-length windows and trying to peer through the blackouts. She knows I'm in here. This is fucking mad. I'm hiding from my sister like she's a bloody bailiff because I'm too chicken to face her and tell her where to get off.

The thing is, I know Grace. Once she has the bit between her teeth, there's no stopping her till she gets what she wants. Right now, she's after my baby. And when it comes to Grace, I've never been any good at saying no.

When we were kids, as far as Grace was concerned,

what's mine was hers. Needless to say, it didn't cut both ways. If I so much as touched her stuff, she'd practically have a cow.

'You don't mind if I borrow this, do you?' she'd say, picking up my new 'Frankie Says Relax' T-shirt or Duran Duran album, and of course I'd be too much of a wimp to say yes, I did mind. Grace's 'Imperative Interrogative', Mum called it. A question that was really a royal command.

I wouldn't have minded so much, but usually that'd be the last I'd see of whatever it was she'd 'borrowed'. If I did get it back, it'd be trashed. Grace was totally anal about her things, but when it came to mine, it was a different story. Jumpers would be returned stretched, records scratched, lipsticks worn down to the nub, and she'd never offer to replace them. I once saved an entire month for a really expensive Dior eyeshadow set, and the first time Grace came back home from college it disappeared. When, on her next visit, I asked her if I could have it back, she airily told me she'd lost it. 'It wasn't any good, anyway,' she said carelessly. 'Boots No. 7 do the same colour, and it lasts much longer.'

Mum said I had to stand up to Grace, but she didn't understand. Grace was my big sister. I *wanted* to share things with her. I wanted to be part of her world. I thought that if I gave her what she wanted, she'd be my friend and share it with me.

Not any more, I think firmly. I'm done with bribing my sister to get her to like me. I've given her everything she's ever asked for, but I draw the line at my own baby.

I hear the rasp of the letterbox as Grace pushes it open and calls through it. 'Susannah? I know you're there. Please, I just want to talk.'

Quietly, I squirm back and huddle further out of sight – not an easy feat with a bump the size of a medicine ball glued to my lap. Two buttons ping noisily off my shirt. I've got to get some maternity clothes soon; I'm literally bursting out all over. My boobs cast such a huge shadow, my feet are going to start sprouting mushrooms.

Just as I think Grace is about to give up, there's the sound of a key in the lock. Fuck fuck *fuck*. Michael must be back from the gallery. Just my freaking luck.

The door opens, and I sign frantically to Michael to tell Grace I'm not there, slashing the edge of my palm wildly across my throat. Without missing a beat, Michael turns back to my sister, blocking her view as she bobs up and down trying to see in. 'You must have missed her, Grace. I'll tell her you were here.'

'But it's really important, I—'

'Help me up,' I hiss, as Michael politely but firmly shuts the door on my sister. 'I'm stuck. My centre of gravity has shifted to my arse.'

'Along with your senses, it would seem.'

I take his hand, and, using it as a fulcrum, slowly lever myself upright. 'What was I supposed to do?' I say crossly. 'She's been round here every day since I left, bugging the crap out of me. She's not going to give up till she gets what she wants. You know what she's like.'

'Then you need to tell her you're not going to change your mind.'

'Give me a break. You don't think I have?'

'No. I don't think you've told her like you mean it. Because, actually, I don't think you do.'

I stick out my tongue at Michael's departing back as he

disappears up the wrought-iron spiral staircase to his loft. What is he talking about: he doesn't think I mean it? Of course I mean it! This baby is the only good thing in my life. I'll never give her up. She's my chance to get things right finally.

But maybe he has a point. Maybe Grace keeps coming over because *she* thinks I don't mean it too.

Michelle's the one who's really my friend, but I have to admit Michael is beginning to grow on me too. I'm starting to see they've got more in common than I thought. They both give good advice, even if I don't always like hearing it. And Michael doesn't judge. He took me in without demanding explanations or offering advice. Nor has he started dropping subtle hints about me finding my own place, even though I've been here nearly a month. I never meant to stick around this long, but I don't feel up to coping on my own yet, and Michael's so easy to be with; at least, now he's got used to me. Women clearly terrify the shit out of him – which is weird, given he makes such a good one – but it's like I'm an honorary trannie or something because of the baby. He knows I'm not going to jump his bones when his guard is down. Shame, really. He could be kinda hot if he wasn't so easily spooked.

When Michael drives back to the gallery later that afternoon, I hitch a lift with him into town. I need some bigger clothes before I split everything like the Incredible Hulk.

He drops me at the covered market, and I head straight to Mortons for a falafel and hummus wrap. I don't know what it is about this pregnancy, but I'm hungry all the time. I've put on about twenty pounds already, and I bet nineteen of that is Ben & Jerry's and soft cheese.

I lick my fingers, still hungry even after wolfing down the lot. Maybe I could nip into Squirrels for some organic yoghurt-dipped raisins or something. It's not snacking if it's organic, right?

My tummy grumbling, I steer my ever-expanding belly down the narrow aisles towards the health food store, trying to ignore the funky clothes shops filled with skinny jeans that (a) I can't get into and (b) I can't afford. I need a real job, not this filler at the gallery. Benefits aren't going to cut it either. Sixty-four quid a week doesn't get you a night at the flicks these days. Honestly, the amount people like Grace pay in taxes, you'd think the government could be a bit more generous.

As I come within smelling-range of Nash's Bakery, my feet stop of their own accord. Screw the organic sawdust. I want one of those custard pies. And a chocolate éclair. And maybe a millefeuille chaser.

I don't realize my nose is actually pressed against the window until I start sliding down it. I straighten up in embarrassment, wiping away the greasy imprint with my sleeve. Seriously. I'm going to be one of those half-ton women on the Discovery Channel if this carries on.

Suddenly I stop wiping, and peer back through the glass. Hold on. What's Tom doing in a bakery in Oxford when he's supposed to be saving little lives in London?

And more to the point: who the hell is the sexy redhead with him?

Tom turns and sees me. He couldn't look guiltier if he was stark naked with his head buried between the redhead's legs.

I back away as he rushes outside to me. 'Don't start. I came here to get away from Grace—'

'I'm not going to. As far as I'm concerned, the baby's yours. And if she brings in the legal heavies, I'll tell them the same thing.'

'Grace won't thank you for that,' I say.

'Grace brought this on herself,' Tom retorts sharply.

To my surprise, I feel a twinge of sympathy for my sister. He's her husband; whatever the rights and wrongs of it, she should be able to count on him.

'Who's your friend?' I ask, nodding towards the redhead hovering discreetly a few feet away.

'She's a colleague from work. Look, I know how it seems,' Tom says, blushing to the tips of his hobbit ears, 'but she's here professionally. For a . . . a consult.'

'What about? Chocolate éclairs versus jam doughnuts?'

'It's personal,' Tom mumbles. 'Susannah, I'd be really grateful if you didn't mention this to Grace—'

I snort. 'As if. We're not exactly BFFs right now, in case you hadn't noticed.'

'I'm sorry,' he sighs. 'I'm sorry about all of it. This is all my fault. I should never have gone along with it in the first place.'

I'm about to point out that it's as much my fault as anyone's, when I feel a familiar twinge in my back.

And then the pain suddenly deepens and intensifies, and in an instant it's moved from *ooh I wonder what that is?* to *oh my fucking God!*

It's not nearly as bad this time. For a start, I'm not in some sweaty, phlegm-soaked mixed ward like I was when I collapsed a few weeks ago at the boys' foster home. This time, I had the good sense to pass out in range of the best Oxford hospitals, and I'm soon bedding down in a bijou little ward with only four beds in it, two of which are empty. It probably didn't hurt arriving with two big-shot London doctors in tow: it seems the redhead really *is* one of Tom's colleagues, and a neonatologist at that. Though that still doesn't explain the illicit pastry purchases.

As soon as the doctors start pumping antibiotics into every available vein, I begin to feel better. They give me some painkillers, too, but because of the baby they're not as strong as I'd like (i.e. pass-out-unconscious) and, to be honest, they barely take the edge off. But the worst part is when they catheterize me. Having a sharp plastic tube shoved up your lady-bits by a nurse with all the finesse and sensitivity of Ivan the Terrible is not my idea of fun.

Finally, I stop swelling up like a jaundiced balloon, and the stiletto pain in my kidney dulls to a kneed-in-the-back sort of ache. More doctors appear to check the baby. She kicks back, and while I don't blame her, I now have heartburn and aching ribs to add to my joys.

The doctors gather in a rugby huddle near the door. I hate it when they do this: they refuse to actually *tell* you anything, and then talk about you in maddeningly not-quite-earshot so you're left to piece odd words and phrases together. From what I can gather, I'm either a seventy-five-year-old nun with syphilis and four months to live, or twenty-four weeks into a high-risk pregnancy with a zillion stubborn toxins doing a victory lap round my body.

Either way, to my intense frustration, I'm once more sentenced to bed rest, tethered into place by leads from a dazzling array of monitors and machines. Which means that when Grace bowls up to my bedside late that night, I have nowhere to run.

'Tom ratted me out,' I say accusingly. 'He promised he wouldn't tell you I was here.'

Grace looks surprised; then livid. 'Tom *didn't* tell me. Michael called my mobile; we were over at Blake and Claudia's. How the fuck did *Tom* know?'

Poor bastard. He's going to be in a world of hurt. Grace only swears when she's really pissed off. 'Never mind that now,' I deflect. 'What are you doing here?'

'What do you *think* I'm doing here?'

'You needn't have bothered. It's the same thing it was before. I'll be fine in a few days.'

'This isn't just about *you*—'

'Yeah. You've made that perfectly clear,' I say bitterly.

Grace pulls up a chair and sits down, her fancy leather bag on her knee. It probably cost as much as a small car, I think resentfully.

'Susannah, you've got to start taking this seriously,' she sighs. 'You're sick, and you're pregnant. You need to look after yourself. You can't just run around doing whatever you want.'

'I was eating a bloody sandwich!' I yell. 'I was hardly bungee-jumping from the Empire State Building!'

Grace ignores my outburst. 'When was the last time you had a bottle of beer?'

I shrug defiantly. Maybe I had two or three yesterday after Michael had gone to bed. Yeah, OK, the doctors said I shouldn't drink alcohol, but if you listened to doctors, you'd need a medical certificate to bloody breathe. No soft cheeses. No raw fish. No peanut butter, no caffeine, no pig's bladders, blah, blah, blah. For God's sake, I gave up bloody cigarettes, didn't I? Women have been getting pregnant and having babies for centuries without freaking do-gooders breathing down their necks, and no one died. Well, OK, they did, but not because of the fucking Brie.

'Susannah,' she says quietly, 'if you carry on like this, you're never going to make it to full term. You won't even make it another week. Do you know what it'll mean if she's born now?'

'She'll be in an incubator for a bit. She's twenty-four weeks, lots of babies survive at that age—'

'No, Zee. They don't. A few, a tiny few, babies survive at twenty-four weeks,' Grace says. 'Most of them die. Their lungs simply aren't developed enough for them to breathe, even with help. They can't suck, swallow and breathe at the same time, so they have to be fed intravenously. They can't cry, because of the tubes in their throats. Those who do manage to make it through the first twenty-four hours have to spend months in intensive care.'

'So?'

She sucks in a breath, and I can see her trying hard to hold on to her patience. 'They have one crisis after another – infections, heart failure, respiratory distress, you name it; and you have to live out every crisis with them too. Can you imagine how hard that is? For both of you?'

'I can do it,' I say crossly. 'I'm not a complete idiot. I have been a mother before, you know.'

Grace absorbs the blow without flinching. 'Then you know that if by some miracle she survives and you get to take her home, it's not necessarily happy ever after. She might be blind, or deaf; even if she seems fine, she may have learning difficulties or behavioural problems. Forget what you read in your magazines. *Listen to me*. If you have this baby now, she'll probably die.'

I'm shocked more than I let on. Grace doesn't exaggerate. It's not her style. If she says I could lose my baby, no matter what else is going on between us, I believe her.

'Susannah, I won't lie to you. I want this baby,' she says. 'I want to be her mother. I know I could make a good one, if you'd just give me the chance. But more than that, I want her to live.' She looks me in the eye. 'Prove to me you're the right person to look after her, Susannah, and I'll support you, no matter what you choose to do. I'll cancel the lawyers, I'll give you everything you need. All you have to do is prove you want her to live, too.'

After six days in hospital, they dose me up with antibiotics (which give me diarrhoea and a violent case of thrush) and release me. I might not like it, but Grace has got to me. I don't want to have a brain-damaged baby. For the next three weeks, I lead the life of a moustachioed nun. No fags, no booze, no sex and lots of sleep. Believe me: lots and lots of sleep. When you cut out all the things that make life worth living, sleeping is pretty much the only thing that's left.

Meanwhile, the Asshole Formerly Known as Blake doesn't send me so much as a get-well card.

If there's one thing I'm good at, it's admitting when I've made a mistake (practice makes perfect, Grace would say). Blake hasn't returned my calls or texts in weeks, never mind actually turning up to see how I am. Screw him. The sex was great – fucking fantastic, actually – but I still haven't forgiven him for the Layla business. And he let that snooty bitch wife of his treat me like a piece of shit. I deserve better. Thanks to the thrush, I've gone right off sex anyway.

True to her word, Grace calls off the dogs. I don't get any

more letters from her fancy lawyer, and she doesn't come banging on the door at all hours of the day and night.

Actually, I don't hear from her at all, which is a bit weird, to be honest. I've got so used to her keeping tabs on me, it's kind of freaky to be left entirely to my own devices. It must be killing her not to come checking up on me.

Somehow, I hold up my end of the deal. I'm so clean-living even the Mormons would have me. I'm taking my vitamins and drinking lots of water and generally behaving myself: right up to the point when I run into Blake and Claudia and their cute coffee-skinned children in Starbucks.

I stand in the centre of the café, gripping my skinny latte so tightly I don't even notice when the foam cup splits and spills hot coffee all over my hand. Blake and his wife are crushed into one outsize velvet armchair with the children playing on a small sofa nearby, and he's got his arm round her, and is leaning down to whisper something in her ear. She turns and laughs up at him, and I see the expression in her eyes, and I know she knows about his other woman, even if she doesn't know about me, and I see that she still loves him and will always love him and is never going to let him go. They don't even notice me, and it's all so gut-wrenchingly, fluffy-kitten adorable I want to throw up; and in fact as soon as I dump the coffee and reach the safety of the toilet, I do.

Afterwards, I go straight back home to Michael's and shut myself in my bedroom. I drink four beers, one after the other, and then I open a bottle of vodka and drink half of that too.

It's not even about Blake. He's just the latest in a long, long line of assholes and losers. Every man I've ever been with has treated me like shit, and I've let them get away with it. I want to tell myself I thought Blake was different, but I didn't, not really. We were never going to run off and play Happy Families with the baby. He was always going to stay with his wife, and I was always going to end up pregnant and alone.

I pass out on the bed, and wake up sometime around midday with a raging hangover. I finish the vodka, and go in search of more beer. The next day, I do the same thing again. And the day after that, I'm back in hospital – only this time, they can't patch me up and fix me and send me home.

20

Catherine

I have no idea if this will work, but I'm desperate, so I'll try anything.

Grace is fast asleep in bed, curled on her side in the foetal position. For the briefest of moments, I stand and watch her, remembering how I used to do exactly the same thing when she was a child. Her cheeks are no longer plump with baby fat, the hair spilling onto the pillow is threaded here and there with grey, and she doesn't suck her thumb, but to me, her mother, she looks just the same.

I shake myself. I don't have time for maudlin sentiment now. Lives depend on me. I lean over my elder daughter's sleeping form, and urgently call her name.

She stirs, but doesn't wake. I try again, louder this time, and Tom rolls over towards his wife, one arm draping her hip as he moves.

I'm running out of time. I'm going to have to do this the hard way. With the greatest reluctance, I climb onto the bed and plant myself firmly on Grace's chest. I have no weight, no substance, of course, but I have to fight my instinct to leap off her before I crush her when she starts to struggle. Grimly, I keep my seat as Grace pants and claws at her chest in her sleep. She won't suffocate. This isn't really happening. I'm just gatecrashing her dreams.

Grace suddenly sits bolt upright, wide-eyed and panicky, and I get up off the bed, my job done. 'Tom! Tom! Wake up! *Tom, wake up!*'

'What?' Tom mumbles.

'I need to get to the hospital,' Grace says, throwing back the duvet and struggling out of bed. 'Susannah's sick.'

Tom is immediately alert. 'I didn't hear the phone—'

'No one rang. I just know.'

He pauses, one arm in the sleeve of his dressing gown. 'You just know?'

'Don't just stand there, Tom. She needs me. We have to go. *Now.*'

Tom knows better than to argue. He is not the ideal son-in-law, or the perfect husband, but he is a man who understands his wife. Certainly better than I ever have. *I've been unfair to you, Grace*, I think, regretfully. *So much of this calamity is my fault.*

Briskly, I rouse myself. No time for self-recrimination now. There will be plenty of time for that later. When I know if my daughter and granddaughter are going to survive.

When I get back to the hospital, Susannah is no longer in A&E. For a moment, I panic, but then I find her upstairs, where she has been admitted to the labour ward. She looks even worse than when I left. Her face is so swollen I barely recognize her, and her eyes are yellow. Her breathing is shallow and fast; a greasy film of sweat coats her skin.

'Susannah? We need to deliver your baby *now*,' the doctor is saying urgently. 'We can't wait any longer.'

Susannah pulls the oxygen mask off her face. 'No!' she gasps. 'I told you! She's . . . too little! I'm only twenty . . . eight weeks. She can't be born yet. She'll die!'

'Susannah, twenty-eight weeks is *fine*. I know you're worried, but the scans show your daughter is a good weight for her age. She'll have to be in the NICU for a few weeks, but we'll do everything we can for her.'

'No. Just . . . give me some antibiotics like you . . . did last time. I'll be . . . fine . . . in a few days.'

The doctor struggles to hide her frustration. 'This isn't *like* last time. This isn't just a kidney infection, Susannah. You have early-onset pre-eclampsia. You and your baby are both very sick. If we don't deliver her now, you could both die.'

'I was fine . . . yesterday. I shouldn't have . . . had those beers, I know that.' She attempts a smile, her swollen face twisting hideously like a Halloween mask. 'I won't do . . . it again. Just give me the . . . antibiotics or whatever I need and let's . . . get on with this.'

Once again, I marvel at how wrong I have been. Just a few short weeks ago, I was quite certain Grace was the one at fault for allowing this insane surrogacy idea to take root. She wasn't ever meant to be a mother, I'd known that since she was a small child. She couldn't cook anything – could barely make toast. Susannah was the loving one, the sympathetic, caring girl who was supposed to have a rosy-cheeked family and rambling old home and a Labrador curled up on the sofa. It was just a mistake, what had happened with Davey and Donny. Life had turned out to be too tough for her. She had never got the breaks that Grace did. If she'd had the same chances as her sister, her life would've ended up just as golden.

But I was wrong. I admit it now. I've made too many excuses for far too long. I've babied and mollycoddled Susannah since she was a child. She didn't need me swooping in like an avenging angel every time she decided she didn't want to cope. She needed to learn to stand on her own two feet, and I never let her.

I missed Grace's ninth birthday. I keep coming back to that. I missed Grace's ninth birthday, *and until she ran away I didn't even know I'd missed it.*

For years, I've allowed my need to protect Susannah to blot out everything, including Grace. I've accepted the front she's presented to the world, and never taken the time to look further. But in the past few weeks I've seen a side of Grace she would never willingly have shown me. I see she wants this baby, but not for the reasons I always thought. Not because she can't bear to fail, or because she wants to tick all the boxes. She *loves* this child. She loves her with every fibre of her being, enough to give her back to Susannah, if that is the right thing.

That was the moment that crystallized everything. Susannah wants this child because she's looking for a second chance. A new start. She's not thinking of the baby at all. Grace is the one doing that. Grace is prepared to give up the child she loves and wants more than anything else in the world, and so I have no choice but to look at her differently. Suddenly my eyes have been opened.

For thirty-four years, I have told myself I had to protect Susannah because her father didn't love her. The truth is I favoured Susannah because David loved Grace so much *I was jealous*.

Guilt pulses through me. David doted on Grace from the second she drew breath, and I felt shut out. I was the one who had carried and nurtured her, and yet it was her father she wanted. He didn't reject Susannah. I withheld her from him. I kept Susannah to myself, because I was determined at least one of my daughters would love me best.

It wasn't David who polarized our family, but me.

I don't know when it became a competition for our children's love, but the more Grace turned to her father, the less I wanted her near me. The more I sheltered Susannah, the less attention her father paid her. Such havoc we have wrought! And as always, it is the innocents who pay.

God forgive me, but He got this wrong. He gave this baby to the wrong sister.

Susannah's eyes flutter, and I move closer to her in alarm. She's losing focus. We don't have much time. Where *is* Grace?

The doctor glances quickly at the monitors beeping next to us. 'Susannah, we can't delay this any longer,' she says sharply. 'Your blood pressure is dangerously high. Your kidneys are starting to fail completely, and your liver won't be far behind. As soon as the theatre is ready, we're going to get this baby out.'

'Just give me some damn pills . . . and leave me . . . alone!' Susannah gasps.

I'm so terrified for my daughter, and my unborn grand-child, I could slap her. So, judging from the expression in her eye, could the doctor. Instead, she nods curtly at Susannah, and whips the curtains closed around her bed.

'Is there anyone who can reason with her?' the doctor demands as she returns to the nurses' station. 'Boyfriend? Family? I don't want to wait until the stupid girl passes out and I can go ahead without her consent. The longer we wait, the more trouble that baby's in.'

'There's a bloke on her next-of, Blake someone, but he's not answering his phone. She has a sister listed—'

A commotion outside the entrance to the ward interrupts us. A moment later, Grace is bearing down on us with grim fury, Tom scurrying helplessly in her wake. He still has his slippers on, I notice, and his soft furry belly is visible between the top of his trousers and his hastily thrown-on T-shirt.

Even in the midst of my anxiety, I find time to worry about Tom. Grace still doesn't know what he's been doing with that red-headed doctor. *How can she not see?* It would change *everything*.

'Where's my sister?' Grace demands, from halfway down the hall. 'Why didn't anyone call me and tell me she was here?'

After the long, slow-motion, anxious wait of the last three hours, in which nothing seemed to happen except for Susannah getting sicker and sicker, suddenly a thousand things seem to happen at once. Grace marches up to Susannah's bed and snatches open the curtains, and tells her, in a tone that brooks no argument, that this baby is being delivered *now*! To the astonishment of everyone – everyone except Grace – Susannah agrees without a murmur. *This is what Susannah was waiting for*, I realize: for Grace to tell her what to do. She is thirty-four years old and she still refuses to take responsibility for herself. How can she take responsibility for a child?

223

My fault, I understand now. I'm the one who never let her grow up. I'm responsible for this.

In minutes, Susannah is being prepped for theatre, and an anaesthetist arrives to give her an epidural. At the last moment, as she is being wheeled away, she holds out her hand to Grace, and without hesitation, Grace takes it.

There's no time to induce labour: Susannah's blood pressure is climbing all the time, and the doctor is murmuring about cerebral haemorrhages and complications; they drape a screen across Susannah's chest, so that she doesn't have to watch her own abdomen being sliced open, and prepare her for a Caesarean section. The theatre is filled with people: the neonatologist arrives with a four-strong team to whisk the baby away to the NICU, the anaesthetist is monitoring Susannah's every breath, Dr Fraser and the junior doctor and numerous nurses and even a few student medics circulate around the operating table; in the middle is Grace, holding her sister's hand, steady and calm and in control, radiating reassurance. *No wonder David is so proud of her*, I think. No wonder Susannah is so overwhelmed.

The doctor picks up her scalpel and waits as iodine is swabbed across Susannah's belly, and then she cuts, swift and sure, and Grace gasps, 'Oh, Susannah! She's beautiful! She's tiny, she's so, *so* tiny, but she's beautiful!' and Ava, my first granddaughter, is finally born.

It takes everyone a few moments to realize that Susannah is still getting worse.

Grace is chattering excitedly to her sister, telling her that her daughter is beautiful, she has ten fingers and ten toes, they're so tiny, she's like a beautiful porcelain doll, only a million times more gorgeous, oh, Susannah, wait till you see her properly! The nurses are bustling around the theatre, tidying blooded cloths into a green plastic sack, returning unused gauze pads to their proper places. The doctor is checking the placenta to make sure none of it has been left behind to cause infection and septicaemia. Even I am a little distracted, gazing at my granddaughter in wonder. The neonatologist has whisked her into an incubator bristling with wires, but I can see already how beautiful she is.

Suddenly a monitor starts beeping, and the doctor looks up alertly. In an instant the brisk, celebratory mood changes.

'Get Mark Jaylor down here,' she snaps. 'Drag him out of bed if you have to. This girl's going into acute renal failure.'

One of the nurses reaches for the phone on the wall. The baby is wheeled from the theatre for the warming lights and high-tech care of the NICU. Grace is gently but firmly escorted out with her, despite her protests. Once she is gone, the doctor doesn't pull her punches.

'If we don't act fast, we're going to lose her,' she says, scooping up the placenta and dumping it into a stainless steel basin. She palpates Susannah's abdomen, her eyes on the monitors. 'Where's Jaylor?'

A figure in green scrubs strides into the theatre, fiddling with his face mask. 'Right here.'

Someone has put an oxygen mask over Susannah's face, but her skin has a grey pallor beneath the yellow jaundice. I can feel Death's presence all around us.

I can't stay here any longer. I can't watch my daughter die.

In the space of a breath, I'm with Grace, standing outside the NICU, peering through the viewing window as a cluster of doctors and nurses battle to save the life of my granddaughter. She weighs less than two pounds; she would literally fit into the palm of my hand. Her skin is covered with soft fur, and is so translucent we can see her heart beating.

Grace spreads her palms against the glass and presses her forehead to the window. 'Please don't die,' she whispers, over and over. 'Susannah needs you. Please don't die, please don't die.'

We all need you, I think. *We are all going to need you to survive this.*

I have no idea how long we wait. It is long enough for Tom to find Grace and take her back to the waiting room, another of those windowless, soulless rooms, where she paces restlessly, unable to keep still. 'It's too much,' she keeps saying. 'Mum, and Susannah, and poor little Ava. It's too much.'

Tom disappears to find coffee. Alone, Grace sinks to the floor and puts her head in her hands and gives way to a deep, aching grief. Her pain is even harder to bear than my own.

In the darkest hour, somewhere between black night and the grey fingers of dawn, the doctor finally comes to find us. Tom is asleep on one of the blocky beige sofas, his head lolling forward on his chest, his mouth slightly open. Grace is awake, but in a world of her own. When I try to comfort her, she shows no sign of hearing me. I know she's blaming herself, convinced that if she hadn't driven Susannah to leave, both she and the baby would be safe. Once, I would have agreed with her. Now I know that Susannah is the architect of her own misfortune. Her life has turned out the way it has as a direct result of the choices she has willingly made. Perhaps she isn't happy with the outcome, but that is no one's fault but hers. It certainly isn't *Grace's*.

'Mrs Hamilton,' the doctor says, 'your sister is stable. We—'

'She's going to be OK?' Grace demands.

The doctor pushes back her hair with the heels of both hands. 'She's stable,' she says again. 'Her condition is no longer life-threatening. I'm afraid it was rather touch-and-go for a while, but I think we're just about out of the woods. She had severe acidosis and her central nervous system was starting to shut down. If we had waited much longer to deliver the baby, I'm not sure if—'

'But she's going to be OK?' Grace says again. 'She's going to get better?'

The doctor sits down on the ugly sofa, and waits until Grace has taken an unwilling seat beside her. 'Your sister has Stage Five kidney failure,' she says gently. 'That means she has less than fifteen per cent kidney function. There may be some limited recovery, but I'm afraid it won't be much. As soon as she's well enough, Mark Jaylor, the head of our renal unit, will need to sit down with you and Susannah to discuss the best way forward.'

'What about the baby?' Tom asks suddenly. 'Is she OK?'

'The baby's doing well. She needs help with her breathing, of course, but she's a good weight for her age. It's just a waiting game now, I'm afraid. If you want to speak to the—'

'Tom,' Grace snaps. 'One thing at a time.'

'I'm afraid Susannah really is still very sick, Grace. She's in the ICU, and she's on dialysis at the moment, because her kidneys can't do their job and clean her blood, so we're having to do it for her.'

'How long is that going to take?'

'This time? Only a few hours. But you need to under-stand: this isn't going to go away. Susannah will need dialysis three times a week from now on. The damage to her kidneys is irreversible. She'll be able to come to the hos-pital as an out-patient, and will be on dialysis for between three and five hours each visit. She is going to need a great deal of support and care.'

Grace stares at her. 'She's just had a baby! How can she go off for dialysis three times a week? How is she expected to *cope*?'

'That's something Mark will need to discuss with you and Susannah. The hospital will give her as much help as it can, but she'll need her family for support. This is going to be a major adjustment for her.' She hesitates. 'Dialysis is usually seen as a short-term option. Mark will explain the details to you, but I can tell you Susannah's best chance at a normal life is a kidney transplant.'

'A *transplant*?' Grace gasps. Her face is ashen. 'She's only thirty-four!'

'The prognosis of transplant patients is usually excel-lent these days. Naturally, the closer we can come with the match, the better. Immediate family are usually the best donors, but failing that, she'll go on the waiting list. I'm afraid I have to warn you that you may have to be quite patient. We do have an acute shortage of donors in this country. But I suspect Susannah will be given priority because of the severity of her condition.'

'I'll give her mine,' Grace says instantly. 'I can do that, can't I? You only need one to live. She can have one of mine.'

'Grace,' Tom demurs. 'This is a big decision.'

'She's my *sister*. It's not a decision. Of course I'll give her my kidney. I'll be a match,' she says to the doctor. 'We have the same blood group. I'm sure I'll be a match.'

'The same blood group doesn't guarantee that you'd be a suitable donor, but it's certainly possible,' the doctor says cautiously. 'The transplant team would need to run a number of tests on both of you first. It's certainly something Mark could discuss with Susannah and the rest of your family.'

I stare at my daughter through eyes blurry with tears. I have never been more proud of Grace. I wasn't sent here to change anything, I realize. There was nothing I had to *do*. I was sent back to *see*. That is what this strange limbo is about. I had to understand that my daughters are neither good nor bad, but a mixture of both. I have only ever seen them through the prism of my preconceptions. It is only now that I can see them as they really are.

'How did this happen so fast?' Grace asks. Her hands are shaking, and she reaches for Tom. 'I know she's had problems with her kidneys before, but how can she suddenly need a transplant? Was it because of the baby?'

'It sometimes happens this way. Certainly the stress of the pregnancy will have played a part,' the doctor said.

Grace looks confused. I pick up on the doctor's hesitation too.

'Is there something else? Is something wrong that you're not telling us?'

'Your sister's blood alcohol level was rather high when she came in,' she admits.

I watch Grace absorb the information, but I can read nothing from her expression. Then, unexpectedly, she smiles. 'Can we see her now?' she asks.

My heart surges with relief. *Thank God Susannah has Grace.* Whatever happens to me, she'll have her sister to look after her.

Tom and Grace follow the doctor to the ICU, where Susannah is recovering. Even though I've prepared myself for the monitors and machines – heaven knows, I've grown used to seeing them around my own bed – it's still a shock to see my child like this. Her skin is less yellow, her face no longer swollen, but she still looks ill and weak, and I feel sick with worry. She may have brought this on herself, but she's still my baby.

Grace rubs her hands with antiseptic gel, and goes into the ICU. I follow and watch as she tenderly leans over her sister, and strokes her hair out of her face.

And then Grace speaks, and I realize I have understood nothing at all.

21

Grace

'I'll give her mine,' I say. 'I can do that, can't I? You only need one to live. She can have one of mine.'

Next to me, I feel Tom stiffen. 'Grace, this is a big decision—'

I shake off his restraining hand. 'She's my *sister*. It's not a decision. Of course I'll give her my kidney. I'll be a match. We have the same blood group. I'm sure I'll be a match.'

I have to be, I think desperately. It's my fault Susannah's sick. If it wasn't for me, she'd never even be pregnant. If she dies, I'll never forgive myself.

I should have supported her when she decided to keep the baby. I wasn't thinking straight. I was so blinded by how *I* felt, I didn't think about what was best for her, or best for the baby – *her* baby. I didn't believe she knew how to be a good mother, or was even capable of it, but she's proved me wrong. Michael says she's turned over a new leaf: she's given up cigarettes, she's stopped drinking, she's eating well and getting plenty of rest; she's stopped hanging around after Blake. A child belongs with its mother. I can't fight Susannah, even though it breaks my heart.

Dialysis. Transplants. My baby sister, so ill she can't even hold her new daughter.

'How did this happen so fast?' I whisper, feeling sick. 'I know she's had problems with her kidneys before, but how can she suddenly need a transplant? Was it because of the baby?'

'It sometimes happens this way. Certainly the stress of the pregnancy will have played a part.'

A sixth sense tells me she's hiding something. My stomach goes into free fall. I heard the nurses talking earlier: cerebral haemorrhages, hypertension, organ failure. You can live without functioning kidneys, but if the liver breaks down, there's nothing anyone can do. Septicaemia. Brain bleeds. Heart failure. Ava could lose her mother before she even knows her.

'Is there something else?' I ask sharply. 'Is something wrong that you're not telling us?'

For a moment, the doctor says nothing. Finally, she looks me in the eye. 'Your sister's blood alcohol level was rather high when she came in.'

It takes a minute for me to process what she's said.

Your sister's blood alcohol level was rather high.

In other words, she was *drunk*.

A bitter, savage rage sweeps through me. Susannah nearly lost her baby – she nearly *killed* her baby – because she was drunk. She's the same person she was when she abandoned her sons. She's incapable of thinking of anyone but herself.

My anger congeals into cold, hard fury. I was right all along. Susannah isn't fit to be a mother. I should never have let Nicholas Lyon talk me into giving her a second chance. I should have trusted my instincts and forced Tom to see the truth.

He has to see it now. I smile grimly. She's shot herself in the foot this time. We will get Ava back. It's just a matter of time.

The doctor leads us to the ICU to see Susannah. I look through the viewing window at my sister, and feel nothing but contempt. I don't give a damn about the tubes and wires going into her body in a dozen places. I don't care if she's on dialysis for the rest of her life. She's brought this on herself. She deserves it. It wasn't just her life she was gambling with, but her daughter's. If Ava survives, she could be permanently brain damaged or disabled. Her life may be over before it's even begun. How could any mother worthy of the name do this to her own child?

Susannah smiles as we walk into her room, and I lean over her bed and gently stroke her hair out of her face. She looks ten years older than she did this morning, but even sick and exhausted, she's still beautiful. Like a Venus flytrap. Beautiful on the outside, but rotting and foul within.

'I understand you need a new kidney,' I say tenderly. 'Been a bit careless with the old one.'

'A bit,' she whispers.

'It's going to be OK, Zee. I'm told you only need one kidney to get by, and I'm probably a perfect match, so you can have one of mine. We can share.'

'Grace . . . I don't know what to say . . .'

'Share and share alike, isn't that what Mum always used

to say? So I'll give you my kidney,' I say, still smiling, 'and you'll give me the baby. What's mine is yours, and what's yours is mine. Share and share alike, after all.'

I had no idea what I was going to say until the words were out of my mouth. But once uttered, I can't take them back. And the truth is, I don't *want* to. Susannah is asking a huge thing of me, a huge sacrifice. All I'm asking in return is that she honours our deal and does what's best for Ava. I think I'm being more than fair.

I'm so filled with bitterness, I have no room for anything else. I watch Tom collect his things from the bathroom and move into the spare bedroom, and I feel nothing. He's fallen under Susannah's spell, as everyone does, eventually. My sister ruins lives: her own, and those of everyone she touches. My mother didn't even know I was alive, she was so wrapped up with Susannah. My father came second in his own home. My nephews are being brought up by strangers because their mother was too busy chasing men halfway around the world. And the baby who should have been mine is fighting for her life in an incubator, unable even to breathe unaided because my sister thought a few beers were more important.

The next morning, Tom returns to our room to get dressed. I lie in the bed listening to him stumble around, his movements as heavy and slow as those of an old man, and I don't even trouble to feign sleep. I hold onto my bright, shiny anger as tightly as if it were a diamond.

The bed sinks heavily as Tom sits down to lace up his shoes. I sense him turn towards me, and I feel his hand hovering above my shoulder, but I don't move, and a moment later, the hand is withdrawn and the bed heaves again as Tom stands.

'She's your sister,' he says helplessly.

'I don't have a sister,' I say.

I wait until I hear the front door slam, and the sound of Tom's feet crunching down the gravel drive. I know I've driven him away for good this time. He won't forgive me for this.

I shower, and pick out a severe charcoal skirt suit that matches my mood, and a pair of low-heeled black court shoes. I don't switch on the radio and listen to John Humphrys slow-roast a mendacious government minister as I usually do. I don't even turn on the television for some news lite. Instead, I dress in total silence, enjoying the freedom from having to think. I'm pleased to note my hand is steady as I put on my make-up and fasten the row of pearls Tom gave me on our wedding day. The worst has happened. I have lost my mother, my sister, and my husband. I will soon lose my best friend. Whatever it takes, I will not lose my child.

Nicholas Lyon is expecting me when I arrive at his office a little before nine. I give him the paperwork he needs to set the paternity test in motion, which has Tom's signature on the bottom. Tom didn't sign it, of course. After living with him for fifteen years, I can replicate it with authenticity. I have never knowingly committed fraud in my life, I haven't even overrun on a parking meter, but I'm no longer worried about the rights and wrongs of stupid rules. Time enough to deal with the fallout when we have established if Ava is Tom's child.

I sit down and balance my Birkin neatly on my lap. 'What happens now?'

'Letters will be sent to your sister and Blake Stabler requiring them to comply with the order to produce a DNA sample. Once we have the results, and assuming that your husband is indeed the father, we can discuss how to proceed.'

'What if they refuse?'

'There is legal recourse, but let us hope it won't come to that.'

I feel sick at the thought of the letter landing on Claudia's doormat. She is my dearest friend; she has been more of a sister to me than Susannah ever was. This will destroy her life.

I harden my heart. *Collateral damage.* What choice do I have?

A week later, my sister is discharged from the hospital. I'm not surprised when, later that day, she turns up at my back door. I expected this. Susannah always thinks she can charm people into seeing things her way.

I study her through the window. She has lost weight, I notice: more than suits her. She looks tired and haggard, and her skin still has a yellowish tinge. She stands in the drizzling autumn rain, waiting like a supplicant for me to let her in, her pretty blonde hair dulled by the rainwater to the colour of putty. In the flat light of an English October afternoon, even her striking blue eyes no longer look remarkable. If I didn't know better, I'd think she actually cared.

I open the door. 'Have you changed your mind?' I ask politely. We might be discussing an invitation to dinner.

'Grace, please.' She steps forward, but I start to close the door, and she stops. 'Please,' she begs, spreading her hands. 'If you won't do it for me, please, think of Ava.'

'Ava?'

'She *needs* me,' Susannah pleads. 'I'm her mother. She needs me,' she says again.

'Do we have an agreement? Are you ready to share?'

'Share?' She laughs disbelievingly. '*Share*? She's my child, not a box of sweets! Have you completely lost it, Grace? I'm not swapping my baby for your fucking kidney! Of course I haven't changed my mind! I'm never *going* to change my mind!'

'Then we have nothing to discuss,' I say, shutting the door.

Susannah hammers on it with her fists. 'Do you know what you're doing to me?' she screams. 'Have you got any idea what my life is like now? I'm chained to that machine for four hours every other day! I'm thirty-four years old, and I barely have the energy to walk upstairs! How can you *do* this to me? I'm your *sister*!'

'I'm not doing anything,' I say coolly. 'You could change this in a moment. You're doing it to yourself.'

I visit Ava in hospital every morning before I go to work, and every evening before I come home. Susannah hasn't been to see her except for once, two days after she was born. She's shown no interest in her child. I knew it would be like this. She's only hanging onto her to spite me.

The only moment I weaken is when Tom moves out. Three weeks after Ava's birth, I come down to breakfast one morning to find him loading up the back of his Range Rover with clothes and books and fishing rods – fishing rods, I think irrelevantly: since when did Tom *fish*? – and emptying his study of all his files and folders from work. I walk silently through the house, thinking that the gaps on the walls and the bookshelves are mirrored by those in my heart. Tom nods at me as he staggers back out to the car through the mud with a cardboard box filled with papers, but says nothing. I nod back. What is there left to say?

Stop him! Stop him before it's too late!

I can't. If he doesn't understand why I have to do this, he's not the man I thought he was. He's not the man I fell in love with.

He returns for the last box, and stands clutching it on the doorstep. 'I'll be staying at the B&B for a few days,' he says awkwardly. 'If you need me or anything.'

Tell him you need him now. *It's all he wants to hear.*

One word from me, and this nightmare would be over. We could go back to the way we used to be. Tom&Grace, the ampersand couple. Finishing each other's sentences, mirroring each other's thoughts.

I know I'll never be given custody of Ava without Tom. And he will never seek it, regardless of whether she's his child or not. There's no point fighting him any longer. I might as well yield now, and accept that Ava is lost. No need to sacrifice my marriage too.

Suddenly I'm eight years old again, and staring at the broken pieces of my mother's treasured jade dragon, her last gift from her father before he died. In my mind's eye I can still see it falling from my clumsy hands, even though it already lies in a dozen shards at my feet. I keep staring at them, my eyes straining with the effort of trying not to blink. I can almost see the pieces leaping back together and re-forming in front of me, like a film being rewound. It's not too late. If I will it hard enough, I can make it happen.

Except it is too late, of course. The moment I disobeyed

my mother and picked up the dragon, long before it had even started to slip from my grasp, it was already too late. Once you set a chain of events in motion, there's no going back.

We were never that perfect couple, I think dully. *We had the perfect life, which isn't the same thing.*

'I'll be back for some more things in a week or two,' Tom says, his voice bleak. 'When I've found somewhere more permanent to stay.'

The door closes behind Tom. I sit neatly at the kitchen table, my hands in my lap. I have no idea what to do, or how to be, without him. So I sit.

An hour later, perhaps two, the door opens again, and I look up. Claudia stands trembling in front of me, clad only in her pyjama sweats and her coat. On her feet are a muddy pair of flip-flops. Her eyes are red-rimmed and swollen. *Not today*, I think. *Not Tom and Claudia in one day.*

She flings a crumpled ball of paper on the table. I pick it up and smooth it out, though I already know what it is. Nicholas' letter, demanding her husband take a DNA test to see if he fathered my sister's child.

'You knew?' she cries. 'You *knew*?'

'Afterwards,' I say wearily. 'Not until afterwards.'

'You couldn't tell me? You had to let me find out like *this*?'

Slowly, feeling about a hundred years old, I get up and put the kettle on the Aga and spoon sugar into two mugs because I don't know what else to do.

'Is it still going on?' she demands. 'Is he still seeing her?'

'I don't know. I don't think so. Michael says she hasn't seen him in weeks.'

'Michael knows too?' Suddenly the fight goes out of her.

She gropes for a chair. 'You all knew, and no one thought to *tell* me?'

'*You* knew,' I reply. 'Not about Susannah, but you knew about the others. You stayed with him anyway. How would it have helped to tell you about Susannah? What difference would it have made?'

The kettle boils, and I pour each of us a mug of hot, sweet tea. I put one in front of her and sit down with my own, too tired and heart-sore even to wonder what comes next. We both curl our hands around the warming mugs, waiting for the steaming liquid to cool, waiting for someone to tell us what to do.

'I know you don't understand why I stay,' Claudia says, after a long silence. 'I'm not sure I understand myself. I don't know if it's love, or cowardice. I don't want to be left to bring up three children on my own, or to sell our house and go back to work; I'd be lying if I said that wasn't part of it. But it's more than that. I know Blake. There are things in his background, things that have happened to him— I'm not making excuses,' she adds quickly. 'It's not OK, what he's done. I'm not saying that. But there is more than one way to love someone. It's not always black and white. Black and white is easy. It's the grey that's difficult.'

We listen to the clock ticking in the hall. I think of my father sitting for hours every day next to my mother's bed; before she got sick, the two of them would go all day without exchanging a word. *There is more than one way to love someone.*

She pushes her mug away, as if it were that easy to be rid of the past. 'You and Tom, you had the fairy tale,' she accuses. 'But for most of us, marriage isn't like that. It's a compromise. Blake and I have a lot that's good. The children, for one. And we have *fun*. That might not seem important to you, but it matters to me. When he's with me, he's with me a hundred per cent. I know I'm the only person who matters. I'd rather that,' she says passionately, 'than the kind of sleepwalking marriage so many women have.'

She means me. I can't remember the last time Tom and I had fun. Sleepwalking? I suppose we were.

Claudia shoves her chair back from the table, then picks up the creased letter, folds it in half, and then half again, and shoves it in the pocket of her Barbour. 'The baby isn't his. You don't need all these tests.'

My marriage may not have been very exciting, but at least it *was* a marriage, I think suddenly. Claudia can dress it up any way she likes, but the fact is that Blake has lied and cheated on her for years. He may love her, but it's a child's love, selfish and demanding. There's nothing *grey* about adultery.

'Claudia,' I say softly, 'I wouldn't have put you through this if I didn't have to. Without a test, there's no way of knowing if Blake or Tom is Ava's father. Even Susannah doesn't know.'

To my astonishment, Claudia laughs. 'No, Grace. I mean he *can't* be. Literally. Blake had a vasectomy as soon as we found out I was pregnant with Kiefer. He didn't want any more kids. He had the snip months before he even *met* Susannah. There's no way Ava can be his.'

I digest this in silence. *The baby is Tom's.* Which means that if he hadn't just left me, she could have been mine too.

'Grace,' Claudia asks, 'where *is* Tom?'

'He's gone,' I say flatly.

'Gone? Grace, *why*? That man would walk over hot coals for you!'

'It seems I offended his moral sensibilities,' I say coolly. 'He was happy to go along with things while they were easy, but when they got tough, he didn't want to get his hands dirty. Don't tell me what he would and wouldn't do for me.'

'I heard about your . . . *deal*,' Claudia says. 'With Susannah. You pushed him too far, Grace.'

'What would you rather?' I demand, my temper getting the better of me. 'You want me to go and give Susannah a kidney, so she can keep on fucking your husband whenever the mood takes her?'

'Yes, if it stops Tom leaving!' Claudia shoots back.

She storms from my kitchen as abruptly as she entered it. I watch her leave, and don't try to stop her. Somewhere deep inside, I know she's right. But my rage is implacable. For as long as I can remember, I've protected and covered for my sister. I've bailed her out more times than I can count, and made excuses for her even when I've known she's not just wrong, but revelling in the chaos she's causing. *Enough*, I think bitterly. Susannah has gone through life thinking only of herself, heedless of the impact of her actions on everyone else. Now she needs to learn what happens when she has only herself to rely on.

But I'm the one who is taught a lesson, not Susannah. I discover that anger doesn't keep you warm at night. I miss Tom more than I could ever have imagined. It is as if my heart has been cut out, my right hand cut off. The only thing that keeps me from rushing to his side and begging him to come home is the knowledge that, if he refuses, all hope will be gone, and I don't think I could bear that.

A few days after he leaves, as suddenly as it descended on me, the red mist clears. The fury that's sustained me for so long has blown itself out. I don't hate my sister any more. I can't quite find it in me to forgive her, either, but in a way, that doesn't matter. The destructive rage has gone, and for the first time in nearly a month, despite my grief, I'm at peace. Love trumps vengeance every time.

I realize it's time to value what I have left. Regardless of her behaviour, Susannah is my sister. I can't hold her to ransom over Ava. Of course I have to help her. I pick up the phone, and call the transplant team; quickly, before it's too late.

When they tell me what my sister has just done, I'm more shocked than I've ever been in my life.

22

Susannah

The baby freaks me out. Ava. It doesn't even look like a baby. Its head is way too big, and it's all scrawny and wrinkled, like a skinned rat. The body is covered with white fur, and it doesn't have any proper hair: no eyelashes or eyebrows or anything. The skin is transparent, so you can see all its veins; you can even see its heart beating like a dark plum in the middle of its chest. The wires and tubes and machines make it look like some kind of sick science experiment. It's disgusting.

Even if I was allowed to hold it, I wouldn't want to. It's a . . . a *thing*, not my daughter. It makes me want to hurl. It's not human. It's not even properly alive.

The nurse leans over my wheelchair. 'What is it, love? You feeling bad again?'

'Can we go now?'

She releases the handbrake, but doesn't move my chair away. The incubator's at eye level with me. I can see this big vein throbbing like some kind of snake in its head. I have to close my eyes so I don't throw up.

The nurse pats my hand sympathetically. 'I know, love, it's all a bit scary to begin with, seeing them like this. All those tubes and wires. But you're not to worry. She's a fighter, your little one. She's in good hands. I've seen kiddies much worse off make it. You just need to concentrate on getting yourself better now.'

I don't want this 'kiddie' to make it. I wish it'd never been born.

I hate Grace. She knows me too fucking well. I feel like a fox in a trap, faced with the choice of eating off its own leg to escape, or starving to death. I can give her the baby and spend the rest of my life a crippled freak of nature: the mother who sold her child for the price of a kidney. Or I can keep it, and say goodbye to any kind of life at all.

Fuck it. I should've stuck to the original deal. Grace would be the one stuck with this freaky cabbage kid, and I'd be the selfless heroine who'd granted her sister her heart's desire. She'd have owed me forever. Donating a kidney would've been the *least* she could do. She'd have been *begging* me to take it, and tossing in a lung and a pancreas too. But now, if I hand it over, everyone will know I'm selling out. This surrogacy crap was supposed to make up for all my fuck-ups, not reinforce them. What will Donny and Davey think when they find out? It'll screw any chance I might have had of putting things back on track with them. I'll lose *all* my kids.

I may not be winning any Mother of the Year awards here, but I loved my sons from the minute they were born. When they handed me Davey, I remember this amazing gush of feelings, all tangled up together: awe and tenderness and curiosity and absolute fucking terror. I never gave my kids up because I didn't care.

Looking in the incubator now, I feel nothing. It's as if it's got nothing to do with me, like it's some stranger's kid. I mean, I know it's genetically mine. I may not be sure who the dad is, but even *I* can figure out the mother.

Well, you'd *think*. The truth is, it doesn't feel like mine at all. If I believed in karma or voodoo or whatever, I'd start to wonder if this whole surrogacy thing hadn't screwed things up from the moment sperm met egg.

The kidney doctor gets a bit nicer once he hears about Grace. Clearly having your sister try to hijack your kid in exchange for a body part wins you a few Brownie points around here. At this stage in the game, I'll take them where I can find them.

'We need to look at your options,' he says, sitting cosily on my bed. 'You're Stage Five, which gives you priority on the transplant list, but I have to warn you, it's not going to be easy to find a match with your blood group. I don't suppose there's any way we can get your sister to reconsider?'

Trust me to be special in a way that sucks.

'Give it up,' I say.

'I'm sorry?'

'Grace. She's not going to change my mind. And I haven't got any other brothers or sisters.'

'Perhaps another family member? Are your parents still alive? Would either of them consider it?'

Dad would cut out his heart and eat it in front of me first. But I suggest Mum might have a kidney or two going spare, especially since she's still doing a mean impression of a vegetable herself. A few days later, the doctor comes back with the results. Good news: she's a perfect match. Bad news: Dad'll give permission for the hospital to raid her for spares over his own dead body.

Except, I think, as they hook me up to the fucking dialysis machine for the third time in five days, *Dad doesn't have power of attorney. I do.*

I don't need a fancy lawyer to explain it to me: even I can see there's a conflict of interest here. But I'm running out of options. I could be stuck on the transplant list for *years*. There's a really pretty blonde girl who comes in for her dialysis every other afternoon, the same time as me. She's twenty-one, and she's been coming here three times a week for six years. *Six years!* She's still a fucking virgin, for Chrissakes! I'll go mad if I have to wait six years for another shag. I'd rather top myself.

If only Grace hadn't backed me into a corner in front of everyone. We could have worked it out. She gives me a kidney, I sign the adoption papers, she hands me a one-way ticket to Hawaii, and everyone's happy. It's not as if I even want the . . . *it*.

I manage to avoid visiting the NICU again. Every time one of the nurses offers to take me, I say I'm feeling sick, or tired, or stressed. They're very understanding.

'I think you're right, love,' one of them confides. 'Best not to get too attached until you know the little one's going to be OK.'

A week later, when they discharge me from hospital, I go straight over to see Grace. It's pissing with rain, and I still feel like shit, to be honest; the scar from my C-section hasn't had time to heal, my boobs are engorged and ready to explode because I can't breastfeed, and I ache all over from the dialysis. It's like they wash my blood and replace it with water. But this can't wait. I've got to get Grace to back down. I need my life back.

Grace watches me through the window, taking her own sweet time while she decides whether to grant me a royal audience.

Finally, she opens the door. 'Have you changed your mind?'

'Grace, please.' No point finessing this. I might as well play the guilt card up front. 'If you won't do it for me, please, think of Ava.'

'Ava?'

'She *needs* me. I'm her mother.'

No response. 'She needs me,' I repeat weakly.

'Do we have an agreement? Are you ready to share?'

Damn it, Grace! I think crossly. Can't you give me a little wriggle room here? If she'd only meet me halfway, let me save face! I can't go through life with my boys thinking I'd sell them for a new pair of eyeballs. She's got to throw me a bone!

To my utter disbelief, my sister shuts the door in my face when I say no. I can't believe she can be this cold! This is *Grace*. My sister, Grace. The same Grace who's looked after me all my life, following me around like a nursemaid, making me wear my coat and checking I've done my homework and handing me tissues when some boy's broken my heart. How can she do this to me when she knows how much I need her? I'm her sister! *How can she do this to me?*

'I don't even *want* the thing!' I wail to Michelle as soon as I get home. 'It's probably going to die or end up spastic anyway!'

Michelle holds out my bathrobe, and I step out of the shower and slide my arms into it. '*She* is not an "it", she's your daughter,' she says sharply. 'It's about time you stopped feeling so bloody sorry for yourself, and started to think about her. She didn't ask to be born three months early, Susannah. You're the one responsible for that. And for your own health problems, too, I might add. Your sister has every right to be mad at you.'

'I knew you'd take her side. Why don't you just go and tell her she can have it, if you think I'm such a terrible person?'

Michelle propels me into the bedroom, and pushes me down onto the stool in front of the mirror. Freeing my wet hair from the neck of my bathrobe, she gently starts to comb it through. 'You're not a terrible person. You're a *frightened* one. Even Grace would struggle with what you've been through over the past few weeks. She's angry with you, but she doesn't hate you. *You're* the only person who does that.'

'Is this the bit where you tell me to let go of the past and get in touch with my inner child?'

'Something like that,' Michelle says thoughtfully.

The next day, she offers to take me out for the day to cheer me up. I imagine a trip to the shops, or maybe even a pampering spa. When we arrive at our destination and I realize what she really has in mind, I freak out.

Michelle, however, is unmoved. 'I don't care if you never want to take her home,' she says. 'You have to accept that you're her mother. Until you do, you're never going to get past your guilt.'

'I don't feel guilty!'

'Of course you do. When you look at her, you see the

proof of what you did. It's why you feel so disgusted by her. You need to get past it if you ever want to move on with your life.'

I refuse to get out of the car. Michelle simply takes out *The Life of Pi* and starts reading. For two hours, we sit in the hospital car park in a Mexican standoff, until finally I give in and agree to go and see it. Michelle accompanies me up to the NICU, but refuses to come in and give me moral support.

'This is a mess of your own making, Susannah,' she says crisply. 'Deal with it.'

For thirty minutes, I sit in the NICU and stare anywhere but at the incubator, then come out and declare myself won over. Michelle, however, isn't having any of it. Instead, she drags me back to the hospital the next morning, and the next. I have no choice but to go with her: I'm tired and sick and frankly too fucking knackered to put up a fight. *Maybe,* I think fleetingly, *if my mother had been as tough as Michelle is, I might not have gone quite so far off the rails.*

Eventually, on the third or fourth day of this, I steel myself to look at it. Only for a moment, but at least I do it without losing my lunch. The next day, it's easier; each day after that, easier yet. There are still times I want to puke my guts up, but every so often, there are times when I almost feel sorry for her too. She's so small, and she fights *so hard*. Every single breath is a battle for her. But respect to her: she doesn't give up. She keeps on sucking oxygen into her tiny, unfinished lungs, and she keeps on pushing carbon dioxide out. In, out. In, out. In, out. Her kidneys pack up, her liver breaks down, she suffers respiratory arrest and repeated infections, but she never stops fighting. *In, out.*

When Ava is four weeks old – I'd have been thirty-three

weeks pregnant – her doctors cautiously declare themselves pleased with her progress so far.

I have to admit I'm relieved. I won't deny I'm getting fond of her, but that doesn't mean I want a spaz for a daughter.

To celebrate, they finally take her out of the incubator for a few minutes and let me hold her. And the moment she's in my arms, I know: *I can't walk away from this.*

'Not out of the woods yet,' I tell Michelle, as we drive home. 'She's still on the ventilator most of the time, but her lungs are miles better. She can't come home for ages yet; they don't usually let preemies out till at least the day they would've been due. But they reckon she's a real toughie. I gotta give her props for that.'

I tense, waiting for Michelle to make a big song and dance because I've mentioned bringing Ava home. She says nothing, and after a moment, I relax. It's not like I've definitely decided to keep her, or anything. I'm just, you know. Saying.

But when I get the letter from Grace's lawyer the following Monday, I freak. Weird to think that the mere thought of losing Ava is enough to drive me postal these days.

It's Michelle who talks me down from the ledge. As she points out, the law is on my side. Two days after we get the letter, she's found a ball-breaking Oxford solicitor who's creaming her jeans at the thought of doing battle with Grace's fancy-ass London lawyer.

'Nicholas Lyon's a decent man, but he must know he hasn't got a prayer with this one,' Siobhan Meaghan says, practically licking her lips. 'It's almost unheard of for the father to win custody in these sorts of cases. Frankly, I'm surprised Nicholas is even pursuing it.'

She hasn't met my sister. Grace will have twisted his arm so far up his back he'll look like a pretzel.

'First things first: a DNA test on the baby,' Siobhan says, snapping her fingers at her secretary. 'Regardless of Mr Stabler's assertion that he's infertile, we want to be sure. Your sister's entire case rests on her claim to the child through her husband's paternity. Might as well shake that tree first and see what comes out.'

The second letter from Grace's lawyer arrived this morning. I'm guessing she got on the horn to him the minute she found out from Claudia that Blake had had the snip. She must have been fucking tickled pink.

I was really hoping Ava was his. His genes are a lot cuter than Tom the Hobbit's, for a start. And I suppose somewhere deep down I was still hoping it'd make the difference with Blake and me. Dumb, I know. But the heart wants what it wants.

Michelle gives me a brisk 'chin up' nod. She knows better than to go all soft and mushy on me. I don't know what I'd do without her, to be honest. Aside from all the practical stuff, like a roof over my head and cash to pay a lawyer, she's the best friend I've ever had. The only friend, really. Growing up, it was the boys who liked me, not the girls, and it wasn't friendship they were after. OK, technically he's Arthur, not Martha. But I've got so used to Michael/Michelle, I really don't notice most of the time which of them is in residence.

I keep it together till we get out of Siobhan's office, and then I lose it again. I read the papers (well, the *News of the World*); whatever Siobhan says now about 'slam dunks', I know nothing's certain once you get into court. And I've hardly got a great track record as a mother. I put my sons in care, and my premature daughter into an incubator. I'm living in a trannie's spare bedroom without a man or a job or a penny to my name. How could any court not pick Grace over me? Even Tom turned against me in the end. I thought he was on my side, but it's his signature on the court papers. He and Grace will get back together and take my baby. They'll take Ava, and there's nothing I can do about it.

Michelle puts her arms around me as I start to bawl. Her expensive blonde wig (real Ukrainian hair, apparently) tickles my cheek, and she smells of Chanel No. 5. She may be a trannie, but she's a classy one, I'll give her that.

'I should just give Grace what she wants,' I wail. 'She'll get Ava anyway. I should hand her over and take the kidney. I might as well get something out of it too.'

'Throw a pity party, why don't you? Grace is *not* going to take your daughter. Grow some balls! Siobhan is writing to your mum's hospital now about a possible transplant from her. If anyone can make that happen, she can. But if it doesn't work out, you're at the top of the transplant list.' She rubs my back as if I'm a child. 'Stop being so negative. You're always punishing yourself. You need to learn to live with the past, and move on.'

Impulsively, I turn and kiss her cheek. In the next second, she's kissing me back, properly, on the mouth. Lips, tongues, everything. Lust strips through me, swirling up my groin with the strength of a hurricane. I'm stunned by the force of my reaction.

I break away, shocked. 'You can't kiss me like that! You're my best friend!'

'Exactly why I should kiss you like that.' She laughs and starts the car. 'Oh, put your skirts down, Miss Havisham. I'm not going to ravage you.'

My cheeks flame. I can still feel that snog in my pussy. Christ! Am I turning into a lezza or something? I've never felt like that when a bloke's kissed me, not even Blake! *What the fuck is going on?*

Michelle calmly drives us home, as unruffled as the Queen on a State visit. I'm like a cat on a hot tin roof. The second she pulls to a halt outside the studio, I'm out and down the garden path like a startled rabbit, before remembering that she has the keys. I put about ten feet between us as she unlocks the door. Was that kiss a one-off? Am I going to be safe in my bed tonight? Or is she going to sneak in and slip under the covers and . . .

I can't help it. Just the thought is enough. Without hesitating, I grab her and kiss her again.

We barely make it to the bedroom. We tumble onto the bed, yanking at each other's clothes, lips and hands exploring, probing, tasting, touching. I'm in no doubt that if it was Michelle who kissed me earlier, it's Michael making love to me now. His cock presses hard against my belly, and I struggle breathlessly with the zip of his skirt. I'm so hot for him that I don't waste time thinking it's weird that he's wearing flounces. He slithers out of the skirt, along with a whisper of silk and lace. In seconds his cock springs into my hand, and I guide him into me as he rips my own knickers away.

My back arches to meet him. I open my eyes, losing myself in his. They're grey and green and flecked with desire. I couldn't care less that they're also beautifully made up with delicate shades of plum and two coats of mascara.

'I don't want to hurt you,' he says, stroking my still-healing stomach.

'You couldn't,' I breathe.

Gently, mindful of my scars and the dialysis stent and my fragile heart, Michael moves inside me. We don't take our eyes off each other. We're barely moving, and yet the sensations in my body are the most intense I've ever experienced. I can feel him from my earlobes to the tips of my toes.

His pupils dilate, and I know he's feeling it too. We're both standing at the edge of Niagara Falls, ready for the wave to sweep us away.

And then it comes, and I realize everything else up to now has been like paddling in a puddle.

Afterwards, we lie for a long moment, still coupled. 'You're my best friend,' I whisper, as he slowly wilts inside me. 'You're not supposed to make love to me like that.'

'Exactly why I should make love to you like that,' he smiles back.

When the phone rings, I resist the intrusion. 'Leave it.'

'It could be Ava,' he replies.

The hospital number comes up on the caller ID. Michael squeezes my hand, and gets up to answer it. I brace myself, knowing that nothing could prepare me for the death of my daughter.

But when Michael puts down the phone, he's grinning like a bloody Cheshire cat.

'You don't need your sister, or your mother,' he says. 'They've only gone and found you a donor.'

23

Grace

I can't let her do it. Even Susannah has a conscience, however hard she tries to bury it. One day, she'll be sorry if she goes ahead with this.

Stealing Mum's kidney! How can she even *think* about it? Mum isn't brain dead! She's not in a permanent vegetative state, like that poor boy who was crushed in the Hillsborough football disaster, or that girl in America, the one they kept alive on a life-support machine for years before the husband finally won the right to switch it off. Mum's just had a stroke. She could wake up at any moment. Susannah can't filch her body parts while she's not looking!

Perhaps I've been too angry for too long, but to my surprise I simply don't have it in me any more to hate Susannah over this. I'm hardly in a position to take the moral high ground, given my attempt to blackmail her into handing over her daughter. And I know if Mum were conscious, she'd be insisting she give Susannah her kidney, and her heart and lungs too if Zee needed them.

In the end, I don't really have a choice. I'm quite certain Zee's feisty Irish lawyer had no intention of taking this to court; it'd be thrown out in a moment, even if Susannah does have Mum's power of attorney. That lawyer knew I'd step in. Smart woman.

I don't like being manipulated, but in this case, I'll let it go. If I'd done the right thing in the first place, Susannah would never have gone down this route. I can't blame her.

The lift doors open, and I step out into the hospital corridor, not even looking up. This place is as familiar to me as my own home these days. Sometimes it seems as if my life has been spent living in the shadows of one hospital or another. Susannah, when she was little. Mum, for the last nine months. And now Ava.

I haven't been to see her for several weeks, not since I found out that Michael was bringing Susannah here every day. I have to accept that Ava is her daughter, not mine. Somehow, I have to find the strength to let her go.

But first, I need to say goodbye. It's time. After today, she won't be my baby. She'll be my niece. It's going to take me some time to get used to that; I don't think the gnawing ache will ever go away.

The nurse at the NICU smiles when she sees me at the door, and quickly buzzes me in. 'Haven't seen you in here for a while,' she says, briskly leading me down to the viewing gallery. 'Have you been away?'

'I didn't want to cause too much disturbance,' I say, 'now that her mother is well enough to come and see her every day.'

'Shame. You just missed Mum,' the nurse clucks. 'She was here not five minutes ago.'

I didn't realize I'd cut it that fine. I don't want to see Susannah until long after this is all over; she has to think I have nothing to do with the transplant. That was my only condition, when I spoke to the transplant team. She must never know I'm the one who gave her a kidney. As far as Susannah is concerned, her donor is nameless, and faceless. Some unlucky soul who met with tragedy and had signed a donor card and just happened to have the same rare blood group as she does.

I rub my hands with antiseptic gel, and put on my face mask, then follow the nurse over to Ava. To my surprise, she's no longer in the incubator, but an open perspex cot, with some sort of warming light above it. I can't believe how much she's grown since I last saw her. She's six weeks old now, though she's still more than a month from her due date. She's small, but despite the wires and tubes still present, she looks pink and healthy, and she's breathing on her own. Her legs and arms have filled out, and her hair has grown thick and curly. It has a distinct reddish tinge. *Tom's hair*, I think. *Tom's daughter. A little miracle.*

'Would you like to hold her?' the nurse asks, reaching into the crib.

I gasp with pleasure. 'Really?'

She laughs. 'Ava loves a cuddle. It's good for these tiny ones, to feel some human contact. It helps them thrive.'

It helps us all thrive.

Gently, she places Ava in my arms. I gaze at her, drinking her in. She's so light, a featherweight wisp of warmth and sweetness. I put my finger in her palm, and she curls five tiny fronds around it. My heart twists. She's perfect. The best of Susannah and Tom and me.

My longing for her is visceral. I feel it in my belly, in my chest, in my fingernails. I would give everything I possess for this child to be truly mine.

But she has a mother, and it isn't me. At least now she will never have to go through the pain of knowing she was given away. Does any child truly recover from that? I drop a soft kiss on her forehead, breathing in her smell. I would do anything to protect this little girl, anything at all. Even let her go.

I hand her back to the nurse and quickly leave, my throat aching with unshed tears. I stumble back to the lift and go down to the surgical floor. The transplant team will be waiting to admit me and run their last-minute tests. In another room, perhaps no more than feet away, Susannah will be waiting for her own pre-op checks. In less than four hours, if all goes well, it will be over. She will have her life back, and I will be left to get on with what remains of mine.

All the pre-surgery evaluations have already been done. Naturally, I scored top of the class. A human kidney has a set of six antigens: substances that stimulate the production of antibodies. Donors are tissue matched for zero to six of the antigens, and compatibility is determined by the number and strength of those matched pairs. Blood-type matching is also crucial, of course. I scored a powerful six out of six. Only an identical twin could have done better.

In the past week, I've been tested for kidney function, liver function, hepatitis, heart disease, lung disease and past exposure to viral illness. I've had X-rays, an EKG and a CT angiogram, during which contrast die was injected into my bloodstream. I passed every test with flying colours. I always do.

Mark Jaylor has already explained the actual procedure to me in detail. You can survive perfectly well with just one kidney, apparently. It just steps up to the plate and performs the job of two; rather like a single mother, I think ironically. He's planning a laparoscopic nephrectomy: instead of simply cutting me open, he'll go fishing for my kidney with long narrow rods through four tiny incisions in my abdomen. It all sounds quite extraordinary: first he'll pump in carbon dioxide to inflate my belly so he's got more room to see. Then, using a videoscope, he'll manoeuvre his instruments into me. Once the kidney is freed, it'll be secured in a bag – rather like turkey giblets, I imagine – and pulled through a fifth incision just below my navel. And then, while my kidney is rushed through to Susannah, he'll sew me up and, in no more than a day or two, I'll be able to go home.

I haven't told anyone what I'm doing, not even Tom. I don't want him to come back because I've given Susannah my kidney. I want him to come back because he's as lost and bereft and miserable without me as I am without him.

I can see now what I didn't see before: I treated Tom as if he didn't matter, as if he was of no account, when the truth is, he's *all* that matters. I want a child more than anything, yes – anything except *Tom*.

I don't want him back because I've finally done the right thing, but I can't help hoping that somehow, doing the right thing will put Fate on my side.

And give me back my husband.

It hurts, but not as much as I expected. I wake after the surgery feeling groggy from the anaesthetic, and the catheter isn't exactly inspiring, but within half a day I'm out of bed, and once Mark Jaylor has established my remaining kidney is working fine, I'm discharged.

He says the surgery went well for Susannah too, though of course they can't tell yet if her body will reject the kidney. That could happen straight away, or years from now. She'll be on immuno-suppressants for the rest of her life. I can't imagine living with chronic ill health the way she has for so long. For the first time, I have a glimmer of what it must be like for her. To know your own body is a failure at the most basic level: sustaining life.

There's no one to drive me home from the hospital. I've told Claudia I'm working on a complicated forensic case in Normandy. Tom moved out of the B&B and is staying at a friend's London pied-à-terre while the friend is on a sabbatical in New Zealand, so there's little chance of running into him in the village. No one else is likely to think twice about me. I shall go home and keep the lights low and the curtains drawn, and lick my wounds in private.

Gingerly, I fasten my seatbelt, feeling as if I've done ten rounds with Mike Tyson. I take it very slowly, and stay off the motorway. The wintry Oxfordshire countryside around me is bleak and grey. Bare branches are silhouetted against the looming November sky. The air of barrenness and desolation matches my mood.

I haven't driven this way for quite a while. I notice that many of the villages I pass through have weather-beaten 'For Sale' signs outside cottages that would normally have been snapped up. Even this prosperous pocket of England has been hit hard by the recession. Tom and I will be lucky to get back what we paid for our fairytale castle, I realize, especially when we take into account the amount we spent fixing it up. Once we have cleared our mortgage, there will barely be enough for two small flats, even in this depressed market.

The thought startles me. It's as if there are two people in my head: one making cool, rational decisions about the practicalities of separation and divorce, and the other watching and listening to her in disbelief, totally unable to believe any of this is real.

Separation. Divorce. I shake my head as if to clear it. Tom and I were meant to be together forever. How *can* any of this seem real?

As I pass the B&B where Tom was staying, I automatically slow. I'm surprised he hasn't taken his car with him, I think, as I see it parked in the driveway. How else has he moved his things to London? He can't have taken them all on the train.

Then the door to the B&B opens, and Tom emerges, and my heart judders in a way it hasn't for years.

He's lost weight. Quite a bit: his clothes are hanging off him. His normally ruddy hair seems flat and dull, and he's walking with the heavy gait of an old man. I recognize that air of puzzled bewilderment from my own mirror. It's as if we both woke up one day and found ourselves in a foreign country, with no idea how we got there.

Just one short year ago, we were looking forward to our upcoming trip to New York to celebrate Thanksgiving with one of Tom's college friends. It turned out to be one of the best holidays we'd had. We spent hours strolling through the Village, picking out Christmas gifts for friends and family and each other. We skated hand in hand at the Rockefeller Center, and snuggled against each other in the cold as we marvelled at the tree. We even took a touristy carriage ride in Central Park. It was like our own rom-com holiday montage, all 'Jingle Bells' soundtrack and picturesque white snow. We might not be honeymooners, but we could still play at loved-up with the best of them.

Neither of us wants this, I think, hope rising unexpectedly in my chest. Tom isn't happy without me. I've never seen him look so miserable. Maybe we can still find a way back to that couple kissing and giggling and eating hot chestnuts in Times Square. I'm not the person I was a few months ago. I know what I've done wrong. Surely it isn't too late?

I pull over onto the rutted, frozen verge, suddenly as excited as a teenager. Enough waiting for things to sort themselves out. I have to do something *now*, before we find ourselves propelled into the world of ready-meals for one and legal affidavits by our own inertia.

I have butterflies as I unfasten my seatbelt, and open the door. Tom hasn't seen me. He's got a box of papers clutched in his arms, and is struggling to get his car keys out of his jacket pocket without dropping them. *It's going to be all right*, I think happily. He misses me as much as I miss him. We can get through this. It's not too late.

And then the door to the B&B opens again, and a stunning woman comes out, a riot of rusty curls spiralling over her shoulders. I watch Tom turn to her and smile, and I see her reach into his pocket for the keys and kiss his cheek with the easy familiarity of those for whom such gestures are routine. My knees buckle, and I have to cling to the roof of my car for support.

I've done it again, I think bleakly. I made this all about me. I stupidly assumed Tom was feeling the same way I did, that I knew what he was thinking, when the truth is, I know nothing about him at all.

*

It's amazing that in a world as interconnected and monitored as ours, with the internet and BlackBerries and Twitter, with CCTV and satnav and Facebook, you can still disappear while in plain sight. But it's perfectly possible, and for the next ten days, I do.

My groceries are delivered, as are my newspaper and my business mail from my office. I work from my laptop on the sofa at home, and quite often from my bed. There are days I don't even bother to get dressed. I unplug the landline and use only my mobile phone to communicate. No one has any idea where I am, or what I'm doing. I don't speak to anyone unless I have to. I cut myself off from the world, oddly soothed by my loneliness and isolation. I don't have to pretend to be in control when it's just me. I can allow myself to feel.

It's not what you think! Tom wouldn't do that to you. Trust your instinct!

I'd rather trust my own eyes.

My mood varies wildly. Some days, I'm calm and organized. I contact an estate agent in Oxford, and email him high-resolution photographs and a detailed floor plan of the house, culled from our own purchase six years ago. As I expected, he crunches some numbers and then suggests an asking price that will barely cover our debts and leave enough left over for two small deposits, but I can't face letting this drag on, so I agree. I arrange to take him a key in a week or two, when I'm feeling more resilient. In the meantime, I start to sort through our things, dividing everything into three groups: items that are clearly mine, such as my clothes and tennis racket, items that are similarly Tom's, and those things, such wedding presents, that we will have to haggle over.

Our finances should be relatively simple to sort out. We'll split the meagre proceeds of the house fifty-fifty, and call it a day. We are both working, and there are no children, of course, so there's no question of maintenance. It should all be fairly straightforward. I can't imagine any of this is going to take long.

Once the house is sold, I'll take a break from work and travel, I decide. My business is doing better now, thanks in large part to the number of companies that are folding these days. I can manage it remotely and leave it to my team to do the day-to-day operational running. I can afford to take several months off if I want to. Locked into Tom's punishing schedule at the hospital, we could never take more than ten days' holiday at a time, far too little to go to so many of the places I've wanted to see all my life. I've always longed to visit China. I can finally do what I want with my free time, without having to factor Tom into the equation. He's never liked antiquing, for example. And he hates trailing round stately homes or going to art exhibitions. I used to go to the Royal Academy every week before we got married. It'll be nice to get in the habit again.

But then there are the other days. The days when I can't get out of bed, when I curl into a ball beneath the duvet and cry until I have no tears left. These days are the ones when I know that I have lost everything, and that even the Great Wall and Millais can't make up for it.

A week after I send the house details to the estate agent, he calls urging me to let him start showing as soon as possible. Our folly of a castle has apparently attracted an unexpected amount of interest on the agency website, despite the tough market. I'm just shutting my phone, having fobbed him off and bought myself another couple of days' grace, when I hear knocking at the back door. I'm tempted to ignore it, but then I remember that my secretary is FedEx-ing an urgent package from London.

It's one of my better days. I've actually managed to shower and dress, albeit in faded jeans and a thick Sherpa fleece. I don't bother to check my reflection before going through to the kitchen. There really doesn't seem to be much point.

It's an oversight I regret when I see Blake on the other side of the paned glass. Automatically I smooth my hair, and then hate myself for being so stupid and quickly mess it up again.

He smiles warmly as if he's expected when I open the door. 'Hi.'

I stare blankly. What can he possibly imagine we have to say to each other? He slept with my sister, and broke my best friend's heart. He kissed *me*. A Mafia mobster has more scruples.

'Can I come in?'

He doesn't wait for an answer, easing smoothly through the door like a snake-oil salesman.

'She's not here,' I say, finding my voice.

'Come on, Grace. I didn't come to see Zee.'

I'm uncomfortably aware of the way my body is responding to his proximity. I busy myself with the kettle to put some distance between us.

'Why did you come here, Blake?'

'Tom's a fool,' he says brusquely. 'He always was too high-minded for the real world.'

'Blake, I really don't have time for this. I've got a lot of work to do—'

This time, I see the kiss coming. I turn my head, and it

lands on my ear. Blake shrugs regretfully and straightens, but doesn't move away.

'I think you should go,' I say nervously.

He ignores me, leaning casually against the Aga as he watches me fluster with the kettle, his stormy grey eyes amused. He looks as if he's stepped from the pages of a catalogue, in his old-fashioned striped rugby shirt and perfectly distressed jeans. He is ridiculously sexy and good-looking. And I am totally immune to his charms.

'Do you imagine Tom will stay on his own for long?' he asks softly.

It feels like a blow to my solar plexus. 'I hadn't thought,' I manage.

'Sure you have.'

He reaches towards me. I flinch, but he simply pushes my tangled hair from my face. 'You are extraordinarily beautiful,' he says simply.

I know it's a line. I know he's used it a thousand times on a thousand women, one of them my own sister. And yet I still flush like a schoolgirl and my heart still thuds uncomfortably in my chest.

'I've wanted to fuck you since the moment Tom brought you home,' he says conversationally. 'I don't know what it is about you. Maybe the way you never gave me the time of day. I used to lie awake at night listening to you and Tom fucking next door. I'd jerk off, imagining it was me in your bed. I only asked Claudia out because I thought it'd be a way to get to know you better.'

I never gave you the time of day because I knew you were out of my league, I think.

The talk of sex has raised the temperature in the room. I can't get the image of Blake touching himself out of my head.

There's a painful throb between my legs, and my nipples tingle with little electric shocks. 'You have to go,' I repeat.

He brushes the pad of his thumb back and forth over my lips. 'Don't tell me you haven't imagined it,' he murmurs. 'I've had blue balls thinking about you since that kiss. You have to know what you're doing to me. You're driving me crazy. I think if I don't kiss you again I'm going to go out of my fucking mind.'

This time, I don't move. I can't. The kiss is hot and sweet, like wine. It sends eddies of desire rippling through my body, and without conscious thought, my arms snake around his neck. His hand slides beneath my fleece, up to my bare breasts, and he pinches my nipples until my legs shake with lust. I barely notice him dance me backwards, his free hand slipping down the back of my jeans and cupping my buttock. His finger slides between my legs and I shudder as he brushes the entrance to my pussy. The back of the sofa is against my knees, and I fold onto it, deliberately disengaging my brain and allowing my body to take over. I don't want to think about Tom and his red-haired girl. I don't want to think at all.

I've only ever had one lover: Tom. Susannah has had more men than I've had hot dinners. Just this once, I want to be like her. I want her life. I want her lover.

I need this.

I raise my arms like a child, and Blake pulls my fleece over my head, and then I stand and let him tug down my jeans. If he notices my healed scars, he doesn't say anything. He's too busy shucking off his own clothes and flipping me onto my belly. His knee pushes mine apart, and he tangles his hand in my hair, pulling my head up so that I arch like a bow against the velvet cushions. It hurts, and I start to protest, but Blake is pushing his fingers inside me, and suddenly I can't decide if I'm feeling pleasure or pain.

His hold on my hair tightens, and suddenly he's pushing his erect penis between my legs. I try to guide him towards me, but he bats my hand away, and spreads my cheeks. Before I realize what's happening, there is an agonizing, searing pain, and he's forced himself inside me and is sodomizing me. It feels as if I'm being ripped apart. I cry out, but he either takes it as a sign of my enjoyment or he simply doesn't care.

His weight crushes me against the pillows. His fingers are still thrusting inside my vagina, and the pressure in my anus intensifies. There is no pleasure here. The warm heady sensations of his kisses a few moments ago seem a distant dream. This isn't erotic or exciting. It's cold, uncomfortable, brutal and humiliating.

His thrusts grow harder and more rapid. I bite down on the pillows until my lips bleed, praying for it to be over. Suddenly he groans, and collapses against me. I keep still, my anus burning with pain. Tears slide between my tightly closed lids.

Blake rolls off me, and reaches for his jeans. 'I knew it'd be good. The Ice Queen cometh. Good, right?'

I grope for my fleece and gather up my clothes. 'I need to shower,' I whisper.

He nods laconically. I flee upstairs, my chest tight with sobs. I have no one to blame for this but myself. I climb into the shower, and scrub myself until my skin is raw. How did I imagine meaningless sex could make anything better? All it has done is make the ache in my heart worse.

Is this what it's like for Susannah? I think suddenly. *This empty? This pointless?*

I stay upstairs until I'm sure Blake has gone. I wrap myself in my towelling robe and go back downstairs to lock the doors. I don't want to see anyone. I don't want to talk to anyone. I just want to crawl into bed and try to forget this ever happened.

But when I walk into the sitting room, Blake is still sitting on the sofa, bare-chested, the smell of sex still hanging in the air.

And standing in the centre of the room, his face a mask of shock, is Tom.

24

Susannah

I may not be a brainiac like Grace, but I wasn't born yester-day. It takes me all of five minutes to figure out the kidney I'm getting is hers.

'Come on, spill,' I tell Mark Jaylor, as they wheel my trol-ley into the operating theatre. 'I know it's her. Where else would a kidney with my exact same rare blood group miraculously come from? I've only been on the transplant list, like, two seconds. No way did I just get *this* lucky.'

'Even if I wanted to tell you, Zee, I couldn't. Rules. You know that.'

'What did you say to get her to change her mind? You haven't just had a baby, have you?'

'What?'

'Forget it. Just my little joke.'

A nurse in pink scrubs hooks an IV to the needle in the back of my hand. 'Ready whenever you are, doctor.'

Shit. I'm really freaking nervous, even with the Valium they've already given me. Like the doc kept saying, every surgery has risks. Some people apparently go into a kind of anaphylactic shock when foreign tissue is implanted in them. Given this kidney's coming from Grace, I'd say my risk is higher than most.

'See you the other side?' I say.

'See you the other side.'

For the second time in as many months, someone is poised with a scalpel over my belly. At least this time, I won't have to listen to Grace going into raptures while they slice me open. Yay for anaesthetics.

I don't really know the ins and outs of what happens next, details are more Grace's thing than mine, but when I wake up, I have a brand new kidney pumping out piss like a racehorse. Actually, I have three, because they don't take out the old crap ones, too much effort and fiddly sewing, they just stick the new one in below them. Should make my autopsy a bit more interesting if I get hit by the proverbial bus one day.

I'm not expecting to feel like I've had a day at the spa, but seriously, I think I'm going to fucking *expire* from the pain. It feels like an elephant is taking a shit on my stomach.

'You gotta give me something,' I plead, as the nurse takes my temperature and examines my catheter like it's the Holy Grail.

'You've already had twice the *normal* dose,' she says snottily. 'Doctor says no more till bedtime.'

As soon as Mark Jaylor appears to check on me, I'm on his case. 'You didn't say it was going to hurt this much,' I complain. 'Can't you give me a fucking epidural or something?'

'If I'd told you it'd hurt this much, you'd have made a

fuss before the operation as well as afterwards. It's not that bad. And you're doing really well,' he adds, scrutinizing the sodding cath bag again. 'Lovely colour.'

The fascination with my pee continues over the next five days. I mean, I've got a nice pair of boobs, if I say so myself, and I'm wearing my best strappy silk négligé (well, Grace's), but no one is interested in anything happening above my waist. Even my second husband, who had a thing for golden showers, didn't show my bodily fluids this kind of attention.

It appears I'm doing brilliantly: 'top of the class', as Jaylor puts it. I wouldn't expect anything less from one of Grace's body parts.

I still don't get why Grace changed her mind. She's savvy enough to know you don't hand over your hostage before the other side has delivered the ransom. Why would I give her Ava when I've already got her kidney safely hidden in my intestines? But if she's not doing this to get Ava, then why? Tom isn't going to come crawling back unless he knows what Grace has done, and she's clearly gone to major lengths to make sure it's kept quieter than a fucking state secret. It doesn't make any sense. My sister isn't generally given to anonymous good deeds. *Something's* going on.

When Jaylor finally discharges me with a sackful of pills, I decide to see Grace and have it out. I've got to know what her game is. I can't spend the rest of my life waiting for the other shoe to drop.

It takes a few days for me to feel strong enough to walk over to her place from Michael's. I haven't said anything to him about it being Grace's kidney: she's keeping it under wraps for a reason, and until I know what it is, I'm not blowing the advantage of surprise by telling anyone, not even Michael.

The next time he's at work, I pull on my Uggs and Grace's winter coat, and tramp down the lane. I'm as weak as a kitten, but I duck my head against the miserable frigging November sleet and persevere. Amazing what a driving force curiosity can be.

I'm just turning into her drive when I notice Blake sidling into the back garden ahead of me. There's no other word for it: he's *sidling*. He looks like he's about to burgle the place: glancing around furtively, and hugging the walls of the house. I don't get it. He's over here all the time – though less so now Tom's moved out, I'd imagine – so why the 007 routine?

Unless . . .

She *wouldn't*. Would she?

Sorry, but this is too intriguing to worry about the niceties. I make my way round to the front door as sneakily as Blake, and lift up the funny-shaped rock where Grace keeps the spare key.

Letting myself into the house, I tiptoe into the dining room, and hide behind the double doors. Through a narrow gap between the jamb and the wall, I see Grace let Blake into the kitchen. I may only be getting a small slice of the action from here, but I don't miss a thing.

The fucking bastard! I expect him to cheat on Claudia, not to mention the rest of his women; that's par for the course with a man like him. But Tom's supposed to be his best friend! He's kept all Blake's dirty little secrets for years. And now Blake pays him back by fucking his wife the minute his back's turned?

I don't blame Grace. This whole baby thing, and Tom

leaving, has been a total mind fuck for her. She doesn't know whether she's coming or going; and Blake knows it and is playing her like a fucking violin. Sleazy asshole. He's got her when her guard is down, and he's totally taking advantage.

I duck back into the shadows as they spill out of the kitchen, his hands all over her. Grace looks like she's not even there: her eyes are closed, and it's like a stranger is making use of her body.

I started this, I think guiltily. I put the idea that Grace fancied him in his head. It was supposed to be a *joke*. I never thought he'd take it this far.

I'm trapped in the dining room, since the only way out of the house is back through the lounge, right past the two of them. I retreat to the far wall and put my hands over my ears. *La la la la la. I can't hear you.*

Finally, the grunting stops. I hear Grace's light feet running up the stairs, and then moments later, the sound of the shower. I don't have to see her to know she's scrubbing and scrubbing, trying to get clean. Damn it. I wish I could've stopped her before this happened. Grace needs love, and what Blake does is sex. Dirty, mind-blowing, totally emotionless sex.

I wait for him to leave so I can get the fuck out of Dodge, but he's sprawled on the sofa, stretching and yawning like he's got all day. He hasn't even put his bloody shirt back on.

I fidget impatiently. *Come on, you fucker! I want to go home. And I need to pee!*

The back door opens again. From my hiding place, I watch in disbelief as Tom walks hesitantly through the kitchen. Christ on a stick! Did he have to pick *now*?

I almost can't watch, except it's too good not to. It's like an *EastEnders* Christmas special: estranged husband walks into his own lounge to find best friend lolling, half naked, on the sofa. Cue wife wandering in wearing only her towelling dressing gown, hair still wet from the shower. Shocks and gasps of horror all round. And *cut!*

Except this scene keeps right on rolling.

'*What the fuck—?*'

'Tom! Mate!' Blake leaps off the sofa, looking guilty as hell. 'Didn't expect to see you!'

Jesus. The man's a moron. I don't know what the fuck I ever saw in him.

Grace is frozen by the door, the blood draining from her face. She looks like she's about to throw up. 'What – what are you doing here?' she whispers.

Tom ignores Blake completely, his eyes burning into Grace. 'I came to see you. To tell you I was *missing* you, and ask if you were missing me.' He snorts. 'Clearly I was way off beam. Well, I'm sorry to have interrupted. I'll let myself out.'

No. *I can't have this.* Grace doesn't deserve have her life ruined because of one lousy fuck. She and Tom are meant to be together. *I can't let this happen.*

Quickly, I pull off my Uggs, take off my coat, unbutton a couple of buttons on my shirt and mess up my hair. I could easily pass for just-got-out-of-bed. It's my trademark look.

Before Grace can do anything stupid, like tell the truth, I stroll out of my hiding place, march up to Blake, and twine my arms round his neck. 'Come on, babe. You said we could go for a drink after. I don't want to stay in all day.' I glace round at Tom as if I've only just noticed him. 'Hi, Tom.'

In a heartbeat, Blake picks up his cue. Clearly he's been in this kind of situation before.

'It'll have to be a quick one, sweetheart,' he says. 'Claudia'll be back at two.'

'Fine. Sorry if we woke you up, Grace. Hope your headache gets better.'

She's gawping at me like a stranded fish. Fortunately Tom's got the same stunned expression on his face, and doesn't notice.

'Grace, I'm so sorry,' he blurts. 'I don't know what I was thinking—'

'Nice work,' Blake whispers, as we quickly make our escape through the kitchen. 'Fancy practising our next move back at your place?'

I remove his hand from my ass and pull my boots back on. 'I didn't do this for you,' I hiss. 'I did it for *Grace*. As far as I'm concerned, Tom would've been well within his rights to beat you to a pulp. I'd have held his coat and watched.'

'I love it when you're angry.'

'Yeah? Let's see how much you love it when I Bobbitt your balls and feed them to my guinea pig.'

As soon as we're out of sight of the house, I tell him to fuck off. It takes a little while for him to realize I'm serious, and then he shrugs and saunters off in the direction of the pub. Lying sleazeball. I hope his willy shrivels up and falls off.

Wearily, I trudge back home. I reckon it'll take about an hour for the jungle drums to start beating. Michael's not going to be very happy when he hears what just went down, but I can't tell him the truth. If I do, sooner or later it'll get back to Tom; there's no such thing as a shared secret. I'm just going to have to keep my mouth shut and hope

Blake does the same. I'm guessing I'm not going to win any Girlfriend of the Year awards. Fuck it. I really liked Michael.

Consider the debt for the kidney repaid, Grace.

Michael is upset, but irritatingly not surprised when Tom unwittingly rats me out. Not Tom's fault: he wasn't to know Michael and I have a thang going on.

I'm hiding out in the studio when, less than an hour after I get home – those jungle drums are powerful loud – he comes over to bend Michael's ear about the latest developments. I hide out in the back studio, so I don't hear the ins and outs, but clearly things between him and Grace are no better, despite my best efforts. What the hell has gone wrong *now*?

'What?' I demand, as soon as Tom leaves. 'Did he and Grace patch it up?'

'He told me about Blake,' Michaels says. 'I thought we had a deal. You said you weren't going to go there again.'

I pick apart a Styrofoam cup. There's not really much I can say.

'I'm not going to make you choose,' Michael sighs. 'I had a feeling something like this would happen. I know you, Zee. But I'm not going to hang around forever. Sloppy seconds aren't my style.'

He *knows* me? Then how come he doesn't know I'm a fucking hero! I just saved my sister's marriage! What about points for enterprise, not to mention selflessness?

Except he has no idea about any of that, of course. I try to see it from his point of view. As far as he's concerned, I just reprised my slapper role with Blake, and it'd be weird if he wasn't pissed off. Although he seems not so much angry as disappointed, which makes me think of my father, and not in a good way. It's bad enough to be in the dock for something I didn't do, but it's a bit much to find out he *expected* me to drop my knickers at the first opportunity. How much of a tart does he reckon I am? Does he think the other night meant nothing to me?

'It's not what you think,' I begin, frustrated at not being able to explain.

'Look, Zee. I get it. You're not a commitment sort of girl. I don't flatter myself I'm any more than a port in a storm. I just wish for Claudia's sake you hadn't gone back to *him*. And I'm a little surprised you had the poor taste to arrange your tryst at Grace's house, but I suppose you could hardly rub my nose in it by bringing him here, for which I thank you, and clearly he couldn't take you home to his wife's bed. That's the trouble when you tup a married man, Zee. No hiding place.'

Tup? Does anybody really *say* that any more?

'I promise, it's over,' I say. This, at least, is true.

'Don't make promises you can't keep.'

'Michael—'

'I have to get to work, Susannah. I'll see you later.'

I feel like total crap as I watch him leave. He must think really badly of me now. I'm on the verge of running after him and blurting out the truth, but then I think of Grace's face when Tom looked at her like she was shit on the sole of his shoe. I'm used to that look; I can take it. Grace has never been disapproved of in her life. She'd go to pieces if anyone ever found out what really went down today.

He leaves, and I'm left to sit and stew at home. Grace calls a couple of times, but I let it go to voicemail. I'm grateful for the kidney and everything, but she's just fucked up the first decent relationship I've had in God knows how long. Maybe the first decent relationship I've had full stop.

Except . . . except how perfect *is* it, when he was just waiting for me to fuck up? It's one thing to be accepted for who you are. It's another thing to be judged by it. It really hurts that he thinks so little of me. He assumed I'd sleep with someone else sooner or later, even before he heard about Blake. Leopards don't change their spots, and old slappers don't turn into born-again virgins.

I thought he had a little more faith in me. In *us*.

I sit beside Ava's cot for a long time after Michael drops me off at the hospital the next morning. It was an awkward drive; overnight, his disappointment has hardened into frosty disapproval, and I've stopped feeling hurt and started feeling pissed off. Since when did he start *judging* me? I don't want to be rescued or saved or forgiven! I thought we'd gone into this as *equals*. I don't need another father pointing out where I've gone wrong, or some kind of martyr willing to look the other way. If I tell the truth now, he'll feel better, but it won't fix things for me. I don't know where we go from here, but I feel in my waters it's not good.

Let's face it: I don't do relationships. Any more than I do motherhood.

'In another couple of weeks, you'd have been born,' I whisper to Ava, tickling her palm with my thumb and smiling as her doll-sized fingers curl around it. 'You'll be big enough to leave here soon. Maybe we'll celebrate our first Christmas together in our own home. Wherever that is.'

An image of last Christmas Day springs suddenly into

my head: Oakey and me at the beach, stuffing our faces with Doritos and smoking some good Colombian skunk and watching the sun sink into the ocean. Not the kind of thing you can do with a baby in tow. Shit, I miss my life. The tattoos, the punters, the freedom to up sticks and go wherever I felt like at a moment's notice. It sucked sometimes, but in comparison Grace's life is so hemmed in and *suffocating*. What the neighbours think really matters to her. How can she *stand* it?

I've been so jealous of her for so long, but not any more, I realize. All those things I thought were so fucking wonderful – the amazing career, the gorgeous house, even the loving husband – it all just means she's *trapped*. Everyone expects her life to be perfect; Grace most of all. She's in danger of letting it all slip through her fingers because she can't accept that life *isn't* neat and tidy. It's a bloody fucking awkward mess.

No, I don't want her life. I want mine back.

I thought I could change, and be the sort of person who came home to the same person every night and cooked dinner and helped their kid with homework. Maybe I could. The truth is, *I don't want to.*

Michael was right. He knew I'd slip back into my old ways, sooner or later. I didn't sleep with Blake this time, but I could have, easily, if he'd gone about it the right way. I'm not cut out to settle down and play house. I'd go mad with boredom. I'm *already* mad with boredom.

Grace would've been a good mother, I think, staring at my daughter. She always tries to do the right thing. Isn't that what good mothers do?

'What's going to happen to us, Ava?' I sigh. 'Shall we go and live in the flat Auntie Grace rented for us? It's near a really nice primary school, apparently. And there are lots of other lovely mothers in the building, she says.'

Ava smiles. The nurse says it's wind, but I know different. She's got an interesting take on life already, my daughter.

'No, I don't think it sounds very me, either. I'm not really a yummy mummy sort of person, am I? I can't see me standing at the school gates in a pretty cardigan and a pair of ballet pumps.' I grin. 'Let's be honest, I'm more likely to be in the back of a 4x4 shagging one of your friends' dads.'

I stay with Ava until the neonatologist comes in to do his rounds. Ava's good company. She smiles in all the right places, and doesn't interrupt. It's easy to think when I'm with her. And I have a lot to think about.

When Michael picks me up an hour later, I ask him to drop me off at Bicester North Station. He doesn't bother to enquire why, so I don't tell him. If he wants to give me the silent treatment again, that's fine by me.

I made the right decision, I think. I can't stand men who bloody sulk.

As soon as the train reaches London, I take a taxi to the passport office, and spend the next couple of hours filling in forms. I don't have an appointment, but the usual arsey Jobsworth must be on holiday, because a really nice woman lets me take a no-show slot on the QT. I need a new passport with one of those chip things in it, or I won't be able to slip into the US without a visa. This way, I'll get ninety days as a tourist; after that, I'll just overstay my welcome and join the millions of illegal workers flying under the radar. Frankly, a little invisibility will suit me fine. When Grace finds out what I've done, she's bound to want to come after me.

My passport won't be ready till five, so I go to an internet café nearby and book my ticket to Florida, then send Oakey a quick email with the details. He must be online, because he sends a reply straight back with the promise to meet my flight; and the offer of a job at the new tatt shop he's just opened in Miami.

Go, Oakey! I think. Maybe this'll work out after all.

Then I hail another cab, and go to see Nicholas Lyon.

25

Grace

'Grace, I'm so sorry,' Tom gabbles. 'I don't know what I was thinking—'

I cut him off, unable to bear any more. 'Please, Tom. Don't.'

'It was stupid of me. I just saw him sitting there on the sofa and I thought . . . I just saw red. You'd never do that, of course you wouldn't. Not with Claudia's husband. I didn't mean anything, please, you have to believe me—'

'I do, Tom.'

For a moment, neither of us says anything. I wrap my robe tighter around myself, eaten up with guilt. How could I have been so *stupid*? If Susannah hadn't been here and had the quick thinking to take the blame, it wouldn't just be my life that would've been ruined, but Claudia's too.

Why was my sister even here?

'Grace,' Tom says nervously. 'What I said, about missing you. It's true. It's been hell without you. I want to come home. Please, can we put it behind us and try again?'

If only he had come to me twenty-four hours ago. Before Blake; before I crossed a line into a place I don't recognize.

What about his girlfriend? I think suddenly. Where does *she* fit into this picture? Has it all fallen apart between them; is that why Tom abruptly wants to come home? Or is he planning to take a leaf out of Blake's book and keep the two of us on the go at once?

How dare he come over all indignant and jealous at the thought of me and Blake, when he's been carrying on with that woman for God knows how long! She was probably on the scene long before he left home. Men never quit one nest until they've got the next one feathered. All the guilt he pushed my way over Ava was just a smokescreen. How could he use his own daughter like that? How could he make me feel this was *my* fault?

I push past him into the kitchen, and pull out the folder my estate agent sent me.

'I've put the house on the market,' I say coolly, handing it to him. 'I'm sure your lawyer will want to have it valued independently. Please let me know when you want to come round, so that I can make sure I'm not here.'

Tom stares at the brochure in his hand as if it's written in Aramaic. 'Grace, please. Don't do this.'

'I can't afford to live in this place on my own. There should be enough left over for us both to start again. That's what you want, isn't it?'

'No!' He flings the folder on the kitchen table. 'That's not what I want! I didn't want to leave; I didn't want any of this to happen!'

'But you did,' I say. 'You did leave.'

'I just couldn't deal with it any more,' he pleads. 'You

were obsessed with the baby. I just needed some time out, away from it all.'

'How do you think *I* felt, Tom? First I find out I can't have children, and then my sister takes away the one chance I have! And you take *her* side! Obsessed? Yes, maybe I was, but can you blame me?'

'I'm sorry,' he says helplessly. 'I'm sorry about all of it.'

'Ava is your daughter. You can't just pretend she doesn't exist.'

'I know that. I'm not trying to. I'll support her financially, of course I will. Whatever she and Susannah need. I'd like to be part of her life, if I can. I don't want her to grow up without a father. But she's best off with her mother, Grace,' he says miserably. 'You know that. You can't hold Susannah to ransom over her baby, you must see that.'

I look away. 'A donor came forward. Susannah has her new kidney. She's going to be fine. She doesn't need me.'

I don't know what prevents me from telling him the truth. I don't want what I did for my sister to change anything, I suppose. I want to see what he's really thinking, what he feels about the real, unvarnished me.

Tom looks startled. 'But that's wonderful,' he exclaims. 'Isn't it?'

'Yes. You're off the hook. Everything's worked out very nicely, hasn't it? For *you*.'

'I don't understand, Grace. Why are you being like this?'

I throw him a look of scorn. 'Did you really think I wouldn't find out, Tom?'

He pales. 'Find out what?'

'Please. Don't treat me like a fool.'

I can see it in his face: *Do I lie, and hope she's bluffing, or do I go for broke and tell the truth and cross my fingers I can get away with it?*

'I was going to tell you,' Tom says finally. 'I just didn't know where to start. There was already so much else going on, with your mother and Susannah and the baby—'

'*Ava.*'

'Ava,' he corrects himself. 'I didn't want to add to your stress. I didn't want you to worry.'

I can't believe he's admitted it. Just like that. I'm in agony over the thought that he might find out about Blake, and he's just held his hands up to an affair without a second thought. And now he's trying to package his deceit as *altruism*?

'You didn't want me to *worry*?' I exclaim.

'I should have said something right at the beginning,' he says quickly. 'But the longer it went on, the harder it became to admit it. I won't go behind your back again, I swear. Grace, I love you. I want to come home. Can't we put this behind us?'

'Just go, Tom,' I say wearily. 'Go. And next time you want to see me,' I add, 'don't just turn up unannounced. Talk to my lawyer first.'

'No,' I tell Nicholas. 'No. She can't have.'

'I'm afraid she has.' He opens a folder, and takes out a letter. 'She asked me to give you this. I'm sorry to have been so mysterious on the phone, Grace. I had no choice.'

'She can't have,' I say again. 'She can't have just *gone*.'

'Read the letter. It might make things a little clearer.'

It's written in Susannah's sprawling, extravagant script and, like Susannah herself, it doesn't beat around the bush.

'*Dear Sis. By the time you get this, Nicholas will of told you I'm gone,*' I read aloud. '*I hope you aren't too mad I didn't say goodbye but I knew you'd never agree to this, you're too stubborn just like Dad.*

'*I love Ava more than anything, she's a sweetheart, but I'm a crap mother and we both know it. I'd of got bored sooner or later. Once a black sheep always a black sheep I guess.*'

I look up, my eyes bright with tears. 'Her grammar really is awful. Too many years in the States.'

Nicholas smiles, and I carry on reading.

'*The best place for Ava is with you and her dad, like we agreed in the first place. I shouldn't of messed about and tried to keep her, I'm sorry about that.*

'*I know you and Tom will sort things out. Take it from me, honesty isn't always the best policy! It just spreads the pain.*

'*I know you'll love Ava and keep her safe. I signed all the forms, Nick has them, you can adopt her and everything and make it official. I hope you keep her name, I named her after Ava Gardner, I always liked her, but I understand if you want to change it.*

'*I don't think I'll be back for a while, I've got a good job with a friend in Miami so I think I'll go there first. When I'm settled I'll send you my address.*

'*When she's bigger tell her I loved her, that's why I picked the best mummy for her I could. Love you, Zee.*'

By the time I finish, I'm sobbing. Once again, Nicholas hands me a box of tissues and acts as if this is a perfectly normal occurrence.

'She signed everything when she came to see me ten

days ago,' he says. 'We'll present her affidavit to the court and ask it to grant you a Parental Order in the New Year. But we don't have to wait until then for you to take her. Susannah's affidavit should be enough to give you temporary custody while we wait for the paperwork to go through. As soon as Ava is well enough to leave the hospital, you can take her home.'

I sit there, too stunned to respond. I don't know what to think. Susannah's played fast and loose with my emotions for so long, I'm honestly not sure what I feel at this point. I'm sure she imagined I'd be overjoyed, and I should be . . .

Why now, Zee? Why did you have to wait until *now*?

A few months ago, I had a husband and a home and a stable family life to offer this little girl. But my life is going to be very different from now on. Tom and I are damaged beyond repair. I love him far too much to share him with anyone. If he'd told me it was just a fling, I could have forgiven that, how could I not after what I've done? But the way he talked about this girl showed me it was far more than that. By his own admission, he shared things with her he couldn't share with me. That hurts more than the fact that he slept with her.

I'm sure Susannah does love Ava, in her own way, but she's treating her daughter like she's a flat or a timeshare you can just sign over to someone else. She's assuming I'll pick up the pieces for her, and fall into line with what she wants, just as I always have. Once again, she's abandoned her children; the boys as well as Ava. Already she's moved on, to the next job, the next adventure. The next man.

I close my eyes, trying to get a grip on the tornado of

emotions. I've said goodbye to Ava once. I've walled up my feelings so deep inside I'm not certain I can reach them. I'm not even sure I want to try.

'She can't change her mind,' Nicholas says, reading mine. 'She knows that. Surrogates are required by law to wait until a child is six weeks old before giving consent to a Parental Order, but once they do, it can't be revoked. No one can take her away from you.'

'But Tom and I— We're not—'

'Divorce has no more bearing on this than if you'd had Ava together.'

I *want* to say yes. I want to seize this precious chance with both hands and never let go, but something holds me back. Never mind what I want. Is it really the right thing to do, for *Ava*? To make her part of a broken home before she's even known what family is?

'Nothing has to be done today,' Nicholas says. 'It's a lot to take on board. The courts are winding down for Christmas anyway. As I said, you've got the authority to take Ava home if she's released before we get the paperwork in order. Why don't we talk the first Monday in January and see where we are then?'

I nod, too overwhelmed to speak.

'My wife and I were separated for a while after our youngest daughter was born,' Nicholas says unexpectedly. 'I had a very stupid affair, and even lived with someone else for a while.'

'*You?*'

'I know.' He smiles ruefully, and for the first time, I see his charm. 'You'd never think I had it in me, would you?'

'But your wife took you back?'

'I never stopped loving her, and she knew that. Our son was born the following year, and Finn – also known as Ooops – eighteen months later. I've never been happier. I don't think she's ever regretted trying again either.'

I know what he's trying to tell me. I want to believe it could happen for Tom and me, too, that my dream of a happy family with my husband and child isn't over.

But life isn't a fairy tale. And I no longer believe in happy endings.

I'm sorting through a stack of old photograph albums the following weekend when the phone rings. I reach for it without bothering to check caller ID, my mind still in Sardinia, where these pictures where taken. I can't believe how slim and happy Tom and I both look! It was the year after we got married. We didn't have two pennies to rub together, and spent most of our time drinking enamel-stripping Chianti at cheap trattorias, filling up on pasta and making love outdoors, since the only places we could afford to stay at were flea-bitten dives where you certainly wouldn't want to get naked.

I tuck the phone in the crook of my neck, and pull out the next album. *Atlanta, 1997.* 'Yes?'

'Mrs Hamilton? Jean Rook here. I'm one of the nurses on your mother's ward. I've got some very good news.' She pauses, aware she suddenly has my full attention. 'Your mother is awake, and she's been asking for you.'

I make the two-hour journey in less than an hour and a half. Dad is already at the hospital, looking as stunned and tense as I feel. Mum's been in a coma for more than ten months. I think we'd both said goodbye to her in our hearts.

Even now, I'm filled with anxiety. What if Mum is brain damaged; somehow not Mum any more? Would it have been better if she'd never woken up?

We go into her room together. As soon as she opens her eyes and smiles at us, I know we have nothing to fear.

'David,' she whispers, her voice papery from disuse. 'I'm so sorry to put you to so much trouble.'

Dad kneels beside the bed and pulls her into his arms. I look away, both embarrassed and deeply moved. I can remember on the fingers of one hand the times I've seen my parents kiss.

When my father finally lets her go, she smiles at me, and I perch on the edge of the bed and take her hand, bruised by the many months of IVs.

'I love you, Grace,' she says firmly. 'Just as much as Susannah. Remember that. I always have, even if I haven't always shown it.'

'Sssh, Mum,' I deflect. 'We don't need to go into this now.'

'We do. It needs to be said. I was wrong.'

She breaks off, coughing, and Dad moves in protectively. Mum waves him away. 'I'm proud of you, Grace. I haven't said so often enough.'

'Mum, it doesn't matter now—'

'I wish I could hold the baby,' she says wistfully. 'Ava. My first granddaughter.'

I glance back at Dad in surprise. 'How does she know?'

'She must have overheard one of the nurses talking. Susannah was in here every day. They all knew about it.'

'You'll be a wonderful mother,' Mum tells me. 'Don't be afraid of it. It'll come to you.'

I squeeze her hand, not trusting myself to speak. My

mother has never said she believed in me before. It means more to me than all the A grades I've ever earned.

'You have to go now, Grace,' Mum says urgently.

'I'm sorry, Mum. Of course, you must be tired.' I get to my feet. 'I'll go and find one of the nurses, Dad, while you sit with her—'

She grasps my hand, her grip surprisingly firm. 'Grace, you have to go and find Tom. You have to go now. It can't wait.'

'Mum—'

'Grace, listen to me. *You have to go to Tom now.*'

Something about her tone stirs a deep and terrible fear deep inside me. I search her face, reading the warning there.

'OK, Mum,' I say nervously. 'I'll go. I'll find him.'

I drop a kiss on her forehead, and for a moment she holds me there, cupping my cheek with her dry hand. Then I straighten up, grab my coat and my bag, and practically run to the car.

I'm already on the road to London when I realize I have no idea where I'm going. Tom isn't answering his mobile. I don't know the address of the flat where he's been staying, or even if he's still there. For all I know, he's moved in with *her*.

No. He's alone. I'm sure of it. Mum wouldn't be so worried otherwise.

I slam my fists on the steering wheel. *Think!* It's Sunday night. Where would he be?

Then it comes to me. *His office.* Of course! When he's upset, he always throws himself into work.

For the second time that night, I drive like a lunatic,

jumping red lights and weaving dangerously in and out of traffic. It's been a while since I drove to the hospital, but I still remember the way. Thankfully, at this time of night, the roads are relatively clear. I pray to God I get to him in time. I don't understand how Mum knows he needs me, but she *knows*, the same as she knew about Ava, the same as she knew exactly what I needed to hear. Tom is in danger, and I don't have much time.

Once I reach the hospital, I abandon my car in a disabled bay by the main entrance, not caring if it gets clamped or towed. The administrative offices are in a squat wing near the back. Most are in darkness this late on a Sunday, though a few lights illuminate offices on the higher floors. The security is minimal; no one stops me as I run down the ill-lit halls, my chest tight with panic. Please God, let me be in time. *Please let me be in time.*

At first I think Tom's door is locked. Then I realize something is blocking the door. I push hard against it, and manage to ease myself into the room.

At first I think he's dead. His face is the colour of porridge, and I can't make out the rise and fall of his chest. I drop to my knees, searching for a pulse. It's faint, but it's there.

Quickly, I grab the phone and hit the speed-dial button for A&E. *If Tom had to have a heart attack,* I think, *at least he picked a hospital to do it in.*

I don't leave his side all night, torn between guilt and fear. Another twenty minutes, the doctor says, and it would have been too late. They can't tell me if he's going to be OK, or even if he's going to wake up. They don't know how long he was unconscious, how much damage there may have been done to his brain. *Touch and go*, they tell me. *The next twenty-four hours will be crucial. You may want to notify the rest of his family.*

I did this, I think. *I brought this on. I literally broke his heart.*

A little before seven, I'm woken by a hand on my shoulder, and realize I've fallen asleep, my head resting on Tom's lap.

'I'm sorry to disturb you,' the nurse whispers, 'but there's someone to see you. She says it's urgent.'

I pull myself up, wincing as the blood rushes into my limbs, and follow the nurse out of the ICU and into another bland, depressing waiting room. *I am so sick of hospitals.*

Someone is already there, sitting on the oatmeal sofa. In this colourless room, she stands out like an exotic bird of paradise, her red hair so vibrant she looks like she's on fire.

She stands up when she sees me, but doesn't hold out her hand. 'I'm Ella Stuart,' she says, 'and I think I owe you an apology.'

'Yes,' I say calmly, 'I think you do.'

We sit down. 'Coffee?' she asks, as if we're breakfasting at Claridges.

I shake my head. She studies her hands for a few minutes, as if gathering herself, and then looks up. 'I told him to tell you,' she says. 'I've kept secrets before, and it's brought me nothing but grief.'

I consider the long, elegant legs, the wide-eyed amber gaze, that extraordinary hair. I believe her.

'If it's any consolation,' she adds quickly, 'the only reason Tom didn't say anything is because he didn't want to worry you.'

'Not much consolation, no.'

'You had so much on your plate already, he didn't want to add to it. And then, when we realized it was serious, it was too late to go back—'

'I'm really not interested in the details of your affair,' I say coldly. 'I don't know what it is you want. I'm not going to keep you from his sickbed, if that's what you're afraid of. I'm not that cruel. But I would prefer it if you made sure we didn't have to see each other again. Perhaps we can work out some sort of schedule—'

'*An affair?*' She gapes at me. 'Is *that* what you think is going on? An *affair?*'

Suddenly, I'm less certain. 'He admitted it. He said he still loves me,' I add, defiantly. 'He said he wanted to come home.'

'Of course he loves you! We haven't been having an affair!' Her expression softens. 'Grace, I'm Tom's doctor, and his friend, but I'm certainly not his lover. There's only one woman Tom has eyes for, and that's *you.*'

'His *doctor?*'

'Well, not exactly. My field is neonatology, not cardio. But Tom's been having some experimental treatment for his migraines – it's a long story,' she sighs, seeing my look of confusion. 'Tom has a patent foramen ovale, or PFO, which is a genetic, but usually not too serious, heart defect. Technically, it's a tiny hole in your heart. I'm sure he's told you. About a year ago, he started having some severe migraines, which a number of studies suggest may be related to the PFO.'

I suddenly remember last January, when the two of us went skiing in Colorado. Tom spent two days in bed with a blinding headache. At the time, we both put it down to altitude sickness.

'There's been some research linking the surgical closure of the PFO to a reduction in the number and severity of migraines, but then Tom heard about a new drug which promised to do the same thing. He wanted to join the clinical trial at the hospital in Oxford, but he didn't want to tell you. There can be some side effects, and he felt you had enough to deal with.'

I didn't want to worry you. Oh, Tom.

As if my Tom would ever have an affair. *A drug trial.* I'd laugh at the absurdity, if he wasn't in a room a hundred feet from me, fighting for his life.

'The drugs had to be administered via IV, a bit like chemo, and they made him dizzy and nauseous for a few hours, so he needed me to collect him from the hospital. I'm so sorry, Grace,' Ella says repentantly. 'We should never have gone behind your back. We should have told you.'

'These side effects,' I say steadily. 'Is that why he had the heart attack?'

She nods. 'It's very rare, less than half a per cent. Most of those were with people much older than Tom. He thought it was worth the risk.'

At some point, I'm going to have to process all of this, and come to terms with the fact that Tom couldn't tell me something so serious, so central to his life, because I was too preoccupied with my own. There was a time we could tell each other anything. I must have been so far away from him for him to feel he had to do this alone. So self-involved that I didn't even notice what was happening right under my nose.

But the blame and self-recrimination can come later. This isn't about me.

Now, I have to be with my husband. I have to be there

when he wakes up, so that I can tell him how sorry I am. So that I can tell him I love him, that I choose him, will always choose him, for as long as he wants me.

My life is suspended between three hospitals. Later, when the doctors come to run more of their tests – 'I don't want to worry you any more than necessary, Mrs Hamilton, but I'm afraid we really need him to wake up soon' – I go outside to the car, which has been clamped but not yet towed, and call my father. My mother has had a good night, he tells me. They've run a dozen tests, and it's still a bit early to be sure, but they think she's going to be fine. I tell him to send her my love, and Susannah's, and close my phone.

Wearily, I rest my head on the steering wheel. There are times, even now, when I wish I was Susannah. She is probably sitting on a sun-drenched beach in Miami at the moment, drink in hand, with no worries or responsibilities. No ties.

I couldn't do it, I realize. I may sometimes be tempted to get on a plane and leave my life behind, but I could never actually do it. It's our connection to other people that makes us human. *You can't forsake the ties that bind*.

My phone rings, and I hold it in the palm of my hand, this silver bullet. For a moment, I'm tempted to hurl it into the gutter, but of course I don't. I never will.

'Yes?'

'It's Lucy at the NICU?' a perky young voice announces. 'Would you be Grace?'

I'm too drained to summon fear. 'Is it about Ava?'

'She's doing really well?' the girl says. 'Doctor says you can take her home today. Isn't that great? So can you come down maybe later? There's a bit of paperwork we need to go through—'

'I'm sorry,' I say. 'My husband is sick. I can't come.'

'Oh, that's too bad. Well, maybe tomorrow—'

'You don't understand. I can't come. Not today, not tomorrow. She's not my daughter. I can't look after her. I'm sorry. You'll have to find someone else.'

I close the phone. And then I switch it off, and put it carefully on the seat beside me.

I choose Tom.

26

Tom

I don't remember any of it, fortunately. Out like a light. One minute I'm sitting at my desk, wondering how the hell I'm ever going to manage without Grace, and the next, there she is, sitting beside my sickbed, my own Christmas miracle. She says I actually came round two days after the heart attack, but I can't remember a thing before waking up to her on Christmas Day. Two weeks of my life lost, just like that.

Came close to cashing in my chips, they tell me. If Grace hadn't found me when she did, I'd have been singing with the heavenly choir.

Extraordinary, that whole thing. I've spoken to David Latham; he says it happened just like Grace said it did. Catherine woke up after ten months in a coma, said Grace had to go and find me, and off she went. I'm not one for psychics and spirits and all the rest of the mumbo jumbo, but I don't deny someone, somewhere, is looking out for me.

I pull the car over onto the hard shoulder, and glance

again at my scribbled directions. Got to be a turning somewhere up here on the left. Can't be far now.

Have to admit, I'm a tad nervous about this little ven-
ture. Grace'd have a fit if she knew I was driving around the
Oxfordshire countryside on my own. The doc said I wasn't
to get behind the wheel for six weeks, but I feel fine. It's
been nearly a month since I came home. I can't sit twiddling
my thumbs forever. Need to start picking up the reins again.
Grace has been a bloody brick, but I can't rely on her to wait
on me hand, foot and finger forever.

When I think how close we came to losing each other, it
makes my blood run cold. I was a bloody fool. I should've
made more effort to understand what Grace was going
through. Ella warned me. She had a similar thing happen
herself a while back. Ectopic pregnancy, I think she said.
Can't have children now, anyway. She and her husband
ended up adopting. She told me I should be a bit more
sensitive, but I didn't bloody listen, did I? I thought Grace
felt the same way I did: a baby would be nice, but if it
wasn't meant to be, we still had each other, and a great life.
I didn't have a bloody clue.

I should never have agreed to any part of Susannah's
ludicrous plan. I knew it was a bad idea. The girl's a flake.
It was bound to end in tears.

Grace says she's run off to America again, without a
word of warning, and naturally she's left Grace to pick up
the pieces. Can't say I'm surprised. The baby's being fostered now, until we can get the paperwork sorted out and
put her up for adoption. Grace's decision, not mine: but as
the father, I need to sign off on it, apparently. Grace says she
wants to look forward, not back.

I rejoin the road, and find myself stuck behind a tractor

spitting chunks of mud onto the road. The rain is coming down in stair-rods, and I can hardly see where I'm going. I slow to a crawl. No point trying to overtake. Grace'd never forgive me if I got myself killed now.

We've done a lot of talking in the last month, Grace and me. Straightened a lot of things out. The business with Ella, for one. An affair! As if I'd ever look at another woman! Mind you, I suppose I was just as bad, jumping to conclusions when I saw Blake half naked in my own sitting room. I was wrong about him and Grace, but I'll be honest, I'm not sure I'm ever going to see him in the same light again. He's cheated on Claudia one too many times. Makes him a hard man for anyone to trust.

When you look at it from her point of view, I can quite see how Grace got the wrong end of the stick. My own fault for keeping the drug trials quiet. Maybe if I hadn't been so cross with her, I'd have said something earlier. I felt she was shutting me out of her life, so I did the same to her. Bloody childish, really. I feel bad about what I put her through. She must've been worried sick. Ella says she didn't leave my bedside for two weeks straight.

The tractor finally turns into a driveway, and I spot the turning I want a few yards ahead. I swing the Range Rover into the rutted lane, and make my way slowly up to a stone cottage at the end. It's a pretty little place, even in January. Smoke coming out of the chimney, and bright red holly berries around the front door. The sort of place Americans would love.

I park the car and get out, glad I didn't bring the hybrid. It would never have made it through this mud. By the time I reach the front door, it's practically up to my knees.

I knock, and a few moments later, the door opens. 'Mr

Hamilton? Do come in. I'm sorry about the mud. We keep meaning to get round to having the driveway done, but there's always something more pressing.'

'Really, don't worry, Mrs Phillips. Couldn't matter less.'

'Diana, please.'

She ushers me through the back to the kitchen. A familiar Aga warms the room, but in every other way, it couldn't be more different from the kitchen at home. Coats and anoraks thrown over the backs of chairs, children's pictures tacked to the walls, clutter and books and papers littering every surface. At least four pairs of wellies are jumbled by the door to the garden. I quite like this sort of family chaos, but it'd drive Grace nuts.

'Did you get the letter?' I ask, as the woman clears a heap of old newspapers from a chair and invites me to sit down. 'I asked them to courier it to you from London to make sure it reached you in time.'

'Oh, yes. We got it yesterday. Everything's fine, no need to worry about that.'

She smiles warmly, and I find myself liking her immediately. I can see why she's in this job. 'She's just upstairs. Would you like me to fetch her?'

'I don't want to disturb her—'

'Oh, no, it's quite all right, she's ready for you. I won't be a minute.'

My heart is beating at twice its usual rate. If I didn't know what a heart attack felt like – a bloody great tank revving its engine on your chest – I'd fancy myself in the middle of one.

Mrs Phillips comes back into the kitchen, and I leap up. She smiles, and tilts her arms, so that I can see my daughter's face. 'Say hello to your daddy, Ava.'

Big blue eyes look straight into mine. A light fuzz of ruddy hair haloes her head. She's so tiny, it's hard to believe she's real. She looks like a perfect porcelain doll.

Unexpectedly, she smiles. In that instant, my heart is lost. I know my life will never be the same again. I will do anything and everything to keep my little girl safe.

I'm staggered by what Grace has given up for me. Whatever my wife may or may not have done in the past, that one act of love wipes everything clean. She had the chance to bring this perfect little person home, and she chose me.

'Do you want to hold her?'

I hesitate.

'The two of you'd better start getting used to one another,' Mrs Phillips laughs, placing her gently into my arms. 'You'll be seeing a lot of each other from now on.'

Tentatively, I cradle my daughter against my heart. 'Hello, Ava,' I whisper. 'I'm your daddy.'

'It's a pretty name,' the woman smiles. 'After the film star?'

I nod, not taking my eyes off the baby. 'Ava Catherine. After my wife's mother. She died just after Christmas.'

'I'm so sorry. But I'm sure she'd have been thrilled you named the baby after her. It's a lovely thing to do.'

Catherine's death took everyone by surprise. She'd been doing so well. As Grace said, it would've been easier in some ways if she'd never come round from the coma. Grace had already said her goodbyes. This way, it was like she had to lose her all over again. But if she hadn't come round, of course, I'd have been toast.

We couldn't find Susannah in time for the funeral. She sent Grace an email a week or two later, full of news and excitement, but she didn't give a forwarding address or even a phone number. Grace had to break the news via return email. She still hasn't heard back.

Susannah didn't even mention Ava. She *did*, however, mention Michael – at least a dozen times. Absence really does make the heart grow fonder, it seems: being away from him made her realize they were soulmates. He's been dropping by to ask if we've heard from her every other day since she left, so clearly he's just as smitten. I give it six months before Susannah's back on our side of the Pond, causing her own unique brand of chaos and trouble.

Mrs Phillips collects Ava's things, and walks the two of us out to my car. 'Have you got a car seat?'

'A car seat?'

She laughs. 'Hold on, let me get you mine. You can bring it back next time you're passing.'

I watch as she expertly installs it into my back seat, and then I gingerly place Ava in it before wrestling with the ridiculously complicated five-point harness. Mrs Phillips waves us off as we lurch back down the lane. She's fostered over a hundred babies in her time, apparently; she's kept track of every one.

I drive home at a slow crawl, a trail of infuriated drivers building up behind me. It's almost dark by the time I reach home. The lights are on in the kitchen, and I can see Grace silhouetted at the sink, washing up. I haven't told her about Ava. I wanted to surprise her.

Carefully, I unbuckle my daughter and scoop her into my arms. She smiles at me, as if she knows where we're going.

Grace turns as we come in, and as she looks at us her face is a picture of disbelief and wonder.

'Hello, darling,' I say. 'We're home.'

Acknowledgements

My thanks to my brilliant agent, Carole Blake, and the infinitely patient and charming Imogen Taylor, one of the best editors in the business. I'm privileged to work with both of you.

All those at Blake Friedmann and Pan Macmillan – Oli Munson, Trisha Jackson, Thalia Suzuma, Sandra Taylor, Eli Dryden: thank you. I know we take it down to the wire every time, and you never fail me.

A special thanks to Simon Pigott of Levision Meltzer Pigott for researching the issues surrounding surrogacy law; and to Katrina Erskine at the Portland Hospital for her advice on the medical issues raised in the novel. Any mistakes are mine and mine alone.

My sister, Philippa, was a marvellous help with this book, enumerating my heinous crimes against her when we were children in colourful detail and with extraordinarily vivid recollection. She has always been the sweetest girl in every way, and the sins of the sisters in this book are entirely fictional. But, just for the record, I *did* give the make-up back.

My father Michael and WSM Barbi provided a wonderful and peaceful retreat in New Zealand for me to finish my final edits. The rest of the family kept their crises to a minimum during the insane days when I raced to deliver the MS on time, for which many thanks.

My children were marvellous about tiptoeing around me when I was in meltdown. Henry, Matthew and Lily: for once, it wasn't your fault.

But most of all, I thank my husband, Erik: for reading every draft and never looking bored, for spotting the howlers before I embarrassed myself in public, for his pithy, constructive criticism; and for not leaving me when I was impossible, unreasonable, paranoid, hysterical, delusional and inconsolable. I couldn't do any of it without you.

TESS STIMSON
Vermont, January 2010